## By Eve Pollard

*Biography*

JACKIE

*Fiction*

JACK'S WIDOW

(co-authored with Val Hudson and Joyce Hopkirk)

SPLASH
BEST OF ENEMIES
DOUBLE TROUBLE
UNFINISHED BUSINESS

# Jack's Widow

~ ❀ ~

## EVE POLLARD

AVON

*An Imprint of* HarperCollins*Publishers*

FIRST EDITION

ISBN: 978-0-06-081705-3
ISBN-10: 0-06-081705-4

*Interior text designed by Susan Yang*

The Willam Morrow hardcover edition contains the following Library of Congress Cataloging-in-Publication Data

Pollard, Eve.
  Jack's widow: a novel / by Eve Pollard.—1st ed.
    p. cm.
1. Onassis, Jacqueline Kenedy, 1924-1994—Fiction. 2. Presidents' spouses—Fiction. 3. Women editors—Fiction. 4. Widows—Fiction. I. Title

PR6066.O394J33    2006
823'.92—dc22      2006048139

07 08 09 10 11   ❖/RRD   10 9 8 7 6 5 4 3 2 1

# LEGAL DISCLAIMER

*Jack's Widow* is a work of fiction. While many of the characters portrayed here have some counterparts in the life and times of Jackie Kennedy Onassis, the characterizations, dates of events, time frame, and incidents presented are totally the products of the author's imagination. Accordingly, *Jack's Widow* should be read solely as a work of fiction, not as a biography of Jackie Kennedy Onassis or as a factual retelling of her, the Kennedy family, the Bouvier family, the Onassis family, or anyone else's story.

FOR

*J.L.T.*

CHAPTER *One*

He had hurt her, betrayed her so many times that she had willed him dead. Often.

Now the November tone of the muffled drum, the black veiling grazing her cheeks, and the mutter of the supple soles of the great and the good marching behind her were proof that her wish had come true.

As the watery Washington sun rubbed its back on the Lincoln Memorial she calmed herself by fastening her gaze on the mane of the riderless horse up ahead.

Her whole life had been a preparation for this moment.

Long before she had become the First Lady she had assumed the qualities of responsibility and reliability.

As the eldest of her mother's four children, Jackie had been programmed. Her basic instincts had always been to lead, to protect. She would not flinch, she would not fail in these last few hours before they laid him to rest in Arlington National Cemetery.

∽ ∞ ∼

Blink.

Everything had changed so fast that it seemed as if all she had done was blink.

Blink.

That bit of shade up ahead, beneath the underpass, would be a welcome relief from the Dallas sun.

Blink.

The air filled with the black noise of bullets and then his flesh and blood spurting, splurging, spilling across her.

Blink.

A last glance at his dear, dead face in the operating room.

Blink.

Kissing his coffin while her two children and her whole nation looked to her for help.

Blink.

Tipped out of the White House and removed from the rituals of state, the men and the manuals of influence.

Blink.

Spirited into a new and unfamiliar home, unable to sleep, unable to cry.

Blink.

If only she didn't have to open her eyes.

Nothing was as it had been.

Even the children seemed different, more excitable, altogether less controlled now that there were so many omissions from the calm order of their previous life, the biggest of these being the absence of their father.

John, the baby—no baby, he's three now, she told herself—had never known anything other than being the president's son, never lived anywhere but the White House. His life would have been in a complete turnaround if it hadn't been for Maud Shaw, the reliable British nanny. During those dark, last days she had carefully gathered up every teddy bear, every toy, every blanket that belonged to her tiny charges and watched over them all until the moment she could unpack them.

Unfortunately she hadn't been allowed to do the same for their mother. Whenever the middle-aged Englishwoman had offered to help she had been rebuffed, very deferentially but very definitely.

Some of Jackie's belongings had followed the sad cavalcade that took them the mile to their new home, but none of the casual clothes that she wore for her daily exercises had yet surfaced. Even her favorite hairbrush was on the missing list.

At first she was too depressed to notice their absence, but as the days turned into weeks she had a growing obsession that these and other familiar objects might be the key to unleashing her emotions. Nothing else seemed to be able to do so.

Whenever she asked where this or that might be, she was fobbed off by the one person that she would have expected to know, her mother.

Janet Norton Lee Bouvier Auchincloss would have liked to tell her grieving daughter the truth about her belongings, but on the night of the assassination she had taken advice from the family physician, who had insisted that for the sake of her daughter's mental health it was imperative that she never lay eyes on the bloodied pink and navy suit again.

Janet also knew that many of the items Jackie was looking for were no longer in the White House.

Even before his coffin had landed at Washington's Andrews Air Force Base, Robert Kennedy, the late president's brother, had arranged for the removal of everything related to him.

Soon Janet realized that, in their zeal, the Kennedys had also gathered up items personal to her daughter. Now they were in cartons in a guarded warehouse especially acquired for their safekeeping.

Janet had been to see them. She wanted to ensure that when the Dallas suit was found it was not sent to the Georgetown house but was dispatched to her own home.

She was assured that her daughter's things would soon emerge, but that it was important that every carton of contents from the presidential home was categorized so that Jack's legacy, everything from his papers to his rocking chair, would be sent to the archivists for the library in Boston that was to be dedicated to his memory.

To Janet the process seemed secretive and lengthy, but ever since they had taken control over her daughter's wedding she knew not to argue with the Kennedy family.

For her daughter Jackie, this new life seemed doubly out of control.

It wasn't just the loss of her husband that made her unhappy, it was the swift change in her position that made her feel that she was doomed to hang on to an existence that resembled a ride on an unstable old steam train rattling along at a feverish pace. In her imagination, a procession of silent, staring strangers insisted on shoveling coal into the furnace that powered the engine. It seemed vital to them that the train must continue to hurl itself along. No allowance was made for her to slow things down.

Part of this rush concerned finding her and her children a new home. The place they lived in now was a gift of diplomacy, lent to them so that they could exit the White House fast. In a few weeks it too would be behind them. Her sister and mother turned up daily with sympathy and real estate information.

Jackie let the two of them push her into an acquisition. Despite the silence from her grieving parents-in-law on Cape Cod, her mother was already working in collusion with them. One telephone call had ensured they would pay for whatever was picked out.

As the moving date drew closer and Jackie showed absolutely no interest in visiting or refurbishing her future home, Janet felt that she had no choice but to tackle the job.

Unable to discuss the house, home furnishings, or any other aspect of her future with her child, Janet decided to reproduce the identical fabrics and colors that Jackie had selected for the private quarters in the White House. She knew that this was a risky strategy. Would reintroducing the designs that her daughter had chosen as the background for family life help or hold up the healing process? Janet had no way of knowing, but she feared that selecting something different that her daughter viewed as tasteless might induce more unhappiness for them all.

Apart from being with Caroline and John, Jackie spent her time reading the newspapers and magazines from every nation that included coverage of her husband's assassination and funeral. As she carefully filed away the best reports in the three languages she understood, English, French, and Spanish, she told herself that she was doing this for the children . . . so that later on they would be able to read how much their father's death had shocked the world. She knew that soon those November days would morph into history. These shrieking headlines showed how it had actually felt. Their immediacy yelled out from every paragraph and picture caption. The scream that had circled the globe.

In truth she was hunting for the words that would move her to tears. A few days later, as the huge cartons, full of their old life as the first family, arrived, she fell on them, hunting for something, anything, that would lead her to the natural mourning she yearned for.

She pounced on the few love notes he had written. He had never been a flowery writer or a romantic one. Even his witticisms were unable to unlock her unshed tears.

Riffling through the mounds of unimportant thank-you notes and putative White House dinner menus she realized that there was much of her past still unaccounted for. As trunk after trunk was disgorged and not a necktie or a cuff link that belonged to him had been delivered, she finally called the White House herself. Upset that their former boss blamed them for the delay, the White House staff advised her to contact the Kennedy family.

In a fury she confronted her mother.

"Why didn't you tell me?" she shouted at the trim fifty-five-year-old Janet Auchincloss. "You know how I feel, you know how desperate I am to find Jack's personal things. You know I've spent night after night looking for things that mean something."

Seeing her daughter angry made Janet defiant. It always did.

Even as a little girl her firstborn had been capable of taking the moral high ground. Their relationship had never been easy.

She interrupted. "On that terrible day, before I could start to come to terms with . . . it—" Janet, in the way of her generation, could never mention death or dying. The word was not allowed past her lips.

She tried again. As always, when she felt her eldest daughter was on her high horse, she was determined not to be bested.

"It was out of my hands. I did what I could. I was advised that we would have to move you out quickly. But even before I could begin to pack, his family let me know that they insisted on doing it all. 'Preserving the legend' was what they called it.

"Anyway, what would you have done with it all? They said that they were keen not to lose any of the papers, the ones that were to go to Boston for the library as we agreed. I just thought that it was for the best." Janet was now speaking to her daughter's swiftly receding back.

The slim widow wasn't waiting to hear the rest. Dressed only in black Capri pants, ballerina flats, and a cream cashmere sweater, she flew out of the house, jumped in the car, and drove off without waiting for the Secret Service detail.

She so rarely went out, and for the past few years she'd never done so on her own.

She looked around at the capital city. The flags were flying for a new president now. She probably imagined it but didn't they look a little different, less buoyant? A little sad and tired?

She noted the Secret Service car had caught up to her. She was not hard to follow since nowadays she always took this route to avoid driving close to the White House. She pulled her sunglasses from the glove compartment and settled down to enjoy the drive out of the city.

Washington in the afternoon had a sunny chill that enhanced the grandeur of the nation's best-known buildings. The Jefferson Memorial and the Washington Monument gleamed.

As she turned into the gravel drive that led up to her brother-in-law's sprawling mansion she reflected that this was another home that had fallen apart. For all its rustic beauty the house looked unkempt. This was not unusual. Her sister-in-law had followed their mother-in-law's example. Loads of children were born in quick succession and the kids basically raised each other. The children turned out to be very close to one another, especially the eldest few who grew up very fast because they became little parents early in life. One or two of them were just starting to be on the wild side of adventurous.

So the sight of two waterlogged sunbathers perching on the steps of the outdoor pool, their matching cushions floating on the pale blue water and a wooden sled left upended on the dipping net of the tennis court was not that unexpected. It was the deflated footballs in the gutters and the silence as she entered the house that were different.

As the back door was on the latch she opened it, shouting "hello" until she got inside. She peered into the kitchen; it was two hours after lunch and the large room was empty. Several dirty plates, cold leftovers, and more than a dozen empty wine and beer bottles were visible.

Jackie began opening doors. No one was in the sitting room or the den. She was edging toward the library when from above she could hear a baby crying and an older child shouting at it to keep quiet.

She went up into the nursery. Here, at least, there was a semblance of order.

The two-year-old sat on a rocking horse, her pink dress the same color as the delicate rosebud wallpaper with its matching curtains. The same fabric surrounded the antique crib in which a six-month-old squealed with hunger.

She and the children's nanny seated themselves on either side of the fireplace. Jackie asked for the baby and the glass bottle and for the first time since the assassination did something that made her feel useful and good. This was so much easier than trying to answer her children's questions.

Under gentle interrogation she discovered that the mess in the kitchen was due to the daily arrival of old pals who had once worked for her husband; they were using the house as a "for-old-times'-sake" club.

On weekends the elder children had taken to spending their days driving around the estate in their father's car. The look in the nanny's eye confirmed her worry; the eldest was only thirteen.

Nanny was too loyal to mention that the children were, like the whole household, somewhat out of control.

Their father, Bobby, sat in his study most of the day with the curtains closed, mourning his brother in the gloom with nothing but a small desk light. He mostly slept there too. His wife, Ethel, seemed only able to rest after lunch. Since the assassination the schedule had been unvaried: extra household staff would arrive in the afternoon when the children were brought back from school. They were essential since the house now needed twenty-four-hour help. They would come in and clear lunch and then prepare supper for the family and the possible twenty extra guests that might, and often did, turn up.

As Jackie walked along the corridor a sign from the nanny made her slip quietly by the master bedroom. Her sister-in-law would be sleeping inside, but Jackie was not going to be deterred from searching for her dead husband's belongings. The White House staff had led her to believe that she would find some of the things that she was looking for in Robert Kennedy's home.

Her brother-in-law, the calm and capable one, was bound to help her.

She continued along the long corridor that followed the line of the house. Outside on the loggia the branches of wisteria, gnarled and bent, framed the picture windows. At the end of the corridor double doors opened onto a huge study.

Gently she tapped on the double doors. There was no answer so she knocked again. The nanny had assured her that this was where Bobby would be.

As there was still no answer she carefully turned the handle. She would leave him a note.

As she entered the darkened room she was shocked to see her husband's leather jacket. It was one of a kind and had the presidential seal tooled on the back.

Her hand went to her mouth as she saw it move. The man wearing it was sitting slumped forward, his head in his hands, a shock of hair falling across his brow.

For a second it could have been him.

As he lifted his head, in a way that so reminded her of what she had lost, she felt tears so plump, so rotund they didn't fall but bounced onto her cheeks, her chin, her neck, and through her fingers as she put them up to catch them.

Bobby stood and they held on to one another.

"For a moment I thought it was Jack." She was clinging more to the jacket than the man, for the feel of it, the smell of it. Jack had worn it so much that it exuded his essence. As she inhaled the scent the horrific reality became believable.

"Oh, Bobby, what will I do, what will I do? I miss him so much. I just can't bear it," she cried. He pulled her close. "I know, I know."

The sound of her crying escalated.

He tried to calm her, took off the jacket and wrapped it round her shoulders.

Like this they stayed together until she had no more tears.

Together they divided his things in a way that brought succor to them both.

CHAPTER  Two

Jackie had always liked N Street. On the day that they were shuttled out of the White House she was grateful that she was returning to familiar territory. The bosky grounds, the neat lawns, the muted gray and blue paint shades on the elegant houses.

They had lived here before moving to Washington's grandest address. Janet had borne this in mind during her house search, especially after Jackie began to tell everyone that her future was going to be "devoted to the children, living in the places Jack and I lived with them."

But even though the new house was just a few yards along the road, the second move, in as many months, did not go well.

There were a few joyful moments when they first arrived. Caroline, thrilled that her bedroom was a replica of the White House nursery, squealed with delight as she opened drawer after drawer filled with her old favorites. John, excited at being reunited with his swing and sandbox, rushed into the garden the moment he spotted them.

There were other familiar bits that resonated with echoes of happier times. Much of the furniture had come from their private quarters in the White House: the comfy linen-covered sofas in pale ivory, the pleated lampshades with salmon pink silk linings that threw a flattering glow.

"I am so pleased you used that color," said Jackie to her mother when she saw that her bedroom had the same pale blue walls and matching fluted drapes she had commissioned at the White House.

As they completed the tour of the house Jackie realized how much care had gone into its preparation.

"Here I've been in my 'misery mist,' while you've gone to so much trouble to make us feel comfortable."

She surprised her mother with a huge hug. "Thank you, thank you so much for everything."

Knowing how much her daughter enjoyed homemaking, Janet left 3017 N Street, NW, feeling satisfied that some sort of corner had been turned.

In a way she was correct. It was early February, so the first Christmas and the first New Year's of her daughter's widowhood had been weathered, but Janet had been misled. Because Jackie, always proud and very private, could not discuss her secret fears with anyone, her mother had no idea that her daughter had barely moved forward in the weeks since Dallas and that in truth the former First Lady wished that they were still in the borrowed home that they had shoehorned themselves into.

For Jackie impermanence had a great advantage: nothing was expected of her. Now she was being forced to proceed. Acceptance and adaptability were, she knew, the stepping-stones to normality, but now that she was forced to take stock, she realized that—as a woman of thirty-plus years, a widow, in a small gossipy one-business town where, through no fault of her own, she had been ejected as a senior member of the ruling elite—she simply didn't fit in.

Another problem was that, for all its prettiness, the new house was completely impractical. It had no driveway, no rolling front lawns, so inevitably, both the Secret Service detail, and anyone who chose to camp out on the pavement just a few feet from the front door were too close.

She suspected that the Secret Service was overcompensating. It was well known that they felt guilty about Jack's death. But to her they were intrusive and seemed judgmental.

Late at night when she played and occasionally even sang along to some of the records of the songs her husband had loved, "Heart of My Heart" or "Won't You Come Home, Bill Bailey?" or Chet Baker's "I Married an Angel," which was the first song that they had danced to at their wedding, she sensed they were close by, listening, wondering what the "mad widder-woman," her own name for her capricious self, was up to.

Ridiculous as it now seemed, she had always felt safe when she was the president's wife. Now without him she was finding it very hard not to feel frightened.

She read all the conspiracy stories about Jack's death. She knew that there were still frequent threats to both her and the children. She felt cornered and the feeling fed her recurring nightmares.

Images that had sieved through her subconscious for years refused to be exorcised.

The most frequent one found her rushing to an assignment carrying a Speed Graphic camera, the cumbersome equipment that she had used when she was single, working as the "Inquiring Camera Girl" for the *Washington Times-Herald*.

She was in a panic because she was late. The job was to cover Jack's second wedding. It was the same every time. She recognized the setting, the rackety Palm Beach Kennedy vacation house, and most of the guests. She also very clearly saw the loving gleam in Jack's eyes as he gazed adoringly at his new bride. She was even able to catch sight of the dress, short ice-blue satin molded around a voluptuous hourglass figure, but unable to get close enough to catch sight of his new wife's face. She always sensed that it was someone she knew.

Other reveries would find her alone in a strange hospital bedroom next to an incubator that was empty except for a tiny plastic nametag labeled "Baby Kennedy," another had her urgently tracking her father down in a crowded bar that he frequented. Before Dallas she was struggling to get through the door against a tide of oncoming congressmen, senators, lobbyists, and other alumni of the political scene. Since November 22 it was smiling Texan policemen that kept her from reaching the barstools and her goal.

The other horror that had been a regular exerciser in her mind gym was the question: Had Jack really loved her or had she been just a useful prop in his political life? It didn't matter now but it was a query that would not go away.

As time passed she barely noticed the first signs of spring, not even when she went riding. She sat in, night after night, now reading anything, in any publication, about Jack's career and their life in the White House.

Old friends came around. They tried their best but in most cases the relationship was not strong enough to accommodate them. Either their friendship was too fragile to cope with losing one of their number or perhaps they had just been Jack's friends.

Maybe, she mused, they would have been pals with any president.

How much did she have in common with them? So little.

She disliked the thought that she missed the White House, but deep down she did. Not the endless political gossip—the insider chat in Washington, D.C., had always been too mean for her taste— but she had relished her role as the president's wife, being useful, being a helpmate. An avid reader she often delighted Jack with nuggets of fascinating, little-known facts.

During his three and three-quarter years in the job she had enjoyed making discoveries that occasionally led him to new thoughts and ideas that could alter his dreams, his plans.

It was a letter from President Johnson that forced her to think of the future. She was galvanized by his suggestion that she should be the next U.S. ambassador to France or Mexico.

Even though she knew that it would probably be wrong to both uproot the children and to upset her brother-in-law Bobby, who hated his brother's successor, the job offers aroused her interest.

"How would you like it if we moved to Paris?" she asked her mother.

As the paint on the walls of the new house was barely dry Janet almost spluttered in shock.

"Paris, where did that idea come from?"

After Jackie explained Janet took a good look at her daughter, sitting on the floor, minus the bouffant hairdo, the high heels, and the perfectly maintained perfection of yesteryear. Jackie had lost weight, they all had, but the former First Lady had lost most. With her wide shoulders, long waist, and slim hips her current appearance was that of a two-dimensional wraith. Janet, already worrying about her daughter's finances, wondered how her eldest would react when she finally resumed normal life and found that none of her perfect wardrobe still fit.

"I don't suppose it pays very well," was all she could manage.

Janet understood enough about their relationship to be careful not to dismiss the idea outright. She would do nothing to make her daughter go abroad for the wrong reason.

"No, but all, well most, of your expenses as an ambassador are paid for," breathed her daughter in reply.

"And, I might make a difference, you know, properly, like Jack."

Janet tried hard not to raise her eyes to the ceiling.

"But you've always been uncertain about politics, disliked them, if we are going to be honest about it," she said. "Remember how you didn't like it when Jack had to say one thing and then do another? You hated it. So how do you think you could handle doing it yourself?"

Even Janet could sense that her voice had risen to a querulous timbre.

Speedily she added, "Not that they don't love you over there and would probably agree with absolutely everything that you suggested."

She could see her daughter was not deterred.

"After everything, I imagine that I could handle that now," she muttered.

"Anyway, anything would be better than being wheeled out as

the Democrats' totem pole for the next fifty years! Just think about it, the children are at the perfect age, it would be so easy for them to become bilingual. On weekends we could travel around Europe and there really is so much I could do workwise."

For the first time since November her daughter was sounding enthusiastic, but still Janet felt apprehensive.

Maybe she was against this idea for selfish reasons. She, of all people, should understand Jackie's need to feel useful. After all, wasn't she herself secretly reveling in it? She had never seen so much of her grandchildren, and having to take care of her daughter again had revived a maternal role that she found very satisfying.

"Of course, there could be problems. If I do well, Lyndon looks good, and if I screw up, well, there goes the neighborhood." Jackie smiled slightly. "Either way the Kennedys, especially Bobby, would hate it."

Sunlight flooded Janet's mind.

She didn't want to lose her daughter, but she realized that she wouldn't have to be the one to keep her at home. She said nothing as she watched Jackie go into the study, select a leather-bound atlas from the shelf, and tuck it under her arm as she readied herself to disappear for her afternoon nap.

On her way out, after she had kissed the children goodbye, Janet allowed herself a short explosive snort.

Bloody Lyndon. Why didn't he keep his nose out of their affairs?


The new president followed up his note with a telephone call. "I don't want to rush you but I'm serious about you doing either of these jobs," he drawled. Jackie recognized that his offer was more than just a kind gesture. Simply pondering how she might tackle either of them was therapeutic. She started to make lists, and as she did so she realized that despite the foreign holidays, her riding, and her shopping expeditions, she had worked hard as First Lady. Whether it was arranging the seating plan for the state dinner for

the president of the Republic of the Ivory Coast or the reorganiza-
tion of the White House garden, she prided herself that she'd had
a hand in everything from the canapés to the canopies at Mount
Vernon.

She had been a tireless, if courteous, fighter for detail. Planning,
organization, and absorption with the fine print of life had always
underpinned her entire existence.

Despite being involved with the setting up of the library in Boston in her husband's name, she recognized that she had much too
little to do and too much time to think.

Even though she eventually declined the two ambassadorships,
she was grateful to her husband's successor because the idea that she
could be of real use, that she was still in a unique position to play a
special role, that she could make a difference, caught her imagination.

It reminded her of the last man who had discovered that her
abilities were exceptional.

Maybe he would be able to find something for her to do. That
night she wrote a short letter enclosing her change-of-address card.

It went, by diplomatic pouch, straight to Moscow.

CHAPTER

Red Square has never looked more beautiful, he thought.

Guy nudged the black turtleneck sweater higher up toward his chin with long, capable fingers embedded in fur-lined gloves. As ever, the glimpse of the Kremlin's skyline lifted his spirits. Even the icy wind left a tinny taste on his lips that he savored.

Do I like it here because it is the most interesting place I have ever lived or is it the work that excites me? he wondered.

It was quiet in the Russian capital this Saturday morning; the few babushkas on the street walked silently, the limp sun had the consistency of a thrice-used tea bag, and even the snow was falling softly.

Remembering his military training, he drew himself up, threw back his shoulders, and breathed in deeply. Although he was accustomed to wearing clothes that would blend in with the Moscow street, everything in Soviet-style drab colors of possum and raccoon, he was already freezing despite the warm interlinings that had been sewn into his coat.

His plans had enabled him to get out of the house without an argument. His wife suspected that since their five-year-old had begun piano lessons on Saturday mornings there was little to keep him at home. He explained that work called and he could not disappoint his oldest contact.

Sergei always asked him in his fractured English, "Please, Guy, the weekends are zo, zo much easier for me. I don't have to go into my office or to any news conferences. Free press," he would say, "no news allowed to happen on Saturday or Sunday! We can meet at my zister's place, I go there for lunch every weekend. Don't vorry, it is my usual pattern," he had said, time and time again.

It was the only part of spycraft that the younger man had managed to teach the fifty-six-year-old.

Within minutes Guy's long strides had taken him to the office. He would have just enough time to read the overnight memos.

After half an hour he had more or less finished. There was nothing special.

About to leave for his rendezvous, he was given an urgent message to go upstairs to collect a special delivery. His heart raced. Anything that was delivered to the office must be serious, must mean trouble.

The message was intriguing, one that he would share with his boss when he came to work on Monday morning.


He thought about the first time he had met her. It was on a day as cold as this, in the decaying grandeur of Prague in 1957.

It was Jackie's first official foreign visit. She was accompanying her husband, Jack, then a senator for Massachusetts, who for the first time had been included in the bipartisan delegation attending the conference of the nuclear club. Four years before, despite deep distrust between the Americans and the British on one side and the Soviets on the other, the three nations had realized that they did have one thing in common: ownership of the atomic bomb. Their shared problem was stopping the spread of nuclear weapons across the world.

In 1953, U.S. President Dwight D. Eisenhower had received a standing ovation at the United Nations when he suggested that some of the stockpiles of these weapons should be given to the world's scientists to discover a dual use for the technology. At a time when the Iron Curtain was callously billowing across Europe, the delegates were amazed to see that even the Russians were applauding. Thus the Atoms for Peace nonproliferation program was born—but it got off to a faltering start. During the first few years the only achievement in the search for ways to harness nuclear energy for peaceful purposes was the decision to hold a small, low-key meeting every year that would include politicians, the world's top scientists, and other experts.

Geneva was chosen as the first place to meet.

It did not go badly and as protocol demanded that the three nations could take turns to decide the venue for the next meeting, in 1955 the British chose London. When Winston Churchill, who had always believed that as few countries as possible should have the ultimate deterrent, was invited to one of their dinners, grown men felt lumps in their throat at his oratory.

As the months went by the Russians suspected that the British and Americans were maintaining their spheres of influence by helping allies like France to acquire the bomb. The United States and the United Kingdom were equally skeptical about the Russians' intentions.

Assuming that the Russians would follow the British example and choose their capital as the next venue, both MI6 and the CIA begged their governments to kiss and make up. Throughout the long reign of Joseph Stalin, the Russian capital had been virtually impregnable to most Westerners.

The mistrustful Russians were well aware that the West was curious about Moscow and had decided to thwart these ambitions by nominating Budapest. The Soviets explained that the Hungarian capital already had the reputation as the most glamorous city behind the Iron Curtain. Unfortunately for them, by the late summer of 1956 this sophistication took the form of a longing for neutrality and democracy. As the meeting got closer the Soviets, sensing that the Hungarians might just be mad enough to rise up against them, hastily canceled it.

The Atoms for Peace meetings might have come to a complete end, but in November the Suez debacle opened all their eyes to the risk of a Middle Eastern despot gaining control of a nuclear weapon, so the three reconvened in the spring of 1957. This time the Kremlin chose Prague.

Installed in the Czech capital's oldest hotel, Jackie was excited if a little worried about her health. Just a week before the trip she had found out that she was once again pregnant.

Less than a year earlier she had given birth to a stillborn daughter, Arabella. Before this she had miscarried with their first child. She was desperate that this time nothing must go wrong.

She was going to take extra care.

So on the third day of the conference she begged off from that afternoon's arrangements for the delegates' wives. In the morning they had seen how the famous glass of Bohemia was created, but her assigned vehicle included a talkative interpreter from Minsk and three enthralled Mamie Eisenhower types. The hour-long trip had made her feel nauseous.

She didn't want to tell her husband that she was feeling unwell as he would be bound to suggest that she return home early, something she was unwilling to do. She loved being with him in these circumstances; even though they were a part of a group she felt there was a coziness, a special intimacy between them.

Perhaps if she had discovered a kindred spirit among the other women she might have been less secretive, but she was by far the youngest and the most traveled of them all. She had visited Europe regularly since she was a teenager. Some of the crass or naive comments from the others in the group told her that they had little in common.

All she needed was a little rest. But when she went up to her room after lunch the sheets were so cold they felt almost damp. She remembered that the radiators would not warm up until after five.

She decided to take advantage of the large open fires in the reception rooms downstairs. This was obviously why Czech café society spent the day keeping the grand salons of the hotel busy with cake, coffee, and conspiracy.

She swiftly changed into an ice-blue cashmere twin set that had been dyed to match her moleskin trousers. Slipping into navy moccasins, she grabbed a new novel and descended to the ground floor.

To avoid meeting any of their traveling companions, she searched for a deep armchair that was tucked away. She found one in a niche behind a tall column where she could sit unobserved. She ordered a large pot of tea and settled down to her book, which turned out to be so dull she spent much of her time gazing into the high mirror ahead of her that reflected the comings and goings of the room. She watched as one glamorous couple, obviously not married, interspersed sips of their large vodkas with much mutual finger-stroking, when her attention was caught by the entrance of two women who, she was sure, were with some Russian scientists attending the conference. Having swept in and noisily arranged themselves, they quickly looked around and, confident that there were no Westerners in the room, began a dialogue in heavily Russian-accented Spanish.

Carefully, using the mirror, Jackie analyzed their clothes, hairstyles, and makeup. Not only did they look far more sophisticated than most females in this part of the world, their husbands were obviously quite senior as they had been wealthy enough to pay for good-quality furs and leather. Their schoolgirl use of the foreign language had obviously been newly acquired from a textbook. So not only had they been well educated, and recently so, they had absorbed the lessons of self-preservation. They knew that it was wise to be careful about where and when they spoke not only their mother tongue but also French, the second language chosen by the majority of those in their empire. A hotel like this was sure to be full of many who had the facility for both languages and would be very interested in anything they had to say.

But they were so sure that no one in the room would understand a word of what they said in Spanish, they spoke loudly and freely.

Jackie, confident that she was situated where she would not be seen by them, stopped being nervous. Even if they did glimpse round her corner she was quite certain that they would never expect an American senator's wife to be able to understand their every word. It was hard not to eavesdrop.

After being served tea, cake, and schnapps, the women launched into a discussion about this morning's visit. Grateful though she seemed for her free gift, one of the women sought the other's advice on whether she thought it more practical to send the sixty-piece Bohemian glass set directly to the next place that they "would call home, rather than drag it back to Moscow."

Conversation about their new billets, a long and detailed one, was so shocking to Jackie that she remained in her hidden chair for a full fifteen minutes after they left to make sure that they did not see her.

Jackie was no politician but even she realized that what she had heard was alarming. Some of the Russian scientists were going off to live in China one week after this conference. Could they have done a deal to share their nuclear-power know-how with the Chinese?

It was vital that her countrymen hear about this. Cool and calm as ever, she knew she must do nothing out of character. There were watchers from the Czech Secret Service everywhere in the hotel, stationed on every floor. After she reached her room she bathed, put on her cocktail dress, and firmed up a plan for Jack's return.

As soon as her husband entered the room she put her finger on his lips before he had a chance to exclaim how extraordinary it was that she was ready for dinner.

Gently she held his hand and pulled him into the bathroom, all the time smiling at him and touching his lips so that he would not speak. Only once the bath taps were spitting out a Niagara of hot water did she begin.

"You may not have noticed two of the younger Russian wives, the tall blond one and the redhead."

He had.

She explained how she had spent the afternoon.

"Jack, I heard them distinctly, next month they and their husbands are off to live near Peking."

His shocked expression was enough for her to recount every word she had heard.

"Would you be willing to repeat this?" He made to move toward the phone, then smiling and nodding, acknowledging that she had quite correctly assumed that the room would be bugged, he laughingly commented that for once he would have just a two-minute bath as he was longing for a scotch, and wouldn't it be great if they could be the first ones down for cocktails.

Standing at the bar in the ballroom, Jackie and Jack appeared to be doing nothing more than enjoying their drinks. The moment that Jackie touched his hand to signal that one of the women she had seen that afternoon had come through the door on the arm of a Russian physicist, Jack gently wheeled them both around the room to join the most senior nuclear expert on the American team. She smiled at the pair while her husband pretended to be whispering a slightly off-color joke to him. As Jack was dispensing Jackie's information, carefully indicating the woman and her spouse, the change of expression on the nuclear expert's face confirmed she had not wasted her time. Seconds later she glimpsed the American scientist sidling out through the large mirrored doors of the hotel ballroom. As they sat down for dinner, some twenty minutes later, he reappeared and slid into his seat on the right of the British Foreign Secretary's wife.

As soon as the meal was over, but before coffee and *digestifs* were served, Jackie was surprised when the tall blond press attaché from the American embassy whom they had met on their first evening came over and reintroduced himself as Guy Steavenson. Within moments he had asked if the senator would object if, even though the night was very cold, he could escort his wife out onto the balcony to show her the view of the Charles Bridge.

Without waiting for her to exclaim about the Gothic towers of stone at each end, Guy explained, in a low voice, that he handled more than press at the American embassy.

"Not wanting to be melodramatic, I wonder if it would be too boring for you if you told me absolutely everything you heard this afternoon?"

She looked up at him. He had a kind but strong face, twinkling eyes divided between white and cerulean blue, lips that seemed more comfortable curved in an upward direction rather than the reverse, and both his pale blond hair and dinner jacket stood out— they had been expertly cut.

Swathed in her mink stole, she recounted everything while pretending to look at the stars.

When she finished he thanked her and asked if she would be prepared to help again.

Still simulating entrancement with what she was seeing, rather than what she was hearing, she nodded.

Staring deeply at her, he said, "If I were to rig things so that you could spend tomorrow together with them, could you cope? I've looked at the schedule, it's a shoe factory in the morning and a children's drama school in the afternoon."

"Try and stop me," she said, laughing.

His eyes are quite hypnotic, she thought.

She did spend the next day as close as possible to the two women. This time they divulged nothing.

That evening, fearing her enthusiasm for the day's work barely masked her exhaustion, the senator, over cocktails, quietly told Guy Steavenson that Jackie was pregnant.

"We've lost two babies. I know that this is important but you have got to let her off the hook now. Tomorrow she needs to rest."

After dinner that night Guy lied impeccably when she playfully accosted him and whispered that she was standing by for her orders.

"Mrs. Kennedy, you have been wonderful. You really don't need to follow these women any longer. We know everything we need to know. What you have done has been above and beyond what we could have expected."

"I've done nothing really."

"Well, you've proved how we linguists will rule the world eventually." He smiled.

"Don't you want to know how many of them are going?"

"The truth is," he lied, "we have discovered that they have called off going on tomorrow's trip. So I am afraid that we have no way of putting you together with them."

She looked at him, the question in her eyes doing all the talking.

Shrugging his shoulders, he moved toward the samovar for some more tea. She followed, having decided on defiance.

It had not occurred to her that her husband had warned him off.

"Well, I am not giving up. Maybe they'll return to their old afternoon haunts. It's worth a try."

There was, he was relieved to think, no way that he could order her not to watch out for the women from the comfort of the grand salon.

She did not see them again until they were all checking in at the airport. They were in the Aeroflot line. Jackie, noting that they and three other couples seemed to have much less luggage than the rest of them, tried to lip-read to see if she could discover any more, but when they were with their husbands they reverted to Russian.

She wondered if Guy could speak Russian. He had told her just a little about his upbringing. How he was good at languages because his grandfather, his only family after his parents had died in a car crash, had sent him off to boarding school when he was thirteen, fearing that his uncontrollable grandson was going to end up in jail.

She would have liked to have told him about the other couples who were also traveling light, but Jack told her to leave that to him. He had decided that they should take no more chances with this baby. "From now on you are to put your feet up. I promise I'll spend more time with you in New York, where you'll be just a few blocks away from the best obstetrician in the country."

As the Cold War iced up and rumors that the French were close to having nuclear capability, the Americans became more determined to push on with the Atoms for Peace agenda.

They called the next nuclear club conference in 1958.

Once again the venue was neutral Switzerland and the senator for Massachusetts was included among the political invitees.

Now that he was seriously thinking of running for president in 1960, he thought it was worth impressing the inhabitants of the smoke-filled rooms of power that though he might be young, he was already involved in foreign policy. No matter that these talks were low-key and not publicized; these influential men would know of their existence and their importance.

Meanwhile America was convinced that to increase their influence the Soviets were selling arms and giving atomic secrets to third world countries.

The CIA was sent in to do what they could to bug and wiretap the Russians' hotel rooms and villas.

Having taken these precautions, the Yanks sat back and waited.

Now, surely they would find out what the Communists were up to. When nothing resulted from their electronic handiwork except discussions about the weather or which shop did the best deals on watches, they were unprepared. It was almost as if the Soviet delegation knew they were there.

In desperation, the day before the conference began they called Prague for help.

Jackie knew nothing of this as she came off the boat from the first of the wives' excursions.

Already she was not enjoying this trip as much as the last. Not only was she missing her baby daughter, but her husband had changed. To get over jet lag, they had, like many of the delegates, arrived forty-eight hours early.

"Do you remember that little café we went to in Prague? In the Art Deco district? I've seen a charming place, not exactly the same of course, but at least not covered in cuckoo clocks, for us to have lunch," she eagerly told him the first morning.

"Jackie." He barely looked up from his background notes. "I'd love to, but there are people here that I never get a chance to talk to at home. My father has fixed up one or two meetings, as well. I'm sorry, but we'll have some time together when we get back."

"I am not sure the presidency is worth it," she muttered but stopped when she saw his disappointed face. "I mean, look at this." She picked up a cerise shantung pillbox hat and perched it on her head.

"Jackie, you look good in it. You look great in anything. We promised, from now on we would both wear hats, try to appear more serious and more mature to the voters," he said, lowering his voice in a theatrical way.

"Why don't you do what I do, just carry it."

"You don't have a handbag to cart around, as well," she said, thinking how this election was changing everything.

Even with an internal band of elastic her headgear would not stay put. The next day, knowing she was going out on the lake, she had tried to skewer it to her hair with several hair grips but it had started to slip. When they came in for lunch she was glad to take it off and leave it on a high wooden shelf in an empty conference room on the ground floor.

She didn't see Guy Steavenson arrive, and would not have recognized him anyway in his disguise as a stooped figure with gray hair and heavy tortoiseshell glasses in an ill-fitting suit who spent the afternoon pretending to be delivering important papers and interpreter equipment around the atrium entrance hall. He watched everything and noted that each time the Russians emerged from their conference room, Jackie's hat on the shelf remained untouched. He continued his vigilance until Jackie remembered to pick it up at the end of the day.

The next morning there was real animosity between the delegations. Constructive talks seemed impossible.

Just before lunch when the small bus that had taken the delegates' wives to a china factory drew up outside the conference center, Jackie was delighted to bump into Guy again.

She wore a simple scarlet wool suit, matching hat in hand. The wind blowing off the lake lifted her hair. He thought that mother-hood had made her even *more* beautiful.

She wondered why he was looking so pale with such dark circles under his eyes but when he suggested that she take him to a small boutique, just around the corner, to buy a layette for his best friend who was a brand-new father, she thought this explained it.

He was glad that the agency had sent for him on the off chance that he could be helpful. He hoped that his good contacts in Swit-zerland (his first posting for the CIA had been in Basel), added to the relationships that had been forged during the two earlier Atoms for Peace conferences, would prove useful.

He had been briefed on the failure of the bugs to gather any in-telligence. His first order was to send an undercover expert out to check on the equipment in one of the villas. It had not been tam-pered with. It was still in place. The only conclusion was that no one had spoken of anything significant in that room.

He had been up nearly all night talking to the other agency members about where and how they had been stymied. They had come to no conclusions. At four A.M. he had finally gone to bed, only to remember that before he could go to sleep he had to remove the gray from his hair. He was drained.

Jackie took a good look at him as they stepped across the tram-lines.

She wondered what his life in Prague was like. As he guided her toward an expensive baby boutique she wondered what was going on, realizing that she knew absolutely nothing about him.

After the preliminaries he had launched straight in.

"We did good work in Prague. Did your husband tell you? The other three that you described, the ones at the airport, they were really important. We soon nipped their traveling plans in the bud." He grinned. "With a tip-off here and an anonymous note there we ensured that their bosses questioned their loyalty."

She felt a moment's dismay. Why hadn't Jack told her?

"Because of their skills they are working inside Russia or at the

Siberian testing stations. I guess less clever scientists are advising the Chinese.

"See how helpful you were? Now I'd like your assistance again. Would you help us if I promise that I'll make sure your husband is informed?"

"Of course"—she grinned—"I'm a loyal American citizen. How can I refuse?" she said.

"Before we leave I want you to buy something and put it in a carrier bag with your hat. Then come and join me in a close examination of those big teddy bears at the back of the shop. There, while we're talking about which one has the most squishiness or will be easiest to get on the plane, we'll swap bags. Okay so far?"

She nodded.

"But I'll need the hat back," she said with a glint.

"I promise," he said, smiling.

"After lunch I will leave the bag at the interpreter's reception desk in the conference hall," he continued. "You probably haven't even noticed it, it's just a table covered in dark gray fabric, with lists and badges on it. Because of security it is always manned. Two lovely girls do it, Irene and Marie-Louise. Simply say you are really worried, that you left the bag somewhere on the ground floor, you have tried the ladies' room but you think you may have put it on the desk when taking your coat off, prior to going into lunch. Push it, make them look under the table, start looking yourself if need be. But rest assured, it will be there.

"You pick it up, take it to the ladies' room, haul the hat out, and in front of the mirror you spend a few moments trying your darnedest to get it on right. There will be other women in there and ideally you will have witnesses. In a perfect world, one of them will be a Russian.

"You fail, mostly because you are in a hurry as you really don't want to risk missing the bus that will transport you and the other ladies to the watch factory, someplace I guess you wouldn't want to miss under any circumstances." He smiled.

"For speed, you simply give up and leave the hat in exactly the same place you did yesterday."

He stopped, letting it all sink in.

"Can you do that?"

Over lunch she thought about him. She'd only met him once before but again he had instilled a sense of adventure into her life.

While the usual three-course lunch was served two CIA officers somehow managed to sew a tiny microphone into the lining of the crown of her hat. Her husband was told of the plan by the courtly American ambassador to Switzerland who had insisted on dragging him out to the frost-covered garden. If the Russians were so aware, who knew what they had bugged!

The diplomat was so busy trying to impress someone who might one day be his boss that Jack had no time to warn her off the whole thing.

She carried out the charade with the hat and eventually it was placed in exactly the same spot as before. This time, when the Russians went into private talks every single word could be heard by the American listeners in a room at the rear of the conference center.

At last the Americans understood. The Russians were waiting for the right moment to stage a walkout denouncing the West. They hoped this would deflect any criticism about their aid to China and with the UN in session act as a smokescreen for their own activities.

The Americans decided that the best way to stop this plan was to fold the talks immediately.

A few weeks later Guy sent her a pale pink smocked dress in Caroline's size that almost replicated the romper suit they had chosen together.

When she became First Lady he was encouraged by his immediate boss to keep in touch.

When he made his twice-yearly visits home on leave Guy would bring her the latest European gossip. They talked about their childhoods. She found it easy to be honest with him about how she felt about her mother and her late father, and he told her how he'd got into the CIA, about how he remembered so little about his parents, and how his grandfather, a wealthy Bostonian with a great deal of old money, had packed him off to a strict school that had a strong military slant.

"It seems cold and callous but he was only doing his best. As a hardworking widower with no free time, he was sure I would go off the rails without it," Guy said.

"Now, when he waves me off to another posting in a foreign embassy I think he regrets it."

Jackie always looked forward to seeing him. Witty, with a store of stories about the Russians, Guy always made sure that he told her how useful she had been, a lesson her husband only learned toward the end of his life.

As it was the first time Guy had seen her since the assassination, he expressed his sympathy and sorrow. Then, breathing on his cupped hands, he said, "It's about as cold as a Siberian winter out there today. Does this mean there are always people waiting outside?"

"Yes, always," she said, sighing.

Now that she was alone it seemed only natural that she should tell him about the problems she was having with security. With his background he would be in a good position to understand.

"They wait at all hours and as the Secret Service can't be sure that one of them isn't a madman we have extra men on guard. The whole thing escalates from there. Since these extra guys are all visible, passersby see them and think, Hey, something's going on, and so it mushrooms. The three of us have started to hate going out. You should come at the weekend!"

To illustrate these difficulties she couldn't resist leaning out of the window.

Immediately a Secret Service man looked up from the garden.

Pretty soon, like naughty children, they couldn't stop taking turns to look out of several ground-floor windows to the resultant semisilent panic of various Secret Service agents.

Bad behavior or not, they got the giggles.

Amazed that she could still laugh, she wanted to do it all over again.

Something in her demeanor made Guy want to indulge her.

He expected her to be low but from the moment he arrived he thought the house seemed to be crushing her, that the somber shadows of the place appeared to add more misery to the mood of the former First Lady.

Innocents caught up in horror and outrage often took years to cleanse themselves of fear and shock. How could she forget the moments when she had held the innards of the man she had loved, had seen the instantaneous removal of all of his dignity, let alone his life?

Guy's training had included a great deal of information about the psychological effect of such a bloody baptismal.

But the heavy drapes and the comings and goings of too many Secret Service staff, all knowing her family's routine, their moments of anguish or joy, seemed to him to be an extra punishment.

As they talked, he realized that for her there were no-go areas in her own home. She didn't stir toward the kitchen for their coffees or for her beloved Newport cigarettes. She relied on staff. He could see this irked her. He knew that in the White House, while she disliked being under a magnifying glass, there was enough space to be unaware of the minders.

He could see that she was a person who had used up all her strength and fire on the nation's behalf. A woman who was now quite capable of being drowned in Secret Service guilt.

It wasn't right.

It wasn't fair.

"Jackie, I know it is easy for me to say but the last thing you should be worried about now are threats.

"Think of it this way, the worst that could possibly be done has been done."

"No, you're wrong," she said harshly, her face creased into a rare tightness. "You are so wrong. So wrong," she repeated.

"Please don't believe in all the stories, like everyone else. Because I don't go out everyone thinks I can't cope with not being First Lady. Not having protocol and pomp and 'Hail to the Chief.' Of course I miss my husband, I'm sad that he could not fulfill his dreams, go on being in the White House, see the children grow up, but there are worse things: they could hurt my children."

"Then you have three choices, stay here with the understanding that these guys are just trying to do their job. They know they mustn't screw up again, but there just isn't the room here for them to operate without your being aware of them breathing down your neck.

"Or move to a larger house, long drive, bigger grounds, less chance of any nutcase being able to join in with the tourists just a few feet away from your front door.

"Or go far away. You love Europe, you speak French and Spanish."

There was a momentary lull while they both stopped to think.

"But then," he continued, "Europe is a problem. The local police will want to help . . . and . . . different countries will have their agenda and maybe try and use you." He raised his hands in despair.

"Not to say they couldn't guard you well."

There was a small silence in the room as they heard yet another tourist bus, with its attendant loudspeaker, drift slowly by.

"No, I don't think I should leave America. There's the children's education and my mother, and the Kennedys." She grimaced in a friendly way.

"Okay, then there is L.A. Big houses, big security are quite common there."

"But"—she smiled—"who would I talk to?"

"Which leaves just one place." He stopped as he stood in front of a piece of modern art that he didn't recognize.

"New York," they said in unison.

"Think of it, you have all the security you have here and more, but it is thirty flights down. You have a driver and a specially adjusted car, faster, yet heavier, safer. You and the children establish a routine, school runs and so on, and everyone guards that bit of your life with no problem. NYPD, and the FBI, everyone gets together. You are less observed. Your apartment block is your fortress. I know these Secret Service guys drive you crazy, and if it is any consolation we have irritated the hell out of them today, but to be honest if I was advising them I wouldn't know what else I would suggest they do."

They talked into the evening, discussing her alternatives. She gave him a kiss on the cheek before he left.


She spent time with her brother-in-law, too much time according to the gossips. She went to as many family Sunday lunches as she could face at Hickory Hill to dampen the stories and to give the children the chance of playing with their cousins.

But it made her feel more isolated than ever. When she married she had entered this gene pool, drunk from it, swum in it, but she could never understand the noisiness and the hearty drinking and eating that went with it. It was not her style.

Guy's suggestion stayed with her when she went to Hickory Hill again the following Sunday and tried to relax in their company. Here everything in life was speedily reduced to a joke. The black humor was fast and ferocious.

It may have been their Irish roots; when things got so bad the only way they could face life was with a laugh and a song. She had certainly enjoyed some of this when Jack was doing the joking and the singing. But their sentimental reminiscences about him, already incorrectly retouched and retold, were too much for her.

Irish eyes may have been smiling but a thousand cuts were slashing at her heart.

To be herself, whoever that was nowadays, she would need to escape.

Within a few weeks she had settled for a home high above the reservoir in New York's Central Park and this time she chose it, and every item in it, for herself.

## CHAPTER Four

Over the years she had come to accept that everything she wore became the subject of comment.

At the beginning she was irritated when stories about her appearance, especially the fortune she was spending on it, were used to score cheap political points. Once she was under real scrutiny in the White House, the fact that absolutely no one had ever suspected how she felt about her looks, that they had never even come close, gave her extraordinary satisfaction.

Because the truth was not pretty.

The myriad contents of the many paper bags from stores like Bonwit Teller, Bergdorf Goodman, Lord & Taylor, plus the monogrammed dress bags and hat boxes from designers such as Oleg Cassini, Halston, and Givenchy, signaled her ambivalence about her image.

This had begun long before she enlisted in a vote-hunting team.

What none of the Jackie watchers had ever realized was that even as a teenager she had given everything that she wore the level of attention that a warrior might use when selecting his armor. All of it—the gloves, the hats, the dresses, the coats, the suits, the necklaces, earrings and brooches—had a role to play, a protective one. They were to be her mask, a fake front, a façade that she could hide behind. It all began where most of our fears are born, at home.

As they disagreed on everything else, her parents had very differing and outspoken views on their firstborn.

Her mother, knowing that her two Bouvier children, though raised in luxurious circumstances, would be poor, inheriting virtually nothing from their father and absolutely nothing from their wealthy stepfather, was desperate for her daughters to marry well, and so repeatedly told Jackie, "Work on your brains and charm, they will win you the right sort of husband." Janet thought that others in the family were far more attractive, while her father insisted, "Jackie, you have the eyes and mouth of an angel, a slightly naughty one. They will drive men wild."

If this wasn't enough to cause their eldest to feel confusion about her appearance, their scandalous divorce made young Jackie a target for gossip that completely undermined her self-esteem.

From her earliest years she had been witness to her parents' constant quarreling. For a while the fights were private, but once they slipped into the public eye—when Janet finally decided that she had had enough of her husband's gambling, his lack of business prowess, and his many infidelities—Jackie was a marked girl.

Divorce at the time, especially among the members of the exclusive Social Register, was such a rare occurrence that after her parents had separated they felt they could not divorce without an attempt at a reunion. Unfortunately this lasted only six months. The marriage was over. Jackie was eight.

Her introduction to unwelcome press attention was a photograph of the entire family that accompanied not just the news of the divorce but an article that included details of the tanned, handsome "Black Jack" Bouvier's adultery.

In 1940 a sex scandal marked Jackie out as in some way different. Jackie never totally recovered from the embarrassment of hearing classmates, frequently joined by their ill-bred parents, talking about her behind her back. Childhood celebrations such as birthday parties, which should have been fun, became a nightmare as they merely produced new people who would stare at her.

Soon it was generally accepted that she was a loner. She was polite, would always join her family for meals, but her chosen hobbies, reading and riding, were solitary ones. She didn't engage in team sports so learning filled the empty hours. She became an A student.

Shielding herself became natural to her. She had friends, but she never got too close. How could she invite girls home when she didn't have a normal family but a house filled with stepfathers, stepbrothers, stepsisters, and eventually half brothers and half sisters? Her confidants were her sister and her eldest half brother, known as Yusha.

She became a defensive young lady.

Her father rather admired her aloofness, but her mother didn't understand her unwillingness to join in with her peers. Because she loved them both she could never bring herself to tell them that her behavior was their fault. She even felt guilty for being angry with them, especially her mother.

Once she was old enough to understand about sex and adultery these sensitivities heightened.

Her fascination with all things French fed her initial yearnings to be well dressed. She longed to clothe her tall, lean figure in elegant but chic simplicity but it was hard to achieve at a time when postwar fashion was teased into terminal cuteness.

By the time Jackie was deemed to be of "young lady" status World War II had just ended. She was locked away in Connecticut for half the year at a girls' boarding school and the vogue was for tiny, blond movie stars with pert breasts like June Allyson. Fashion meant frocks with a fully packed bodice, cinched into a tiny waist atop a circular skirt with its accompanying flurry of swirling petticoats.

Nothing could be further from the simple silhouette that she sought.

She could have turned to her mother for advice, but as so often happens, forced to be a spectator at the continuing fights between Jack Bouvier and his ex-wife, her sympathy flowed toward the absent parent.

In her late teens, though she was not interested in boys, her father's regular admonitions to "be a mystery to men," had been highly successful. She knew that she would be the subject of even more unwelcome snickering if she held herself apart from this new world of flirting and teasing.

As a fairly unsociable being, she didn't know where to start. At the time it was accepted that teenagers met one another under parental supervision, but even when she had the opportunity she was still far too hesitant, concentrating more on avoiding doing anything spontaneous that might send out a signal for pity from her peers, or even worse, allow them to look down on her. Reticence held her back for months until success occurred, quite by accident.

As soon as Jackie could walk she was sat on a horse. From early childhood her weekends were spent riding. She was so keen that she persuaded her grandfather to pay for her favorite mount, Danseuse, to be stabled near her school during term time. Like her mother, she had been winning rosettes since she was tiny. Competing in equestrian events was second nature to her.

At sixteen she was entered in the local Connecticut gymkhana in the dressage event. She enjoyed the competition, which was based on guiding a horse through a series of complex movements by the subtle shift of her hands, legs, and weight.

After dismounting she was surprised to see that, for the first time, many of her classmates and girls in the senior grades were among the crowd.

As an outsider she had not realized that the more precocious of her fellow students had discovered that sporting events like this were the perfect occasion to meet boys from the local schools and colleges, as they were sanctioned by both parents and the headmistress.

As she moved through the crowd she was aware of attracting male attention in a way that had never happened to her before. She wore the formal uniform of dressage. A severe habit of a tight jacket in black velvet, a pairing of fabric and color then regarded as highly sophisticated for such a young girl. Beneath was a white shirt in thin silk with a matching stock, the long slim scarf traditionally worn wrapped tight around her throat, knotted at the collarbone beneath it. The event over, with her jacket open, the scarf hung between her breasts. Taut jodhpurs with high riding boots and gloves completed the outfit. After the exertions of the ride her eyes shone and her skin glowed. She removed her riding hat and released her gleaming brown hair from its regulatory snood, letting it tumble in the breeze.

Jostling around her were the older boys, the ones who already had all the accoutrements of sophistication such as their own cars and wallets full of their fathers' money. As she reacted to their jokes and impudent quips with a mixture of embarrassment and delight, she realized that it was not her brave horsemanship that had aroused the attention of her classmates' idols.

She saw interest entwined with lust in their smiles, but no spite. They were not laughing at her, but with her. Curious to discover just what she had done to attract them she spent time dissecting her appearance.

She looked in the mirror and saw the strong image of a fit young woman barely bridled by her masculine, form-fitting clothes that accentuated her slim hips and long legs. This was nothing like the girl who usually spent her days in simple yet unobtrusive blouses, skirts, and cardigans.

Nor was it in any way similar to her peers, who attempted to look like their mothers in supposedly grown-up clothes and heavy peach-pink lipstick. This was the tailored style she had been looking for, one that relied on a good cut and a simple design that simply followed the lean lines of a disciplined body beneath it.

From then on her pursuit of equestrian excellence was as much about winning looks as silver cups.

She also scrutinized the pages of *Vogue, Harper's Bazaar, Seventeen*, and other fashion magazines to look for a way to make facets of her riding "look" into everyday reality. Amid their glossy pages she found one star and one style that echoed her dreams.

Equally blessed with huge eyes, shiny hair, and a tall, boyish figure, Katharine Hepburn also had oodles of aristocratic style. In public and private life she was always attired in the classics: pearls, silk shirts, crisply tailored trousers, and restrained evening wear.

Failing to find some of these things in the stores, Jackie hunted for a dressmaker that would help her follow her role model. Subtle and understated, the outfits that emerged were serious and successful—like the blossoming woman inside them.

Her father had been right all along. Attracting men was not all about large bosoms and trying too hard. Beauty was empowering; *unapproachable* beauty even more so.

"If you are beautiful, and by the way you are going to be a knock-out," he told her when she was six, "you can do anything. Be anybody."

He repeated it to her and her sister like a mantra.

"If you look great you can take chances. Be special, be different, even difficult. Every day, in so many ways, a beautiful woman can get exactly what she wants."

At last the bits of her lonely life began to fit together. Being naturally mysterious seemed to encourage men.

Because her father had been so perceptive about this she was in awe of him. When she was away at school just the prospect of a visit from him would make her starve for days beforehand.

As she and her sister grew old enough, he took pleasure in pointing out beautiful women, not only commenting on how well they had adorned their natural beauty, but admiring the quality and provenance of the jewels or clothes they had selected. These were to be their role models, as were younger women married to older successful men. Her father thought May–December relationships were highly practical.

When the three of them were together he would give his daughters little tests to show them that a pretty face, good figure, and the confidence to turn on the charm could improve life a hundred percent.

"See that table over there," he would whisper, "it's the best in the house. See if you can get the maître d' to give it to us. He's bound to. You girls are going to decorate the dining room for him."

A New York dinner with Daddy was quite an ordeal. Hair, nails, teeth, and clothes had to be flawless. A patter of intelligent if coquettish conversation had to be forthcoming, including a repertoire of gentle jokes, so that he wouldn't fly off the handle and castigate his daughters as dolts.

He never stopped grooming them. Like eager puppies, yearning for his approbation, they jumped through all his hoops. His idea of how a young woman should behave became second nature to them.

He was a good teacher. Before she was much beyond twenty, both men and women would go that extra mile to please the soft-spoken beauty. But when she entered the public arena with Jack she took it upon herself to be far more analytical about her image.

Despite, or perhaps *because of*, her marriage to the flirtatious senator, she still lacked confidence in her appearance. She could not stop from obsessing about what she saw as her problem areas: wide shoulders, wavy hair, big hands, and long feet. She attempted to eradicate these feelings of inadequacy by a lifetime of incessant dieting and spending a lot of money on her hair and her clothes.

Now that she was married to a millionaire, she owned dressing rooms full of French couture, furs, and jewels that were typical of their well-heeled set. But the Kennedy publicity machine and her own good sense made her pinpoint very early on that the media was changing politics. More people would see her, and her husband, in a newspaper or a magazine or through the growing power of television, than would ever go to an election rally or a debate.

She made a cool appraisal of her wardrobe. Anything overtly luxurious was dispatched to the bank vaults or to cold storage. From now on all her clothes would look so simple that any housewife in the land would feel that she could comfortably wear them. In truth every garment still cost many hundreds of dollars as each one was handmade by the finest designers to fit and flatter her—but because they were uncluttered they seemed very affordable.

She wanted women to admire not envy her.

She found experts who advised her on camera-happy colors. It may not have been intellectually challenging, but if it was simply a matter of tacking down collars so that they would lie flat or sticking nonslip rubber soles on top of expensive leather ones to ensure that she wouldn't trip, it was worth it.

Her appearance was so faultless that even her mother-in-law was impressed and passed on a tip from the British royals who had their dressmakers sew tiny weights into the hems of dresses and skirts so that they wouldn't fly up.

What started as a way of looking approachable on camera became a way of life. Even the large sunglasses, worn to hide tiredness or unhappiness, became her signature.

Foiling irritants like the newly named paparazzi and persuading Jack that it was not just the rhetoric of political speeches that swayed opinion—his style mattered, how he looked was important—was interesting to her. She persuaded him to memorize parts of his speeches so he could look the audience in the eye and learn foreign phrases that would please the crowd.

Soon this ploy had become something more. Looking immaculate was the beginning, but the hours of preparation acted as a shield. Having intimate knowledge of exactly what the day held for her gave her some feeling of control, that she would never be caught looking flustered or nervous.

And now that she had to attend the great occasions of state alone she added a further layer to safeguard herself.

She went into what she called "dream mode."

She had discovered this by accident. It was the way she had coped with his funeral.

Exhausted but finding sleeping pills gave no rest but simply clogged up her veins, she found that she needed all her concentration to keep a tight hold on the children or to follow the steady pace behind the coffin. She was determined not to cry in public so she made herself block out the noise, the crowds, and the military music. Because she had planned every detail of the day she knew where to stand, when to turn.

In front of the world she appeared calm.

After this technique had helped her endure that terrible day she made a habit of using it whenever she was "on parade."

Over the last year the dream mode had been severely tested.

Utilizing it at the launch of a destroyer named for him, she had been able to keep her emotions in check when presented with his old navy dog tag that he had left on his last naval voyage.

It worked really well at the dedication of a new airport when she was presented with a gift of a previously unseen photograph. It was of the two of them looking carefree lolling in a gondola. It had been taken by the in-house photographer at the Cipriani Hotel in Venice. Although all those years ago they had waved him away, he thought that they were such an attractive young couple that he put the picture in his shop window to brighten it up.

There it had sat, in a quiet passageway off the Grand Canal, until the Italian-American community had unearthed it.

The dream mode would come into its own tomorrow.

She had wanted to spend the anniversary of Jack's death alone with the children, on Cape Cod or somewhere they had all been happy together, but her husband's successor had persuaded her that because the assassination had been such a shock, the country needed a day of mourning to heal its soul.

Even though she was not keen about attending, she knew that the hundreds who had worked with him, academics, speechwriters, economic advisors, many of them now stuck in nowhereland—having been thrust into outer darkness and ejected from the center of power—would agree.

To survive the day she began to compartmentalize her emotions. As she left her apartment she began to propel herself into dream mode by putting all her critical faculties on hold.

"Do not question anything," she told herself as she entered *Air Force One,* sent especially to New York to collect her. As she entered the cabin she couldn't help but recall earlier times on this plane, the children's excitement when taking off, the navy leather she had selected for the seats, the makeshift lift, kept out of the public eye, for when Jack's back was so bad he couldn't walk up the stairs. Anything but that last trip back from Dallas with his body in a casket.

"Do not worry about anything," she repeated to herself as the president's plane landed.

She had been advised of all the plans weeks before.

As far as she could tell nothing overtly tacky was about to occur.

The technique saw her through the eulogies at Arlington Cemetery, but she lapsed into it fully when once again she was sitting in her old spot, the left-hand back of the presidential limousine. For a few moments she couldn't stop herself pretending that if she turned from waving to the crowds lining the streets she would be able to look to her right and he would still be there.

As they pulled into the drive of the White House, she almost could make believe it was just over twelve months ago and they were going home. She looked up at the columns of this beautiful building. At least they had really, truly enjoyed their time here. She knew every corner of the place. Her mind filled with the sound of her husband summoning the children into the Oval Office, the memories of Caroline doing handstands on the lawn.

She immediately made herself stop thinking like this. These were dangerously emotional thoughts.

*I wonder how they have changed things? Focus on that, focus on that,* she told herself angrily.

She knew that she appeared withdrawn and quiet but that was a benefit. Cutting herself off in this way meant that no one dared intrude on her silence. She didn't have to make small talk.

She remained in dream mode when she was shown up to her suite. She had redecorated this room in elegant white-on-white stripes. Simply replacing the blowsy mismatched chintz had made the sitting room and bedroom look so much larger and lighter.

She started to remember a laughter-filled moment that had taken place in the corridor outside when Jack had started to tease her about some aspect of the White House makeover, and for a moment she tried to remember what it was.

"I have to forget about that now. I can afford to have feelings when I go back home. Not before," she said under her breath.

It was only when ten minutes had passed and no one had come up to escort her downstairs to meet the visiting dignitaries that she wondered if her cool exterior hadn't been rather too successful. Perhaps the president and his wife thought she wasn't up to facing all the guests.

Down there were her friends, her allies. It was rude to keep them waiting for her like this. She found the phone and tried to remember how the White House switchboard worked.

When she got an answer, from a new operator, she was quite surprised that when she asked to be put through to the First Lady she was informed that the president was on his way up to see her.

"No, no, really. I don't want any fuss," she said.

"Tell him I'll come right down. I do, of course, know my way and—"

Surprisingly the switchboard operator interjected.

"Please, ma'am. Please stay where you are. I have just been informed by his secretary that he'll be right up. She says it is important that you wait for him."

She smiled. Like many powerful men, he had deliberately chosen a tough disciplinarian as his personal secretary to keep everyone in line, himself included.

She had heard that unlike the more relaxed behavior of her predecessor, this secretary insisted upon knowing exactly where the president was at all times.

So she sat and waited.

When she had redecorated the White House she had installed bookshelves in all the bedrooms. She idly started to look through a book full of Michelangelo's drawings.

It took nearly six more minutes for the president to appear.

Surprisingly, he was with the attorney general. They looked gray and extremely nervous.

As they entered neither of them smiled.

She looked at them. For a second no one spoke.

Not another tragedy on this day, she thought.

"Not something else bad?" she whispered.

She had left the children with their nanny at her sister's house in London.

"The children?" she blurted out.

"No, no, no," said the president. "They're fine. But I am afraid Nicholas here does have what might be some"—he hesitated—"very unwelcome news."

"Well," Nicholas said. "It seems that this morning . . ."

He paused as the door opened and the First Lady slipped into the suite. The president looked daggers at her for the interruption.

First Lady and ex–First Lady nodded to one another.

"Well," Nicholas started again. More slowly this time. He looked back at the door.

The president, without looking around behind him at the door, barked: "Shut the door and let no one else in."

A hand emerged and closed the door.

He nodded at his subordinate to continue.

"Well"—he looked straight at her—"the facts are, Marilyn Monroe died this morning."

Wishing to look away from two shocked brown eyes, he withdrew a piece of paper from his pocket.

Good God! she thought. The blond bombshell has finally exploded.

Instantly, a well-known picture of her husband and the sexy film star filled her mind.

It had been taken at a Democratic fund-raiser. She was in the lineup and he was shaking her hand looking down, seemingly equally attentive to her upturned eyes, nose, and breasts. To be fair there had been nowhere else for him to look. They were being served up on a platter.

Everyone here in this room had been in the audience of that fund-raiser when later, wrapped in a tiny scarlet dress, with a long side slit that had been dipped in diamonds, she had breathed out a song. She had been part of a cavalcade of stars saluting the new chief. Some columnists wrote that although the curvy Monroe could hardly have worn less, the movie star's appearance had been largely overlooked because the new First Lady had looked like royalty. But a few months later the actress starred in a new movie about politics and the White House.

Billboards across America had featured advertisements for the film. The poster consisted of a full-length picture of M.M., as she was known, wearing a swimsuit made of nude-colored chiffon strategically splattered with gossamer sequins. She was emerging from a cake painted with the Stars and Stripes. Behind this scene were cartoon drawings of famous presidents, the most prominent of which looked a lot like the current holder of that office.

This started a round of rumor and innuendo in which her concert appearance was reprised in light of the poster.

At the time Jackie had dismissed it all, explaining that the filmmakers were obviously encouraging this publicity. Anything that could be used to link the supposedly sexiest woman in the world with the powerful U.S. president, especially as he was so attractive, would mean money for the box office.

Some of the published articles were highly annoying to the White House, not least because they had a germ of truth in them.

The one given most credence was that the president liked the movie so much that he had moved his bed into the White House cinema. The truth was that he had installed a new hard, single daybed in the room so that he could rest his bad back while watching movies. Since he had always kept his various medical conditions as secret as possible, there was nothing the White House could do to refute these stories.

Some of the sleaziest gossip columns would from time to time inform their readers that red, white, and blue bouquets delivered daily to the star on her latest film set were from the president.

Jackie knew that this was rubbish. She might have worried if the pieces quoted that the actress had been receiving books.

Books he sent, flowers, never.

Occasionally the gossip columnists would record sightings of the pair. But she didn't worry. On the dates in question her husband had been with family members. Although she knew that he was not monogamous before becoming president, she expected that as nowadays he was surrounded by the whole retinue of White House staff, often including Cabinet members, there was safety in numbers.

So it was not until two slightly fuzzy pictures of just the outline of that famous M.M. shape appeared in one of the supermarket weeklies that she began to worry.

Apparently the photographer had positioned himself across the road from the Biltmore Hotel in Los Angeles where the president and his retinue were staying. Aiming for what he presumed was the presidential suite, even though he couldn't see much through the half-drawn curtains, he thought he would run off a roll of film using his new long lens.

There were two photographs of the actress. In each the straps of her evening gown had been pulled down so that it was clinging to the tips of her nipples. She was being held by a man whose face was out of focus but who had his naked arm around her waist.

In one of them her head was tipped back, eyes closed in rapture. In the other she was mischievously putting her tongue out and smiling up at her unknown partner.

Upset and suspicious, Jackie challenged her husband with this. He denied everything.

He also tried to reassure her by adding that, nowadays, there was no way that he "could cat around and not get found out."

For hours she had raged at him and his ability to hurt her.

The president swore that the photographer had picked the wrong suite.

"Look at the pictures," he snapped. "Note there are no pieces of paper, empty coffee cups, or dirty ashtrays visible. You of all people know what it is like. The speechwriters, Phil, Dave, and even Deck, come in and out of the bedroom. You know that even the bathroom gets a trashing.

"Just to remind you, the weather was bad and we got to L.A. late. We had a quick meeting and a final discussion on the speech I was going to make at breakfast the next morning. I can get you minutes of those, by the way. Then we headed out for the dinner but we were late so we just had the hors d'oeuvres and went straight into the speech. California, as you know, is really important to us so we hung around, pressed the flesh, had a few chats. Artie reminded us that when they give in that state they give big-time, so he introduced us to some of the guys he thinks will do so. By that time we were absolutely starving, so we went to the Crosby place to eat. Lots of people, but she wasn't even there, and I was with my *sister,* who is sticking to me like glue, my other sister who has just bought a house in La Jolla, two speechwriters, and Deck, Paul, Steve, and Jim, not to mention the Secret Service guys and so on and so on."

The minutes of the meeting were delivered the next day. He sent them to her in an envelope covered with his kisses and hearts drawn by their daughter. By then not only had he been very loving toward her, he promised that before the next election they would return to Venice. She loved him and wanted to believe him. And she knew that unless she assumed that most of his staff, not to mention his family, were conspiring in his adultery, there was absolutely no way of discovering the truth.

"At eleven-forty-nine this morning Miss Monroe's resident housekeeper, a Miss Consuelo James, went to her bungalow to rouse Miss Monroe," continued the attorney general.

"She was due at Paramount for an important lunch meeting with senior executives and her agent, Folksie Campbell.

"On that agent's advice, Miss James was told to wake Miss Monroe up.

"She knocked at the door and when no one answered she looked through the window. Although she could see a body in the bed, she could not see who it was.

"She shouted but this garnered no response.

"On the further orders of Mr. Campbell she was asked to get the gardener to break the door down. Whereupon she found Miss Monroe dead."

He looked up. Slowly he added, "There were pills on the bed. They think they were barbiturates but they are checking all this now. Foul play is not suspected."

Since no one said anything he felt it right to fill the silence.

"Famous. Beautiful. Only thirty-six years old. Why would she want to kill herself? Today of all days."

"Damn shame," he said to no one in particular.

They all looked at Jackie.

"Yes, very damned," was all she could think of saying.

In his quiet drawl, the president interjected. "The story will hit the news wires very soon."

She knew they, too, had all been remembering the pictures and the gossip. They were not close friends but she had known them all for years.

"I'm sorry to have been the bearer of bad tidings," added the attorney general.

He gave her a small bow as he left the room.

"Is there more?" she asked her husband's successor in a very quiet voice.

He raised his eyebrows as if to balance his thoughts.

"Apparently there was a letter. Miss James has it. Don't worry, we are doing everything in our power to get hold of it. And as soon as we do I'll make sure it's checked—and destroyed if there is anything in it, anything at all, that *any* of us wouldn't like."

He put his hands on her shoulders.

His wife sat watching warily in the corner.

"This may be nothing to worry about," he continued.

She refused to let him see that she was in the slightest way bothered.

"Of course not." She smiled and stood.

"Don't you think we should join them all downstairs?" And with that she picked up the tiny black jacket, fastened the six pearl buttons, and followed President and Mrs. Johnson, suddenly feeling like an interloper in her old home, a stranger in her own country.

CHAPTER *Five*

Not one of the four hundred guests assembled in the East Room, not even the one who had given birth to her, could tell that the former First Lady was more upset than the already somber occasion called for. For the first time as a widow, she descended the red-carpeted stairs flanked by the military color guard.

The sympathy factor toward the late president's widow was so intense that few dared even approach her. Guests assumed that just returning to this house, this place that had meant so much to her, would be enough to drive a sane person to the edge.

Sensing this, she took advantage, knowing that she had less than an hour before the news of M.M.'s suicide emerged. With a do-not-disturb expression firmly fixed on her face she began her silent safari, searching for her prey among the best and the brightest of America.

The new president had obviously decided to use the occasion not just to commemorate the anniversary but to luxuriate in the halo effect of surrounding himself with as many of his successful countrymen and -women as possible. Business scions and political leaders, sports stars and actors, mixed with the cultural icons who had made up JFK's old gang.

The decibel level of the hubbub convinced her that many had brought hip flasks full of whatever they needed to deal with today's graveside service at Arlington National Cemetery.

In her low-heeled, rubber-soled shoes she made good speed through the State Dining Room, the Green, Blue, and Red Rooms, desperately trying to remember exactly who had traveled with Jack to Los Angeles that weekend.

None of her in-laws could be found. Because of the time she had spent upstairs she didn't know if their absence was to avoid shaking hands with Jack's successor, or whether, through the many tentacles that the family possessed, they already knew about the star's death.

Within minutes she realized that it was not only his family who were missing.

Others too were absent.

She could find none of their inner circle, the men and the women who had spent both the high days and the low ones with them in the collaborative girdle that surrounds every leader before and during success. These were the group that had shared their most intimate moments. They had often been too clingy for her liking but they were part of the essential background noise of his presidency. Even as Jack's girlfriend, she knew that she had to accept their devotion. They had been with Jack for years, on all the campaigns, through many of his illnesses, in the small hours when nuclear bombs threatened. They had waited outside the operating rooms when their babies died; they had downed yards of Black Velvet as they brushed the snow from their shoes on the first day that she had been hostess in this room. They were the cheerleaders, the sympathizers, the empathizers, the jousting knights, the jokers, and most importantly, the fixers.

Finally, she found one.

One who had gone west with her husband.

The tall, boyish figure of Declan O'Donnell was emerging from the men's room. Was it her imagination or had he made a perfect pirouette and gone into reverse the minute he saw her? One second he was there, the next he had returned to whence he had come from, the one place she couldn't follow.

She decided to wait.

Declan, a bachelor so beloved by the ladies that he was known as "All hands on," had been best friends with Jack since they were in college together. While the Kennedys were of relatively recent Irish immigrant stock—all of Jack's great-grandparents had traveled steerage to the United States—Deck was at the core of the Shamrock establishment related to various wealthy landowners. Declan had seen something exciting—call it ambition—in the young student that he knew was missing in himself. The two had studied and gone into the navy together but mostly they had had fun together. Deck, an early orphan with a large inheritance, seemed to have been bred to understand to perfection the innards of a martini, a Hispano Suiza, what makes a woman good in bed, and the name of every maître d' in New York.

So trusted was he that he knew all about Jack's many illnesses. The first one being Addison's disease, the failure of the adrenal glands, which led to exhaustion and pain and had to be constantly monitored and treated with cortisone. Second were Jack's severe back problems, which not only meant that he could often only move on crutches or while wearing a corset, he also had to undergo several highly dangerous operations that could have left him crippled. Of course, this was all kept out of the public eye, behind the scenes.

Declan also knew about Jack's chlamydia, a sexually transmitted disease. Publicly, his doctors described it as "nongonococcal urethritis." Yet even though it was treated with antibiotics and other drugs, it was recurrent and was the one known thing to stop him from "anticipating marriage" with whomever he could find, and later, when he was a married man, curtailed what Jack referred to as his "girling."

Ever since their teens they had often bedded the same women. Jack would seduce them and then they would fall into Deck's arms when "Potatoes" (as the older man always called his friend) had discarded them. Of course, the girls rarely realized exactly what was happening. The dashing pair would roll up in Deck's latest sports car to collect them, then, occasionally after just one date, Jack would ask the girl out again and during dinner, if he had his eye on someone new, would do his disappearing act, leaving Deck to pick up the pieces. Slowly they would fall for the gentler, sweeter man.

From day one Jackie had learned to accept Deck as part of the Kennedy equation.

More poignantly, in the early years of her marriage, Deck would be the one to drive her home when Jack vanished. Carefully ignoring her anger and pain, he would brilliantly pretend that Jack probably had a very good reason for having to dash back to the office. He never admitted that his pal was the "low, contemptible bastard" that Jackie called him but would always attempt to dredge up some excuse for his friend's behavior. More feeble than feasible, nonetheless these well-bred, considerate lies had been part of the putty that kept the marriage together until Caroline was born.

Deck's wealth meant that he had no need of a job. He occasionally wrote pieces for small literary magazines. Often engaged but never married, he was always able to drop everything to drive down to Hyannisport, fly off to the Riviera, or sit at the back of the train on campaign trails.

He was very well read and took great pleasure when a word or phrase that he suggested crept into his friend's speeches. He didn't care if the speech was delivered at the local Boy Scout meeting or on Capitol Hill. He was just happy to be of service.

When Jack Kennedy's heart stopped in Dallas, Jackie knew that it might as well have been Deck's. His life, his extravagant hobby, the worship of his president, his friend, was at an end.

In the first few days he was the only visitor allowed to pass through the curtain of bitterness and tears that surrounded the president's parents. When he returned to Washington there was a deep emptiness in his life. He was lost. The first Christmas, just four weeks after Dallas, without his friend, he found that he had nowhere to go. Jackie's mother was watching over her daughter and invited no one except close family. An old fiancée suggested that Nevada was the place to escape. He was encouraged to lose himself in a land where there were no clocks, no snow, no sentimentality. Once there he didn't look back.

Jackie had seen him only once or twice in the last year when they had both turned up at her brother-in-law's Sunday lunches. He was godfather to her daughter and to one or two of the cousins. He charmed the children, all of whom called him "Uncle Deck."

Before he heard the news about Monroe, she had to talk to him.

She puffed away at a cigarette while she waited for him to emerge. Having nowhere else to stub the butt out, she deposited it down by the side of a tub of white hydrangea encased in a majolica jardinière, one she well remembered acquiring, though not for this purpose. She marveled at what her life had come to, skulking around her old home trying to find out the truth about her late husband's sexual affairs.

In her mind she went over and over what Jack had sworn to. The hurt it summoned made it all seem like yesterday. She was sure he had mentioned Deck. His great buddy had been there.

Not that long ago, and yet it seemed like another century.

She noted that as he opened the door he checked both ways to see if the coast was clear.

When she stepped out in front of him, he jumped.

As she drew close to him she could tell from the shaking hand holding his cigar that Deck, Mr. Cool, was nervous.

"Hello, Deck," she said quietly.

Before he gave her a kiss or had a chance to mention his pain, her pain, today's ceremony or anything else, she murmured to him.

"Do you want to do your last kind act for your pal Jack?" She pulled him to her and kissed his cheek while tugging him gently toward a roped-off area, back into the quiet end of the corridor.

"You know . . . you know I'd do anything," he stuttered, realizing where they were going and slowing down.

She was forced to stop well before the door of the private quarters. She could see he was worried about them being alone.

"But shouldn't you be mingling with everyone, shouldn't we be back in there?" He nodded toward the wall of talk.

"Unless you're running for office." She raised an exaggerated, amused eyebrow. "I don't feel that I *have* to do anything," she said and smiled, trying to put her old friend at ease.

He was reassured by her calm voice but still remained immovable.

She tried another way.

"I'd like to know why half of these people are here and what they had to do with Jack. I'd like to tell that damn Texan just how grateful he should be to be following in the footsteps . . ."

She could see this was getting through, but as she continued to try and steer him into the quiet corner he was still hesitant.

He obviously knew. She felt stupid. Of *course* he would know. His new West Coast contacts were bound to include the police. They would have tipped him off.

She would have to appeal to every shred of love he had for her dead husband. She suspected that he had no special feelings for her; she just happened to be the one that Jack had chosen. Deck would have been just as lovely to anyone else.

Even after death he would be on her husband's side.

She realized that it was vital he had absolutely no idea that she knew about the frenzy about to engulf her.

"The current administration," she muttered sarcastically, "lured me here by saying that now that the people have got over the shock of last year and the scars have begun to heal, the country could mourn Jack with dignity.

"I obliged," she continued with a flash of bitterness.

"All three TV networks are showing it this evening. So the whole country can watch.

"But we who really loved him, my dear Deck, we have done enough. And what we are going to do now, just like the old days, is walk through the party, say our goodbyes, drive off together, meet up with the others, and really remember the good times.

"Haven't you noticed"—she forced herself to smile—"everyone

in the family has already gone? I wouldn't join them until I had found you."

She was mentally crossing her fingers, hoping that just because she hadn't found them that this was true.

Apart from being seen to mourn their brother, he knew that Joe and Rose Kennedy had other sons wishing to become the elected leader of the free world. As a piece of public relations it was essential they had to be seen attending the presidential reception after the service by their brother's grave. Tonight's moving TV images and tomorrow's newspaper photographs of their return to the White House would not only remind the nation of the private loss of a family, but would also reinforce the Kennedy dream, that the tragic events of last year were just an interruption before they reclaimed the keys to 1600 Pennsylvania Avenue.

As to the flattery, Deck didn't stand a chance. Black Jack had made her an expert many years ago.

So despite the president's wish that she remain, and the First Lady's suggestion that Jackie take a little nap upstairs, it took only a few minutes for them to say their farewells and slip away in Deck's black sports car.

They had no idea that just five minutes later the president received the call.

In her last note, Monroe had left nothing but bequests to various friends' children and an apology to those friends for seeking "the easy way out."

Also included in the envelope was a color photograph. Just the telephone description made the most powerful man on earth's throat dry.

It was of Marilyn barely fitting into a teeny baby-doll-style negligee of peau de soie, in palest pink.

In one hand she held a copy of the *Washington Post,* open to an inside page, the headline referring to the nationwide success of the film set in Washington.

Behind her was the clear outline of the headboard in the Lincoln bedroom in the White House. In front of her, lying on the pleated cotton bedspread, were various private presidential folders both open and closed with their highly recognizable letterhead.

On her knees, kneeling forward, the star is smiling, looking up. Her outstretched hand is being held by the photographer.

The interlocked fingers are a little out of focus but there was little doubt who they belonged to.

Consuelo James contended that the note and the photograph had been addressed to her and were therefore her private property.

The president thought of the widow who had left so early and the nightmare of the days ahead.

CHAPTER *Six*

For the rest of his life Deck would wonder how he had ended up in his car with just the former First Lady by his side.

For some reason as he left the White House driveway he headed north.

Had she suggested it? Or had he taken that route because it seemed the best way to avoid photographers?

For the first few minutes they drove in silence. He expected that her Secret Service men would catch up with them at any moment. When a few minutes and several miles had swirled by without their appearance, he consoled himself that they had been taken by surprise as much as he had.

How had he been dragged off on this wild-goose chase?

Twice he asked her if they were going in the right direction.

All she did was nod. It was a while after they left the capital when he realized that they were not meeting up with the others. But she was so quiet, he felt he had no option but to continue.

Maybe she had just seen him as a way of escape, he thought. Maybe the day had just driven her over the edge.

She had been right about one thing, the streets and the roads were empty. Just as they had sat in front of their television sets last November 22 so the nation had collectively returned there just twelve months later.

He asked if she wanted more heat. He was worried about the cold. She hadn't left his side in the White House so she was wearing no coat over the little black suit.

She only smiled in response.

He moved to switch on the radio but she put her hand out to stop him.

"No noise, please, not after that," she said.

He was right, the quick escape, the silent treatment now. Today had spooked her.

He would have to choose his words with care.

He had no idea where they were going.

This, being alone with Jackie, was just what he wanted to avoid.

Like most people Deck didn't know what to do with death. Both his parents had died when he was too young to learn. Like most people he was uncomfortable, didn't know what to say, how to act, what to do.

After Dallas he had written, of course, not only to Jackie but to Rose and Joe and Bobby and Ethel too.

He had known them all for so long. It felt as if a member of his family had passed away, except that he wasn't, strictly speaking, re-lated. Sadly for him, when they were mourning he rarely got the call; in this the Kennedys were self-sufficient. There were just so many of them, who needed more? So the Bobby lunches and dinners were a godsend.

At first he felt that he was only grudgingly welcomed, because he didn't rant and moan enough about the new president. Deck was aware of this but he just couldn't bring himself to dance to another brother's tune. It was only when he proved to be the most accurate of storytellers, the one who remembered all the little details, that he truly gained acceptance. He could always be counted on to describe exactly what had happened on this or that occasion. Suddenly Bobby understood what his use to Jack, other than being an adaptable good-time guy, had really been.

Deck would throw his mind back to fish out another story about Jack. Then he would prepare and hone it to perfection for the next day.

Many of the narratives were from the navy or college days. He was delighted when he realized that many of these uproarious adventures were new to them all.

One-upmanship, which was after all the essential Deck, got him through.

It was over at Bobby's house that he had encountered Jackie and the children.

She had been friendly but cool, leaving the lunch table to walk around the icy garden with the little boy.

His opinion as she watched him entertain the group with a story about Jack's courtship of her was that she was hostile. Even though she knew the outcome of the tale he was telling, and that both she and Jack came out well in it, he was sure that she hated his knowing the truth about her marriage.

An incredible image had been spun out of beautiful photographs, making the whole world think that the bullets in Texas had ended a passionate love affair.

Even if, right around this table, there were others who knew it wasn't so, none of them had known it as well as Deck. The myth of Camelot, the fairy-tale love of this couple, was being earnestly peddled.

He owned too many secrets.

Since then he had sent a Christmas gift to his goddaughter, but like all well-brought-up girls of seven it was Caroline who sent the thank-you note. Except for sending a good-luck card to Jackie when she moved to New York, he had had no communication with her for months.

Quietly Jackie interrupted his thoughts.

"Deck, I know that you loved Jack."

After the long silence in the car he was relieved that her breathy voice had total control.

"And I know that he was very different . . . very, very different from most other men." She noticed Deck wince.

"He was, I realized more and more as our lives went on together, very special. And only someone as exceptional as yourself would have given up so much of your valuable time to him.

"You could have been doing so many more lucrative things but you generously gave up your time to help Jack. We all recognize that. I was just talking about it to *belle-mère*." (Jackie had adopted the French name for her mother-in-law. It satisfied Rose and, as importantly, Janet.)

Deck was devoted to Rose even though his pal had always said what a cold mother she had been to him. Filled with momentary happiness and lulled by Jackie's tone, he was shocked by what she said next.

"Deck, I don't know if you ever knew, but I knew about Jack and Marilyn."

Deck looked straight ahead, concentrating on the road, as if they would crash if he flicked an eyeball in her direction. "Yes, Deck, it's true," she lied again. "I know I used to get upset when Jack would wander off with some girl . . ."

Her voice suddenly lost its balance and went down an octave.

"I was so young, so childlike, so immature . . . but as time went on, I understood." She was giving him no chance to interrupt.

"Jack's life, the pressure, the illnesses—"

"When did this happen?" he blurted out.

"Let's just say that over time I realized that these women, they were not a threat to me, that they couldn't endanger what we had together."

"But you made such a fuss," said Deck almost to himself, trying desperately to remember what the big fusses were all about.

"Well, I couldn't just ignore it," she snapped.

If he was to believe her, to trust her enough to tell her the truth, she knew she must keep hold of her legendary calmness.

She tried to take the drama out of the situation.

"But that was at the beginning. Jack and I had long ago reconciled to living in a more . . . adult, European way."

She turned to face Deck, a tall man even behind a steering wheel.

"Didn't he ever tell you?"

Deck so wanted to believe her. He cast his mind back. He remembered nothing of the sort.

Impatiently her voice cut into his memories.

"Dear Deck, think about it, how else could I have coped?"

He slowed the car down. His mind was not on the road. He was recalling the giggles of two sensational debutantes who tittered nervously when he and Jack led them into the immense quiet of Joe and Rose's empty Hyannisport house. The Kennedy parents were conveniently in Europe and he and the senator had been out looking for trouble. They had locked themselves in so that no one would be able to disturb them. He could still hear the retreating footsteps of a servant, or perhaps it had been Jackie herself, after trying and failing to open the front door.

He heard Jack on the ship-to-shore telephone lying to her about the work he was doing as they lay on teak sun loungers between two brand-new blondes just off Cap d'Antibes on the French Riviera.

He speeded up again, keen to change gears and have a second or two to think.

Perhaps this was right. He knew that from the very beginning of their marriage Jack had played around.

On reflection, he supposed that no woman could have dealt with Jack's constant flirtations without having a deep sense of insecurity unless there had been some sort of agreement. Hell, just watching the man chatting to his neighbor at dinner you could see that he was sex on legs.

But if so, why did Jack worry so much about getting caught? Deck wondered. He recalled times when it seemed that half the White House needed to be drafted into the deception.

As if she read his mind, she posed the same question out loud and, just as fast, answered it.

"Why did Jack worry about my finding out? That was just part of the game."

And if so, why did he not tell his old pal Deck? God, the lies he had told Jackie over the years.

Jackie continued. "He was embarrassed. When I found out that he had been fooling around while we were in the White House he promised me that from then on he would change his ways, especially when I told him how impossible it would be for me if anything ever got out."

Deck could hear the implied threat in those few words.

"When you think of what Jack wanted to achieve . . . if it was there he just couldn't say no."

Deck knew then that she was lying. Anyone with just a passing knowledge of Jack's life would have known that none of it happened by accident. It was always he who made the moves. Whether it was politics or passion, everything that happened came down to his energy. A great deal of forethought on his part ensured that he had a constant replenishment of sexual partners.

"Honestly, Deck, this is not just some idle chitchat. It's important, really important for Jack's sake, for his memory. We have to get this right."

Whoah! What was with the "we"? What did she mean? Here he was thinking that she was taking an uncomfortable stroll down memory lane, which was bad enough. What was with this switch to the present?

He turned and looked at her and made as if he were going to speak when she continued earnestly.

"Deck, we have known each other for years. Please, will you be honest with me now?"

Deck licked his lips. They were very dry. He had to be very, very careful now. What did she know? Where should he start?

"Look, Jackie, what's the point of raising all this now?"

There seemed nothing and no one in the world except them and the car. She remained silent.

"Well." He cleared his throat and paused. "My throat's on fire. There are some cough drops in the glove box."

While she hunted for them she said, "So strange to be back. Then next week there's the big fund-raising concert again."

So that was it.

"This isn't about that picture of Marilyn with Jack?" he asked her like a stern headmaster.

He could see that she was waiting, imploring him with those eyes.

He could picture it clearly, Marilyn's upturned face mirroring Jack's smile.

Swiftly his imagination flicked up the other pictures of Marilyn in his mind, Marilyn in the Los Angeles hotel.

Marilyn with her eyes shut in pleasure or her tongue playing between her lips, her engorged nipples, her body arching back.

Suddenly it seemed like those two sexually provocative photographs were glowing, dancing in the headlights before them.

His reverie was smashed by the pain, as sharp as broken glass, in her voice.

"No, Deck, it's because she killed herself today!"

Before he had a chance to recover she continued. "Lyndon told me at the White House a few minutes before the reception started. The police are convinced it's suicide, they found pills, barbiturates I think he said, by the body. Her maid found her at home. Sometime tonight the news will get out."

Deck was stunned.

"My God" was all he could say. He had always liked Marilyn, who was brighter than most actresses. He recalled that despite his frequent visits to Los Angeles he hadn't seen her since the assassination.

"There's a letter. Lyndon says he's going to see what he can do to stop it getting out."

Suddenly she sounded tired, the fight and the feistiness draining away.

She knew that she had shocked him. That he had had no idea.

So what else was he hiding from her?

For a moment or two he said nothing. Only the slow, mellifluous engine was audible.

He sighed.

He so wanted to comfort her. What was best to say?

"You know it meant nothing to him." Jesus, he thought, dead for a year and I'm still lying for him.

The widow put up her hand as if to say, No more lies please.

"That sounded like such a lie, I agree."

He said nothing more for a few minutes. He felt like a cornered rat.

"I guess that whenever he went to Los Angeles—and remember, he was always asking you to come—she would make herself available. She was always there, on her own. She even took over several suites, under assumed names, of course, at the hotels we stayed in, so she would be sure to be on the same floor as us.

"One time she did so and we came back overnight. He wanted to get back to D.C. . . . Heavens, she swore at him.

"She was the sexiest Hollywood star of her generation. Like any man would be, he was flattered. It was like a fantasy."

Deck's rueful smile told her everything. Her husband and the star had shared a romance that had lasted as long as his presidency. Surely Marilyn would not have killed herself today without leaving incriminating evidence.

"So, it *was* Jack in those photographs in the hotel," she muttered quietly.

"Probably, I guess so . . . Okay, so yes, but don't think that it was anything but sex. He was with us most of the time and we were all working in the suite as usual, writing speeches, meeting the local party bigwigs, same as always."

"And," she said, very quietly.

"From time to time he would just vanish."

Suddenly he was brought back to reality.

"He loved you, you know that. You and the children were all that he—"

"Don't Deck. Just don't," she interrupted.

"Shouldn't we go back?" He glanced at her. "Everyone will be looking for you. Your mother, the Secret Service." Deck noticed a nervous whine in his voice.

He didn't want any more questions. This whole thing had been a setup. On the one hand he felt he had let down his old pal, and on the other, as he sat here with her, it all sounded so shabby, so tawdry.

She was looking out of the window, her face turned away.

He stopped worrying about the dead and for the first time gave proper thought to the living.

Jack and he used to think sex was their right. Hell, what was the point of having good looks and money unless you put them to good use.

Fidelity was for women and men not lucky enough to have their advantages in life. He had never given it a second thought, until now.

Angrily he said, "Today, the ceremony, it was a mistake. Lyndon had no right to ask you to do it. Just upsets us all over again."

Bitterly she answered, "Oh, Deck, don't do what they all do and knock Lyndon. Trust me, today won't have been half as bad as tomorrow is going to be."

There was silence as they both imagined how the suicide would be covered in the newspapers, the radio, and the television.

"Maybe she says nothing in her note," said Deck, ever the optimist.

"There will definitely be questions about why she especially chose today to die, and those pictures will be shown all round the world again and there will be endless innuendo about Jack.

"If she has written something about Jack, who knows what else will come out," she muttered to herself.

She turned to look at him, her face awash with hurt and anger.

"Except you know what else, don't you, Deck? You know everything."

She turned away and looked out of the window.

When no answer was forthcoming she said, "Oh, don't bother to answer. I suppose your male—sorry, *boys'*—code won't allow you to."

There was a wedge of silence in the car. He put his foot on the accelerator. Wherever they were going, the sooner they arrived the better, as far as he was concerned.

He remembered so much. Even if he hadn't actually been with Jack, should some sexual dimension have been breached, anything from a girl playing footsie under the table to full-on mating in a Washington apartment, his friend would always keep him in the loop.

Her breathing was labored. "From now on it's *me* you can watch out for.

"Just make sure you point out any other woman Jack knew who might try the same publicity stunt as Marilyn. Don't forget to remind me of who is getting old and poor and just might have to sell her story, or which Hollywood star so badly needs to haul the public out of their easy chairs into the movie theater that she'll tell how Jack Kennedy kissed her lips and whispered love words into her ear.

"Perhaps you can tell me exactly *how* you helped Marilyn get through security and how her little messages reached him? I seem to remember in the early days, with one or two notable exceptions, that you were always very keen to have his castoffs. Perhaps you even nudged him toward Marilyn because you wanted her yourself?" She was shouting.

By now she was semikneeling on her seat, flailing at him and obliterating his view. She began to hit him, anything to make him speak.

He put his arm up so as to fend her off. The car shook from side to side as he tried to see where he was going.

He braked and slowed down but didn't speak and didn't stop.

"Jackie! Stop hitting me. Who will look after your children if you kill us in this car?" he asked her.

"Don't you dare try and be so high-and-mighty and responsible with me," she yelled.

Then she fell back into her seat. How pointless. It wasn't Deck she wanted to kill. The man she wanted to murder was already dead.

"Maybe if you tell me exactly what happened I can learn something. After all, aren't you supposed to be the greatest storyteller of all time? Aren't *you* the one who can remember all the important little details? The who, when, where, and how, and how damn often. Why don't we"—she opened the other glove compartment—"find some paper and a pen and do a list."

As she scrabbled for a pen he could see that she was crying.

For him this was the most upsetting. This was the woman who had not shed a public tear, ever. Now she was shaking, sobbing, her whole body retching in misery.

Deck knew that nothing he could say would make it better, only worse. That she had never, ever, had an agreement with Jack about his private life was clear. Even worse, she obviously had no inkling that there were so many more women than she knew about who had played their part in Jack's secret world. Not only had her husband taken the decision that as president he was not going to give up sex on the side, he had not hesitated to turn virtually everyone around him into coconspirators.

In his parallel universe many on his staff had not just helped him run the country but had colluded in his deception. Some knew more than others but their aid had enabled him to entertain other women behind her back anywhere he wanted. For the first time he was forced to acknowledge that it wasn't just Jack who had betrayed her.

He pulled over and scrambled out of the car. The night was bitter.

He leaned back in and spoke to her shivering back. "I'll go up ahead into that diner. I'll see if I can get us some coffee while you calm yourself.

"Then I'll take you home."

She didn't even acknowledge him through her tears.

"Jackie," he started, wanting to say that all this had nothing to do with her. That whoever Jack had married it was inevitable that the good-looking, all-powerful multimillionaire son of a multimillionaire adulterer was never going to be a saint, and that the way he had behaved was as much a part of his genetic makeup as his eyes, or his nose. But he could see that this was not the time.

She had every right to be furious. Her pain was not just about sexual jealousy or infidelity.

Once she had been forced to accept that Jack would make no effort to be faithful, he should have gratefully acknowledged his debt to her. From the moment that he ran for office she could have divorced and destroyed him at any time. Deck tried to put himself in her shoes. She had every right to feel angry and bitter. To be reelected, Jack would have needed her. She had been an outstanding First Lady. At the very least she deserved to be treated with respect and entitled to the truth.

The terrible aftertaste of her marriage, the one that she would always be left with, was that Jack had not only taken her love for granted, he had taken her for a fool.

As he entered the diner he was aware of a large sports car moving toward him in the empty street behind him.

Turning, he saw the former First Lady at the wheel, tears flowing unchecked down her cheeks.

When she saw him she didn't stop, but sped past.

She was obviously going to drive more than a hundred miles home to New York without him.

It was eight P.M. The TV programs on today's memorial service were about to start.

If the nation knew that the calm and collected former First Lady was speeding down the highway alone, sobbing her heart out, they would never believe it.

He was worried about her safety but realized that if he raised the alarm he would never be trusted by her or the family again. The police always tipped off the press. If the newshounds picked up this information it would end up as part of a juicy amalgamation with the Monroe suicide.

Her guardianship of Jack's legacy would have been a complete waste of time. It would give those who disliked Camelot, and all it stood for, more ammunition.

He had to find a local cab that would drive him along in her wake. He could say that he was too drunk to drive. It was his duty to ensure that she got back safe. He would check with her doorman that she had arrived. Over the next day or so he would somehow retrieve the keys to his car. It would not be easy; after tonight he did know too much. He had seen her with her defenses destroyed.

He doubted that she would ever want to see him again.

## CHAPTER Seven

Marilyn's suicide made the front pages of all the newspapers the next day, but since the press was concentrating on the graveside service for the dead president, despite the extraordinary coincidence in the dates of their deaths, her name was not linked with his in the eulogies and obituaries.

Jackie knew that this was the calm before the storm. Tomorrow, free of their pious mask of mourning, the tabloids would take full opportunity to chew over the state of Marilyn's mind before she elected to die on the anniversary of the slaying of the late president.

The former First Lady knew that if they had just a sniff of the existence of a suicide note, even if it was only marginally more interesting than a shopping list, the story could bubble for weeks. Unlike yesterday's events, which signified the end of something, the subject of the actress's untimely suicide had legs.

President Johnson had called this morning to assure her that he was still hopeful that Consuelo James would give up the letter.

He hadn't talked for long because he was in a quandary. He didn't feel it was right to assure her that the suicide note contained nothing for her to worry about without revealing what was in the photograph, which he still had not seen himself. As he was still confident that he could use his power to stop the image from ever becoming public, it seemed equally worth trying to ensure that the widow would never find out what it showed.

He had come to this decision for several reasons. Overriding all considerations was his admiration for Jackie. He thought that she had been through enough. Secondly, he thought that Jack Kennedy's sexual shenanigans denigrated the status of the presidency, especially as they seemed to include using the White House itself for his louche behavior. Lyndon was no angel but he still thought there was a certain way that a man should behave. As a poor boy who had done well he had always had huge contempt for the playboy Kennedys.

He was also jealous. He had just won a landslide victory and yet the dead man could still reach out from the grave and grab what Lyndon felt should be his headlines. When he felt proud of an accomplishment, his efforts were often trounced by a front-page story about the Warren Report, the official inquiry into the death of JFK (everyone seemed to have forgotten that he, LBJ, had set it up), or vying for space against an article about yet another place being named in JFK's honor. And if it wasn't the dead president getting ink, his brother Bobby, the new senator for New York, was in the news.

Lyndon Johnson was fed up with being in their shadow. Now he was caught up in another Kennedy mess. His attorney general warned him that there were legal difficulties in suppressing Marilyn's suicide note and the photograph because, as both of them had been addressed to her maid (the actress had even written Consuelo's name on the back of the photo), when the coroner released them, Miss James could do as she wished with them. At this very moment a government lawyer was on his way to L.A. to see if a deal could be done.

"Perhaps the maid has someone she wants to bring over from

Cuba, Italy, who knows from where?" was his first instruction. "Maybe this and some money can shut her up."

Jackie knew none of this. Nervous of what more she would discover, she was nonetheless proud of herself for having been brave enough to challenge Deck. Having grown up in a house of arguments, she usually did anything to shy away from scenes.

But it was all too much for her.

Maybe the note would die with the blonde but there was always someone who talked. She wondered just how far the ripple of betrayal had spread among her family and friends. Several times she went to the phone, tempted to call her in-laws, especially the ones who had been in L.A. with him on that trip. The Kennedy tribe had long been trained to circle the wagons and go into defensive mode if any one of them was under attack. As a relation she might be able to breach their defenses, but she needed to be sure that she selected the right person. After all, it was quite possible that her sisters-in-law were equally in the dark about Jack and Marilyn.

Glued to their spot on top of a pedestal, they could not bend, or even sway in the breeze of freedom, a situation and state enjoyed by their husbands. They remained protected, almost imprisoned, often completely unaware of what any of their men were up to.

Because of this Jackie knew that from a practical point of view, it was highly unlikely that her sisters-in-law would have placed Jack under the close scrutiny that she had been forced to do from the earliest days of her marriage. It had been a complex game that the pair of them had played. He was furious if he ever caught her prying, but over the years she hadn't been able to resist keeping a watchful eye on him at parties, dinners, and any other places where he might meet new women. Right away she could mark out which type he went for. She prided herself on her ability to abort an introduction or to swiftly separate him from his target by attracting her husband's interest in something or someone else.

His sisters wouldn't know anything. More importantly, she doubted they would have the imagination to suspect their brother had—as Jackie had convinced herself he did over the last twenty-four hours—unnatural sexual needs.

When they were first married they had had countless arguments when Jack had refused to be bound by their wedding vows.

At first he would try to brush off her worries by lying about where he had been, but as time went on he tried to persuade her that his infidelities meant absolutely nothing and that they would never threaten their marriage. Religion and a sense of family would never let any of his "girling" impose on their life together. He felt that the United States was puritanical and tried to persuade her that in Europe things were different. After all, the more devout Italians and the French, who prized family and heritage above all else, rarely remained faithful but seldom divorced. Relying in equal measure on her low self-esteem and her abiding love for him, he attempted to persuade her that coming home in the early hours after vanishing with a girl at a party meant absolutely nothing. He claimed that his inability to resist the occasional one-night stand was the result of being a longtime bachelor; he had been thirty-six when they wed. His way of jousting with illness and pain was to find sexual release.

"It means no more to me than having a cool drink on a hot day," were his exact words. "Just a little palliative for the old ache in the groin," was another description. "No more important than an aspirin."

However much he tried to reassure Jackie, there were many times when she felt the situation was unendurable, although once Caroline was born in 1957, both Jackie and her husband knew that she would never let her daughter suffer the same miserable childhood she had. She could never subject Caroline to divorce.

That Marilyn had been seeing Jack for so long was a big shock. All night she had tried to piece the thing together. Marilyn had not been a casual fling, she had been Jack's mistress.

How often did he see her? How often did he talk to her on the phone? Why did he fancy her so much? What did she do for Jack that made her so special to him? What did they say about her behind her back?

Jackie was no prude. Jack had persuaded her to view some pornographic movies; they had been to see one or two raunchy films. If only she could convince herself that the affair with Marilyn was because of some strange sexual kink.

She alternated between anger and tears. She felt so helpless, her fate in the hands of Lyndon Johnson and some film star's maid.

Despite her ambivalence toward her in-laws she took comfort from their phone calls. All morning they had been phoning to praise her for handling the memorial service with her usual aplomb, citing this or that from last night's TV programs or this morning's newspapers. Admittedly it was the female side that called. To try and find out what they knew she gently prodded them all, including her mother-in-law, to discuss what they expected the press would say about Jack and the dead actress. All believed that this would be a one-day wonder, that the date was just a coincidence.

As the morning passed, with no further word from the White House, it was a desperate Jackie who called the eldest surviving Kennedy brother. She could think of no better person than Bobby to advise her. He had, after all, relinquished the post of attorney general quite recently and he could tell her what influence Lyndon could bring to bear on Consuelo James. Equally important, if she decided to tell him what she knew, she was sure that he would keep this shocking piece of information to himself.

By lunchtime she had left two messages. It was dark outside before he returned her call.

He began by apologizing for leaving the White House reception early. "I just couldn't handle it, seeing him there when it should have been Jack . . . I'm not surprised you got out of Washington so fast. You're better off in New York."

He spent time complimenting her for the way her children were growing up so well and how brilliantly she had dealt with everything at Arlington. Then he said that his contacts in the newspapers had told him that tomorrow they were going to go heavy on the fact that Marilyn had chosen to kill herself on the anniversary of Jack's death.

"I'm glad to have this chance of warning you. I don't imagine the story will amount to much, there'll be the picture of them at the concert and that stupid film poster, but Jackie, don't weaken now, try to just ignore it. Do what you always do. Don't acknowledge any filth that those scum write," Bobby told her.

"The papers are probably angry at something that Lyndon's done, or that he hasn't done, so they want to get at the Party and this will give them a useful excuse. And of course, it's a way of getting at the family, or at me, sabotaging my political chances."

When she quietly asked if he knew why the star had chosen the anniversary to kill herself, Bobby reacted angrily.

"Of course I don't. The stupid woman was probably drugged up to the eyeballs."

Jackie asked him again if he knew anything, anything at all, that connected Marilyn and his murdered brother.

The slight twang in her brother-in-law's voice got more noticeable.

"Look, Jackie, I knew her too. They could say something about her and me, but they don't dare because I'm alive to answer back."

Jackie interrupted, her voice low and serious. "You sound worried, Bobby. Surely they won't be able to write much if they only have the picture of her shaking Jack's hand, the film poster, and the coincidence of her death yesterday?"

"Well, I wasn't always with him." He was more hesitant now. "Especially not in L.A. Marilyn was fun, a good-time girl who loved to party."

There was silence.

She refused to break it.

"Supposing, just supposing, he got out of line." He sounded less angry now.

"What exactly are you saying?"

"Absolutely nothing . . . but supposing . . . you know, she meant nothing to him, she was just a, ah, convenience to him."

"Oh, that again, so you all say it."

"What do you mean?"

"Just something Jack used to tell me."

"Jackie, I admit he was no saint but he loved you."

"So you did know about it." She spat the words out.

Why had she even spent a second worrying that he didn't know and that she would have to tell him all about his precious brother and his mistress?

"Jackie, calm down. It meant nothing. Remember that. He was always asking you to go on the road with him. Getting upset just plays into their hands. As you've said, the papers have got nothing . . . and she meant nothing, zilch, to him."

Jackie decided not to bother to tell him that Deck had spilled the facts.

"I'll call you tomorrow. When you get down here for Thanksgiving, come over? We'll arrange to go out somewhere, all of us."

So whatever the papers say, we'll all be seen together and everything will look hunky-dory, which will be good for your career, thought Jackie. This family!

"We'll tip off someone we know, some reporter we can trust, get some pictures taken," added Bobby.

Unbelievable! More lying pictures. The whole Kennedy edifice was built on photogenic falsehood.

"I don't think so," said Jackie firmly. Why not put him under the same pressure that she was coping with?

"Bobby, Deck has told me everything. He had no option. The woman has left a suicide note."

She wasn't sure but she thought she heard a gasp from the other end of the phone line.

"Lyndon says that he is trying to deal with it . . . What do you think he will be able to do?"

She said this in such a matter-of-fact tone that it was some seconds before he responded. She interrupted his spluttering avowal of apology.

"Bobby, we haven't got time. Is there anything that Lyndon can do, without making it more of a story?"

"Well, he is hardly going to ruin his reputation for the Kennedys, is he?"

Although Bobby believed that the president must be taking some delight in this situation, he said nothing more.

"Let me think about everything, look up some law books, and call you back within the hour."

Jackie hoped he would call Lyndon and help stop the story from getting out, but during the next hour all her sisters-in-law called her again and told her yet again how Jack loved her and how he had confided to them how much he admired her.

Poppycock!

Now not only did she know that he had continued to be a habitual womanizer, Jackie realized that she alone would have to deal with it.

Should she put out a statement? Saying what? Should she call up the newspaper owners, speak to them off the record? In the old days they had been very helpful. She could ask that they watch what was written for the sake of her children.

No, they would be as sweet as peaches on the phone and then the word would get out that she was groveling.

*Never.*

Should she ask to meet Consuelo James and try and beg or bargain directly with her?

Too risky; it was bound to get out.

Later, Bobby called her again. Both he and the family lawyer felt that if the government legal team could not coax the maid or frighten her into releasing the letter and picture, no one could.

Next morning even the serious journals featured, among others, the photographs of her late husband meeting the woman that she now knew had been his mistress for years.

The ravishing blonde was also pictured with her first and second husbands and her last costar. Most of the stories referred to the remarkable coincidence of Monroe committing suicide on the first anniversary of Jack's death.

The next day the children returned from Europe in time for their birthdays.

As they were going to spend Thanksgiving with Janet at Merrywood, they had their parties early. Luckily both of these celebrations took place at home.

In front of her children's friends, assembled nannies and mothers, Jackie once again entered dream mode.

She laughed, ate crustless cucumber sandwiches, and birthday cake. She joined in with laughter at the clown booked for her son and the magician she had hired for her daughter.

It was during one of the latter's tricks that she stepped outside the drawing room to take a call from President Johnson.

Sadly he explained that he had been able to do nothing about the note. "I assume you are coming down to your mother's for Thanksgiving? Could the attorney general visit you there?"

"More bad news?"

"Why don't you just enjoy the rest of Caroline's party," said Lyndon, and was gone before she could follow up with supplementary questions.

The most powerful man in the land knew she would be horrified by the picture that he held in his hands.

He felt it essential that she should be surrounded by loved ones when she saw it.

When he arrived at Merrywood, Nicholas Katzenbach, the attorney general, quietly suggested to Janet that it would be a good idea for her to be present at his meeting with Jackie. In the cathedral quiet of Hugh Auchincloss's library he slowly withdrew the picture from the heavy white paper envelope with its presidential seal and placed it on the low glass coffee table. Jackie bent forward, painstakingly absorbing its content. Involuntarily she fell forward, emitting an anguished whimper followed by the entire contents of her stomach.

The two of them. In the Lincoln bedroom in the White House. For days she had been unable to escape her self-made images of the pair. She imagined them chatting longingly and lovingly on the phone, dancing alone together, kissing and reading and walking, arms around each other, along a beach with a West Coast sunset gilding Marilyn's perfect limbs. Hurtful, romantic images of the kind that she had always wanted for herself.

But she was totally unprepared for this.

Two hours later she emerged from her room and asked to be left alone with her children. She gave them their baths and read them to sleep. For the first time the dream mode failed and she sobbed into their soapy curls.

Finally, at midnight she allowed her mother into her room and was told that the White House had rung to inform her that Consuelo James had sold the photo to one of the supermarket gossip magazines.

CHAPTER *Eight*

A few days later the photograph was published.

In the interim Jackie had been unable to go out.

If it were just hurt and embarrassment she was feeling, she would have defied the photographers and journalists lying in wait for her on the street downstairs. After all, these emotions were not new to her. She had been dodging them ever since she was a girl.

The photograph revealed the extent of his ardor. Not content with maintaining M.M. as his mistress for year after year, his heedless irresponsibility meant that he had not only played while out of town but he had taken crazy risks at home. Defiling their inner sanctum seemed to mean nothing to him. He had wanted her enough not to care.

It wasn't just pain she felt; it had become clear that her belief in her "specialness" to him was delusional.

There was no real Jack and Jackie. It was a fraud. Even when he became president he could not be loyal to her. How he must have been laughing behind her back, his intellectual wife with such useless radar, his empathetic partner who found such reassurance in her own imagination that he didn't even have to lie to her.

These thoughts shattered her confidence, not just in everything she had achieved but in what she believed she now stood for. Her life as a role model for the nation had rested on the shakiest of foundations. How on earth could she continue?

Because her self-esteem had been burned off, first by her parents, then by her unfaithful spouse, when Jack had first won the presidency she shied away from her role as First Lady.

She made it clear to White House staff that she was not going to change.

"I want to be called Mrs. Kennedy, not First Lady," she told them.

She also stated that she intended to continue to concentrate on her children and her hobbies.

Although she had given press conferences while her husband was running for office, once installed at the White House she stopped.

"The press always covers my official engagements and is kept abreast of my projects and I prefer not to answer personal questions, so that leaves little for a press conference," she explained.

She felt such a fool. She hadn't raised the subject of Jack's behavior once they were in the White House. In the past she had always found talks about his "girling" so painful, leaving a pall of misery over them both for days, so she assumed, now that he was never alone, that his Casanova ways had stopped. He still flirted outrageously in front of her and she guessed that from time to time he still managed to go "off piste," but she was comforted by many things in their new situation that she thought would keep him mostly on the straight and narrow.

For one thing he was keenly aware of the continual scrutiny he was under from both the Secret Service and the police. She was sure that he would never put at risk the high office that both he and his family had fought for so hard.

Even if he could square things with their loyal security guards, he knew he could not rely on all sections of the press.

It was true that American newspapers were deferential and not intrusive into their leaders' private lives. As far as Jackie could tell, as long as their elected representatives did not misbehave financially they were content to leave their other off-duty activities unreported. This meant that other than having their hand in the till, politicians could put other parts of their anatomy wherever they liked. Elements of the foreign press were far less supine, but Jackie had no idea that as soon as he was elected JFK had given orders that they were to be kept as far away from him as possible.

Jackie also reckoned that Jack would be worried about giving anyone the opportunity to blackmail him. Having sexual secrets that could be unearthed by the enemy in the middle of a ferocious Cold War was so risky.

She convinced herself that he would not want the people that he had handpicked to work with him, in particular the men that he respected, to know that sexually he was out of control. In front of them she imagined he would want his private life to mirror the same lofty ideals that he pursued while in the greatest office of state.

So she made the decision that apart from the dullest of jobs, which she continued to parcel out to her mother-in-law or to the vice-president's wife, she would attempt to embrace more First Lady duties. She put her heart into not just refurbishing the residence for her family's comfort, but restoring it, inviting world-class artists and musicians to entertain there, making the White House not just a powerful destination but a glamorous one.

Everything that she had been and everything that she had done, both with him and for him throughout his presidency, was predicated on what she thought of as his "new loyalty."

How was she to know that he didn't care if his praetorian guard of speechwriters, economists, and other experts found out that beneath the elegant charm of the youngest president of the United States, there was just a greedy sexual predator? She added up how many people in the White House would have known of Marilyn's visit. Anyone who entered would have had to leave their name with the men on sentry duty, then been signed in. As she slowly ticked off the names, his secretary, the sergeants on the desk, the private quarters housekeeper who changed the sheets, the list was endless, Jackie arrived at the shocking realization that having those around him in the know about his relationship with the Hollywood sex bomb was obviously something he positively relished. It gave him a buzz, a sexual frisson.

Throughout the thirty-four presidencies before Jack, the way in which the White House was used—whether it had been welcoming or forbidding—had been an accurate litmus test of the personality of the incumbent, and occasionally, of his wife. Part of his legacy would forever be tainted by his cheating.

She wanted to vent her anger to him, so decided on a visit to Arlington but this time without the cameras.

Late at night, when members of the public were not allowed in, lit only by flashlights, two Secret Service men led her to his grave.

There she hurled invective at him, but fearing her protectors might still be in earshot, she could only hiss the words under her breath.

She told him that from now on she would do only what suited her and she would do just the minimum to make her children think they had lost a decent father.

"But I am not going to peddle anything else good about you.

"You bastard. You liar.

"You betrayed me and I didn't deserve it, I loved you.

"I just wish that I had never met you.

"The sordid secrets you have left have destroyed my life.

"Did you never think of anyone but yourself? . . . Me . . . The children . . . ?

"I owe you nothing. Nothing!"

Somehow the whole episode did little to extinguish her sorrow. Who could be angry with an eternal flame?

To the outside world she forced herself to appear indifferent, making flippant jokes about the dead movie star, but privately she felt her paranoia growing. She found it hard to accept that her husband had cared for, possibly loved, another woman. Emotionally, as well as physically, she had not been enough for him.

It offered small comfort when she realized that neither had the blond goddess. Just two weeks after the Marilyn story subsided, another one emerged.

First there was the president and the prostitute. The woman, a high-class hooker, had been so bowled over by doing business with the leader of the free world she ended up charging him nothing, so he went back for more, twice.

Then some two weeks later it was the president and the princess. An elfin brunette, she had lost everything when her small country had been snaffled by the Chinese. One person, her ex-butler, discovered the joys of capitalism by fleeing to the U.S. and selling the letters he had found in the royal bedroom.

Then there were the memoirs of a policewoman. She had met the president while on duty, guarding him on a trip back to his original homeland, Ireland. Every facet of the lovemaking with the most successful member of the Fitzgerald clan was laid bare in public.

She was followed by a stunningly curvaceous Italian who pretended to be a writer and politician but was famed for giving the best parties in Rome.

Jackie continued her self-imposed purdah but forced herself to ridicule these stories when she spoke to friends and family. But when a pretty maternity nurse, hired to help with night-time feeds for the premature baby John, stepped forward, it all became too much. How could she have been so stupid?

Virtually every month she had been married to him, he had been with someone else.

And everyone around her must have known. How could she keep socializing with them? How could she ever keep facing the people she saw at parties every night who had probably been scheming behind her back for years? If only she knew who they were.

However she tried to hide it there was tension in the house.

She made sure the newspapers arrived after the children had gone to school. Caroline could read, but even little John wondered why his daddy was still on the front page so often. Remembering just how distressed she felt when she had been the same age as Caroline and her parents went through their very public split, she arranged for the nanny to take them to and from school in the car, hoping that the little girl would not see the headlines on the newsstands.

Slowly she started to become what she had tried to avoid: bitter.

She couldn't face asking anyone but her sister for the truth. She had a horrible suspicion that Lee might have been closer than she should have been to her brother-in-law.

When Lee visited from London she felt she had to know.

She started by asking if Lee knew about Jack's conquests.

"I knew as little as you," was the cool reply. "I often suspected something was going on. I mean, it wasn't something strong, just a feeling.

"Whenever Jack came to Europe he was friendly and came to dinner, but he always had to leave early. I can remember teasing him once and asking if he had a girlfriend tucked up at the embassy, but you know him . . . he told me nothing. I just figured there was a crisis going on that I was too feebleminded to know about."

Jackie thought her sibling was being too casual and lighthearted and remembered that Lee herself had played around when married to her first husband.

Maybe her sister didn't think it mattered, or did she really know something?

It was infuriating.

"Why on earth didn't you say something, warn me?" Jackie asked.

Sardonically, Lee remarked: "Even you must have suspected that some out-of-town branches of the family were very keen to lay on parties for big brother. I have no proof, but don't you remember how exhausted he was after seeing his relatives in Florida or California?

"Let's face it, what was he doing out there that was such hard work?

"Still, he was consistent." Lee got up to refill her glass of white wine and passed her sister yet another cigarette. "He was always the same from the moment you started seeing him. Extremely charming, the sort of man who never let a decent-looking woman walk by without giving her the hard stare."

Jackie started to reproach herself for not having done anything about it. Lee was right, he was far too interested in other women. He was also careless and believed he was bound by no rules. He often cut phone calls short when she came into the room but not so quickly that she could accuse him of anything. If she did ask who he was talking to, his usual response was that he was talking politics.

Suddenly the comment about her Californian in-laws caught her off guard. Something was trying to force its way into her memory.

With exquisite pain it came back to her, the misery just after he died when she couldn't find so many of his things, not just his clothes but his diaries, his medicines, his address books and notebooks, all his pieces of paper. She should have guessed then. His family knew he had secrets. Loads of them. So without so much as a by-your-leave they had judiciously ransacked their home the minute he was dead.

She was furious now that she understood how ruthlessly they had taken advantage of her grief to step in and save him from himself one last time. Any incriminating evidence had to be removed before the new incumbent moved in.

She remembered an upset Nurse Shaw when two of their smoothest operators, young men obviously working for the attorney general, Bobby, had ushered her away from some of the rooms in their private quarters. How gullible Jackie had been in later accepting their apologetic excuses. Even the White House logbook had not been left behind.

"Oh, come on, Jackie, don't be so hard on yourself," said Lee. "Your husband had just been shot. And when he was alive, you were always having babies."

"Or losing them." Jackie's eyes filled with tears as she remembered Arabella and Patrick.

"Let's face it. Guys like Jack ran around because they could. They had the money, the looks, and no one ever said not to. In fact, judging by his father, the reverse. The world's a great big bowl of sexual adventure for them."

Emboldened, Lee said: "Also, you could've left him. You had the power, you had the children."

"And have them grow up like we did?" said Jackie. "Sent round like parcels from one parent to the other, from one city to another, never fitting in? Never knowing which parent you were going to upset next? I just couldn't do it to them. It was okay for you, you were Mummy's favorite. You were the pretty one. You got married first, even though you were younger. You did everything first, I seem to remember."

Jackie started to wonder, Was she so mad because she thought that her own sister had slept with him?

"Yup, and I split up first and it was the best thing I ever did. So don't give me the whole divorce and guilt bit. You still wanted to be his wife even when his adultery was staring you in the face You wanted the excitement of being with—what did *Life* magazine call him—'Washington's most eligible bachelor.' "

She was now putting on a fake accent and speaking with the Boston inflection that all the Kennedys used.

"You could have got out early when he treated you abominably at the beginning. But even when he left you in the lurch at parties, or flew off for a little R and R on the Riviera, you stuck with him. Then you got lucky, really lucky, because whatever else he was doing, this boy went all the way. So you became the most famous woman in the world after the Queen of England."

Lee was circling the room now, pretending to acknowledge the crowds and curtsying to her elder sister.

"And then all Momma and I had to do was answer all those boring questions about your eyes, your clothes, your hair.

"So he had a mistress . . . or many. At least you know now," she said, holding up the tabloid with that day's piece of scandal. "And he wasn't faithful to her either!"

"How can you be so cynical? After we went to the White House, then after Patrick . . . I really thought things were better between us."

"Then you shouldn't have left him for days at a time and come cruising on Ari's yacht."

So she was still riled up about that, thought Jackie, just because the Greek had showered her with the most expensive jewels and not Lee.

For the sake of peace she changed the subject.

"How do I get over the past? I feel I don't know who is who and what is what anymore. I don't know who I can trust, who is my friend—"

"Jackie." Her sister's voice was more serious now. "Apart from me and Yusha, you don't really have friends, remember? You never did. You're the cool one, the one who needs nobody. Yes, you make all the right noises, but apart from me and some of the others in the family, you haven't ever really bothered."

At this Jackie became incensed.

"Of course I have friends, I just never needed 'friends' to get me out of scrapes, to cover for me when I was sneaking out of the house and seeing another man. Correction, other men!"

"I don't have to listen to this." Lee stood up. "You're not the First Lady anymore. It's late, I'm jet-lagged, I'm going."

"Stay right where you are." Jackie moved to the door. Taller and bigger, she stood with her arm across the doorjamb.

"I want you to tell me—"

"Honestly, I just want to get out of here. He played around but he's dead; you're alive. Deal with it."

Jackie stiffened; she would not let her pass.

"Think of it this way." The women were as close as possible without touching. Lee continued, "He was just looking for a pulse. Something he didn't have at home." Then she made as if to duck under her sister's arm.

Jackie automatically stopped her by grabbing her wrist.

For a moment it seemed like they had gone back in time and were a two- and a six-year-old pulling each other's hair and wrestling on the ground.

"Leave me alone, Jackie, I've told you I knew nothing." Lee eased her arm from her sister's viselike grip. "But I always suspected him."

"So what stopped you from telling me?"

"At exactly *which* presidential moment was I to whisper my worries in your ear?

"Hell, at that fund-raiser there was nothing clearer. Marilyn was making her move and she was succeeding. But you were playing the Fairy Queen, while he was eating the Sugar Plum. Be honest, you could have been brave and tried to get him in line. Pity you were so busy with the West Wing flowers you couldn't see straight. Ooh, and I forgot, nothing sordid ever happens in Camelot. Still, why don't you ruin the rest of your life hating everybody, sitting here avoiding everyone you know and reading all this." She pointed at the paper on the floor. "Yes, it seems like most of them knew what was going on, but he was in charge, he was the boss. That's life. I expect lots of them do think that you were cold and aloof, Miss Perfect, Miss White-gloves. And they blame you," she hissed. "What a pity it is that I am the only one in the world who knows that you *are* capable of passion," she said, rubbing her arm with feeling.

"I won't enjoy watching you drive yourself mad sitting here night after night wondering who let him stay where, who introduced him to whom, who was sent out to buy them presents—yes, face it, there must have been lots of those."

Jackie knew that she had gone too far by physically attacking her sister and she couldn't altogether blame her for enjoying her discomfort. Yet her rant had sparked a brainstorm. If anyone could, Guy Steavenson might be able to find out who had been Jack's pimp. And who else had been his girl.

"If you know more than you're telling me I'll find out in the end," she shouted at Lee.

Lee stopped and turned: "You know, those bullets could have killed you too. You've got two adorable children, tons of money, and every male from here to the Euphrates in love with you. Help yourself and for heaven's sake go and see a shrink. I can think of no more suitable case for treatment."

~ ❧ ~

Over the next two weeks, Jackie forced herself to go out with the cream of the Manhattan elite, "the ladies who lunch."

Now that she had the sympathy vote, they were more likely to share their misfortunes with her than before.

Without giving away her interest, she made it her business to find out if they were in therapy. It was while sitting in a chair at Kenneth's, her hairdresser, that she finally heard one talk about a good psychoanalyst.

The woman had married into one of New York's old-money families. Her husband's high status and wealth gave him, like many of his friends, the belief that he could indulge in inappropriate behavior at will.

"I had to get help—he has girlfriends. I discovered when I was eight months pregnant," her friend whispered under the drying hood. Jackie had welcomed her into her private room at the salon for just such a chat.

"I thought that once I had the baby everything would return to normal. But no. His thrill is to get them to have lunch with him wearing no underwear, then they do it in the car. He likes the feel of leather . . . it's disgusting. Mostly he heads out to the estate and does it on the way. Sometimes he gets back and takes another one out to dinner and does it all over again.

"He's been seeing some of them for years. He gives them money, opens accounts for them at Tiffany.

"I can see what you are thinking . . . so why don't I leave him?

"Well, there's our son, Junior. And let's face it, Jackie, who's ever going to invite me over when I'm alone? Yes, I'm smart, I've got a degree, but by comparison to him, 'no contacts, no class,' as his mother always says."

"So that's why you started to see a psychoanalyst?" Jackie carefully inquired.

"Yes, there I can unburden myself. I can tell the doctor anything and he can never, ever tell anyone else. Those are the rules," she uttered brightly.

So Jackie made her decision, chose a man whose name she had heard mentioned favorably, and started twice-weekly visits just a five-minute walk from her home.

David Goadshem was handsome, black haired, and six foot three. He had the advantage of being from New York's Lower East Side, coupled with the warmth of a Viennese mother whose family had actually known Dr. Freud before World War II.

His first job was to persuade her that the real Jackie was a strong, capable woman.

"For example, you have been describing over the last few weeks your ambivalence about going to the White House, then how you dealt with it. Don't you see, in the end you took your demons, all the things you hated about the place, the protocol, the lack of privacy, and made them work to your advantage, you owned them."

He asked her how she coped with the really bad moments.

"Well, as I did when I came here for the first time," she said, smiling, "I preplan it, I 'dream' it. I imagine it so clearly, not just my part but how I am going to have to interact with others."

He chuckled. "You may not be aware of it but this is a well-known way of handling all sorts of trauma. Some therapists almost hypnotize their patients to give them the courage to act in this way. It is a mental escape hatch. And you found it for yourself."

As her confidence grew, he gave her "permission" to feel that she could deal as she wished with anyone she thought had betrayed her; she owed them nothing, "and that includes your in-laws."

He also tried to explain the unaccountable urge some men had for forbidden sex rather than sexual love.

The therapy helped her immensely so Jackie figured that she owed it to her sister to perk up her ideas and arrange a family lunch for her before she, and her husband, the prince, returned to London.

On the morning of the lunch, one newspaper gave Jackie her first pummeling. A detailed article, tracking each time she had been absent from the White House, almost blamed Jackie for the president's many adulteries. It did not mention that these absences were often due to pregnancy, or the health of other members of the family, including the president's own father.

It was the last straw.

At the lunch, at the end of her small speech wishing her sister farewell, Jackie announced that she was withdrawing from public life for a while.

As she saw Lee down to her car, more fans than ever clustered round the doorway of 1040 Fifth Avenue. Whatever the newspapers and magazines wrote, the Jackie effect lived on.

## CHAPTER Nine

Jackie wrote to Guy asking for help. Now that she had learned to unburden herself to her psychoanalyst, she found it therapeutic to put everything she felt, or suspected, down on paper.

As she had written that she had withdrawn from social life, he sent her a pair of powerful binoculars, as used by the CIA, to cheer her up. The message on his note concluded, "Look through these for now. I believe I will be able to help you look further when I get home." He made her feel hopeful.

When she was bored she would train the binoculars on the waiting reporters and photographers, fifteen floors below. She took pleasure in frustrating the ones that she loathed, that she recognized from their head-and-shoulder snapshots tucked next to the bylines on the most aggressive news stories about her. She would wait inside until just after they had given up and gone home.

As for the ever-present photographers, it was silly, she knew, but she loved it when it rained. They got soaked, as no self-respecting doorman on Eighty-fifth Street would let them shelter under his awning. When there was a heavy shower she occasionally took the opportunity to escape, camouflaging herself with a trench coat, headscarf, and large sunglasses. She knew that if a snapper was still hanging around, any picture he took would be like so many others already in the file, it would not be used.

Immaculately dressed in black (or occasionally white, chosen because it was the alternative color of mourning in many countries), the Jackie that had been emerging to attend the ballet, the opera, and some intimate, private lunches and dinners, folded her wings and crept back into her chrysalis.

The city missed her, the newspapers most of all.

Weeks turned into months and stories of Jack and his women still appeared, but none had the power to shock like his romance with M.M. Without new titillating details, or a glamorous photograph, the "Prezcapades" might begin on page one but soon ended up on the inside pages.

She assumed from Guy's hopeful note that despite the fierce competition between the CIA and the FBI, he would be able to ascertain many more of Jack's little secrets.

She recalled how intensely all the Kennedy men had disliked FBI boss J. Edgar Hoover. She had once bumped into the short, pugnacious man strutting into the White House as if he owned the place. At the time she had ascribed it to familiarity; he had after all worked for every president since Coolidge. But with hindsight she understood that the confident gait was the result of knowledge. He knew that of the three of them around the table, including the president and his brother, the attorney general, he, because he knew their secrets, held the most powerful hand.

Jackie yearned to see Guy. She hadn't worked out what she was going to do when everything was revealed, but she felt that at the very least she wouldn't lie awake and worry that she was being too kind to someone who had betrayed her trust. Her pride balked at that.

When he arrived he presented her with a large pot of caviar from his local Moscow store, gave her a quizzical look, went to the window, and tried out the binoculars for himself.

After slowly surveying the gaggle of photographers below, he returned them to her.

"I'll get you a telescope next time," he said.

"They are even more powerful and they will show you every wart, every pimple. With a bit of luck it'll eventually make you lose interest in them all."

She interrupted, "Or even better, they'll lose interest in me."

"And." He only paused for a second for breath as if not acknowledging her comment. "The stars probably look very good from up here."

She poured him a glass of white wine. As they chatted about his son's school progress, and exchanged information about her latest trip to the Adriatic, she thought how handsome he looked. Even though she always told him to dress informally when he came around, he wore a navy suit. Years ago she had teased him that he bought a certain shade of pale blue shirt in Jermyn Street in London because they matched his eyes.

"I bought a couple when I was passing through," he said, "to celebrate the promotion."

After offering her congratulations she asked, what did it mean, would he have to leave Russia, had his paycheck doubled? She was interested in the agency. An old friend of her stepfather's had once suggested she think about joining when she left college.

She had made an effort for him. She wore a simple wool sheath in a fine black and white houndstooth check. Her hair was gleaming and full. Her only adornment was her usual three-strand pearl necklace and matching earrings.

He did not comment on her hands, bare of her wedding or engagement ring.

"Instead of wasting time when I arrived yesterday I decided to take advantage of a friend. I found out that I could look at everything that J. Edgar has in his favorite, very large box file, the one marked PRESIDENT OF THE USA. So I got down to work."

Her grin of grateful delight reminded him of the enthusiastic senator's wife he had met in Prague.

"Believe it or not, he's already got some stuff on the latest one, but dear lady, we are not interested in that.

"Before we start and I tell you what I've discovered, you've got to tell me how you want me to do this."

"What do you mean?" she asked.

"Well, supposing I find someone you really like is in there?"

"There are bound to be some friends, people that I *thought* were my friends . . ." Her voice trailed away to a whisper.

"Well, this is the moment when you really have to think about it.

"Most of the stories so far have been about dames at the lower end of the market. Now that I have been able to rummage among Mr. Hoover's files, the situation is bound to change. After all, Jack had nothing against wellborn women, which means that we must expect to find some women more like yourself."

"You mean my sister?" The minute she blurted it out she regretted it.

"Actually . . ." There was a long pause while he consulted his memory and even checked the small black notebook he always carried.

"No. Not so far. But I've only had a chance to give the files a quick look. I meant Nantucket, the Upper East Side, Newport, Ocean Drive, Vassar, Spence, Chapin, and so on. You've got through the worst, is this really what you want?"

She was impressed. He was being sensitive while also being completely businesslike.

She confessed about her paranoia; every time she met an attractive woman she imagined her making love to Jack. She explained her conjectures were driving her mad. Since she had failed to drive them out of her mind she felt that finally knowing everything would be better than not.

"Okay, so how do you feel about the boys, the jolly old friends who helped him? For instance, how do you feel about Deck now?"

"Well, of course I always knew that he was never really my friend. We were strangers washed up on the dirty, sodden fields of the JFK fiefdom.

"But I have to remember that he is Caroline's godfather, there is still that link.

"I know that I should have had no expectation that he would ever be honest with me, I know this kind of *omertà*, this loyalty, is the way you men work, but he could have helped me so much.

"I was so nice to Deck . . . and his mad Irish sister. Always welcomed him in, often when I wanted to be alone with Jack and the children. I know it is naive of me to have expected him to behave in any other way, I just feel so used, so stupid."

"But Jackie, just imagine what might have happened if Deck had told you what was going on. You might have left your husband and then you might never have done the things you have.

"Because you stayed in the marriage your husband became president; he could have never done that if you had left him. Then, by quite reasonably assuming that once he was in the White House he was a reformed man, you did wonders, some great things."

"I've thought about that a lot. I guess if our marriage had ended he wouldn't have become president but then I would not have had Caroline and John." She glanced over at a new photograph on the demilune mahogany table; the picture featured both of them grinning, astride their ponies.

"Once we had Caroline I was in for the long haul."

Over the next hour they went through the little notebook. He had used it to jot down names and times. If some hurt or upset her she gave no indication of it except for the occasional "oh" of surprise that escaped from her. Even baby Patrick's death had not stopped his father from a speedy return to the welcoming arms and breasts of a stranger.

The other surprise was how many women frolicked with her husband the minute his wife and children flew off in their helicopter. It was clear that this was going on so frequently that some of the men, distinguished, clever ones, whom she thought of as happily married family men, could not fail to know.

"From what we know he probably kept some of them in the loop by letting them join in," said Guy.

When he saw her eyebrows rise, he said:

"What you have to realize is that guys like that, not famous, not rich, middle-aged, probably very clever but not skilled in seduction techniques, can't get hold of a girl who looks like a model or a film star unless it's a presidential edict. This is fantasyland for them."

No wonder Jack had been so successful at keeping all of this a secret, she thought.

Guy was watching her carefully. He knew that the information he was giving her could easily allow her to slide back into the same sort of depression he had seen when he had visited her at the disastrous new house in Washington.

"Look, let's call it a day. If you like I'll bring you the rest tomorrow."

He moved over to her side of the table and sat next to her.

His training at briefing and debriefing foreign agents could come in useful now.

"If this is depressing you, maybe we should stop right now."

"I couldn't be more depressed than when I saw that picture of Marilyn. Frankly, now all the stuff about the rest of the women has come out I don't feel so bad. It seems he wasn't loyal to her either; the numbers, the frequency, it makes him look worse. He seems to be what the ancients in literature used to call a satyr, I believe. It looks as if he were completely out of control, driven to excess, and it contrasts so badly with his image." She leapt up and went to the desk in the corner of the room and produced a magazine from the bottom drawer.

"But look at this. Because his sexual antics were so at odds with the way our life appeared, there's some truly horrible stuff—I wouldn't dignify it by calling them stories—starting to appear about me now."

"Just ignore them, they think this stuff sells."

"No, there's more!" She started to pace back and forth in front of the shimmering fire.

"There's this other theory that I was power-hungry, that I wanted to be First Lady so much that I was in on it all, that I deliberately colluded to pretend that we were a happy family, that my European background and attitude to life mean that I thought infidelity was unimportant, the sophisticated way to behave. Or there's the other theory, that I'm really stupid."

He sensed that she was on a roll, one of anger and anguish. He decided to stop it.

"C'mon. That's all garbage," he interrupted loudly.

"But they are taking away my past. My life. *Our* life.

"I used to deal with the stories by thinking that life, *real* life, was taking place somewhere up here"—she indicated her shoulders— "and had no relationship with what they wrote down there. But now that my life with him is over . . . they are taking it, even the good bits, away."

He stood up and went over to her.

"You must forget this. We need you, the public, the country needs you. Don't let these bums get to you, everyone knows that this is all ridiculous. Give it time. People will begin to understand that he was not what he seemed, that he was prepared to risk everything for a lay, and I don't mean just losing you, I mean everything. Just think of what the Russians could have done with some of this if they had known about his screwing around during the Cuban crisis. Arghh, it doesn't bear thinking about."

The open fire crackled, and they were both mesmerized for an instant, thinking back to those dangerous days.

"Now, more than ever, you have emerged as the star of this show, the Kennedy show, in fact the whole presidency itself. I know you won't like this but if I was an advisor to you—"

She cut in, "But you are. Apart from my mother there's no one else I really trust."

"Okay, if I was properly advising you on how to run your life and how to protect the image of the 'numero uno widow' in the world, I would say that so far you haven't done a thing wrong.

"Everything about you has been perfect. From the way you planned the funeral to everything you have done since."

Slowly Jackie started to shake her head.

"No, now that it has all come out it's obvious I wasn't enough for Jack."

"So, more fool him!" He stopped looking straight into her eyes and wheeled around to sit back in his seat.

"Remember, soon the historians will start to look at how smart he was at the rest of it. They will be measuring his accomplishments. Whatever they think of his achievements in the future they will have to acknowledge that sex was his weakness, that he was unable to recognize the jewel that he had and that he wasted a lot of his time and energy pandering to his sex habit."

Had he gone too far? Guy was relieved when she stopped pacing and sat down next to him.

"Life moves on," he continued. "Even his greatest admirers will have to admit that in this day and age he just didn't have the correct attitude toward women anyway. In his mind they were never his equal. He used them as nurses or whores; either way they were there just to satisfy his overactive ego. He's gone, so now his presidency will have to face the jury of world opinion. But for you, this is no time to retreat or to dump your husband."

She looked at him in a puzzled way.

"What I mean is, when I first arrived you were telling me that you went to Arlington the other night and told him you were through. And I notice that you have taken your wedding and engagement rings off."

"Well, I only did that yesterday," said Jackie.

"Don't you understand that every time you are seen to be cherishing his memory you look greater, grander, better. Putting the pieces together for your children's sake, trying to cherish the good moments, the times the four of you were happy. Every time you lead Caroline and John in prayer, anywhere in the world, people look at you and think, There is a saint.

"Believe it or not, what you do now is important to America."

She pulled an unbelieving face.

"Look at the wider picture. This country badly wants not to feel guilty. Many of those who think it's their right to carry a gun will wonder, Am I a bit to blame for a nut like Oswald? Did I make it too easy for him?

"You, by staying here, by trying to do the best for your children, are a beacon.

"You can't be that if you just bury yourself.

"You stay inside, hiding yourself away from the world, stop doing your charity work, stop putting your energy into the library they're building in Boston, stop showing that you still care about America, and people will start thinking, Maybe the newspapers are right, maybe she isn't what she was cracked up to be either.

"Remember, they've been burned. They were taken in by Jack. A pretty regular sort of family guy, they thought. Or at least that is how he was sold to 'em. Now they find he has these skeletons in the closets, in the drawers, behind the faucets . . . everywhere.

"Just like yourself, they don't want to be taken for a ride again.

"If you aren't out there, they will wonder what you're hiding.

"Then they might believe that you *did* go along with a lie, posing for all those pictures and features about the perfect family. That you did want power at any price.

"Yes, I know it isn't fair. Immediately after his death, yes, you were given the allowance to be truly upset, to retreat and cry for your man, for the future that was taken away from you. But now, over a year later and a lot of dirty linen after . . . if you hide away you lose your stature.

"Every day in this great country of ours, I would take a guess probably half a million women discover that their man has been fooling around. For them it has to be business as usual. They have to take the children to school, care for their elderly parents, go to the PTA and the supermarket.

"So at best they will think that you are behaving like someone who is so grand she feels that she can just dump her responsibilities. That you are behaving like a spoiled princess.

"At worst they will assume that the gossips are right. Because you have the power to raise money and bring in thousands of dollars to charity—you know that your name does that—if you can't be bothered to turn up you will look heartless, cold, and disinterested."

He could see that she was unsettled by his words.

He gently rested his hand on her arm for a moment and looked into her eyes.

"The last thing I want to do is frighten you. But get outside of yourself and see how this might appear to Mr. and Mrs. Middle America."

Jackie looked at him, huge eyes out on stalks.

"Sorry, but you did say you like the truth.

"Out there." He pointed at the window in what he knew was a slightly melodramatic style. "It is so much worse for those who are ill, poor, lonely."

He could see he had shocked her, so for a moment he turned his back and looked out of the window.

"I'm sorry, I've been rude and harsh," he murmured.

"No," she answered, "I know that you are doing it for the best of reasons. I'm going to think about what you've said."

"Tomorrow I promise you that I'll bring you the rest, everything that's known about your late partner and his catting around, and you will have to decide how you process that information.

"My last piece of advice: you have a great understanding of animals and know that they do best in their natural habitat. Well, yours isn't within this very elegant apartment, however large it is.

"Let's face it, the kitchen is a foreign country to you."

The old joke lightened the mood.

"Your natural surroundings are center stage. Your natural attitude isn't bitter and twisted but making things happen, doing things, and helping others.

"Jackie, you're our greatest asset, please don't waste more time worrying about what was, think about what is and what could be."

Within minutes he was gone.

When he arrived the next day and produced the notebook she leaned forward and put it back in his pocket.

"I've changed my mind," she said.

He paid close attention as she paced back and forth in front of the fireplace.

He noticed the beauty of the room, which she had arranged so that when sunlight spilled through the window the antiques, the silverware, and the mirrors glowed.

"I sat here for hours after you'd gone. I went over everything you said. I turned it over and over in my head. You'll be glad to know you've changed my mind on a lot of things.

"I want these stories to die."

She looked into the middle distance and he knew not to interrupt.

"So don't tell me what is in that little book. Please just keep it all to yourself. Someday when I am a very old lady I might ask you for it, so keep it safe, but for now, it's over."

He got up to congratulate her but she waved him down.

"Guy, this is so difficult. Let me get it over with.

"As you suggested I got to thinking about ordinary Americans, about those people who voted for us, for me and Jack, not just Jack.

"Everyone thinks I am apolitical. It's not true. I know that I can do things that matter, and I do have things to do. Yes, I am going to go out, be active, but not just in the way you think. Not just to parties and VIP stuff. The only way to get over this is to shock people, but this time in a good way. I want to do something that makes a difference.

"And you are going to help me to do it."

CHAPTER

It was modesty that made her turn her back to him. It had been a long time since she had done this.

Slowly she bent over and carefully eased the sheer stocking up her leg. It was so quiet she fancied that the electric buzz between her skin and the flimsy nylon was audible. Once the inky black fabric was taut two tiny portions were clamped into the silky suspender that rested high on her thigh.

She began the same routine with the other leg. Apart from her stockings she appeared naked to him even though she had already slipped into her bra. All her lingerie, the tulle, satin and organdy, even the silken threads that held them together, was hand-dyed in Paris to match her skin to perfection.

She could feel that David, David the doctor whose mind and now whose hands had roused her out of her misery, was watching her.

Still naked on the couch he realized that they had not even had time to pull the curtains. Thank heaven his office was not visible from neighboring buildings. The only interloper had been the rare shard of late-afternoon sunshine.

"You know this is very bad. If we continue to behave like this you are going to have to find yourself a new psychoanalyst." He laughed as he attempted to pull his hair into some sort of tidiness while taking a cursory look for his shorts.

Without turning, she said, "Well then, you'd better find me a handsome one."

The smile in her voice gave him all the encouragement he needed. He got up and pulled her into his arms.

Playfully he kissed the tip of her nose, her lips, then on down to the hollow in her throat.

He slipped behind her and held the strands of her deep brown hair roughly aside while he paid close attention to each of the tiny bones at the back of her neck.

She thought how much better the sex was than with Jack.

The appointment had begun as normal.

Ever since she had started therapy she had always been prompt for her twice-weekly appointment. It fitted neatly into the time between the end of lunch and her children's return from school.

At the beginning she had been Jack-obsessed but gradually the thirty-nine-year-old psychiatrist had calmed her, engaged her thoughts, and led her from panic about the present into having the honesty and the inquisitiveness to behave like all his other patients and lead him through the road map of her past so that he could attempt to explain the workings of her mind.

She had thought him very attractive from the moment they met. But it was with the same regard that she might have for a curtain fabric or a vase. Her emotions were entirely bound up in the loss of her husband and his hidden love life in the parallel lane of their marriage.

At first the sessions did not go well. Years of being guarded kept her from being frank and speaking openly, but then life conspired to alter her attitude. She realized that the idea of maintaining control was foolish self-deceit. The continuing press disclosures about her husband's betrayals meant that trying to retain a façade of containment would not work. So she opened up and gradually he persuaded her that her husband's behavior was in no way related to any failure on her part. Then he went to work peeling back the deeper layers of her unhappiness, starting with her position as an extremely youthful mediator in her parents' miserable marriage.

For David Goadshem this was not only what he had trained for, this was what he knew about.

"Are all families so destructive?" she asked after they had spent many weeks analyzing the various effects that the Bouviers, Auchin-closses, and Kennedys had had on their offspring.

"Freud thinks so. I think that understanding why we behave as we do is the first step."

She began to anticipate their sessions with pleasure. At Easter she sent him the gift of an Audubon print he had briefly mentioned and later a book of drawings. She was intrigued, perhaps curious about him.

David Goadshem knew that there was nothing unusual in that. He had been doing this work for ten years and it was expected, had even been discussed at medical school. It was inevitable that some female patients, especially those who had never had a man who really listened and talked to them, would start to see their psychoanalyst in a romantic light.

There were rules about sexual relationships between patients and doctors, rules he had never broken. The trajectory from living with his grandparents, who were still mentally dwelling in the shtetl outside Krakow, to medical school had been too steep for him to ever put his livelihood at risk. From the day he set himself up as a psychoanalyst he had never faltered, not even when some of his most glamorous clients arrived dressed as provocatively as possible and made it plain they were available. Not even when one of them had brazenly stripped on the couch.

Also, although he treated her in exactly the same way as all his other patients, he could not help feeling a little protective toward the former First Lady, so the thought of ever being involved with her did not occur to him.

It was a strange retrograde session that altered things. After months of even progression she arrived obsessively chain-smoking, more anxious and nervous than ever before. The previous evening she had heard high-level Hollywood gossip about a biopic that was soon to go into production based on Marilyn's life.

It was as if she had returned to the bleak, dark days of her early visits.

"The rumor is that it's going to say that Marilyn was the love of Jack's life."

"Okay. Let's do what we used to, let's ask ourselves, Did Jack ever say he wanted a divorce?"

"No."

"Did Jack behave differently to her or was she betrayed like everyone else?"

Lying in her usual position on the couch, she couldn't see his face but found his voice compelling, determined yet failing to be completely unemotional. For the first time ever she sat up, turned, and stared at him. Examined him.

He couldn't explain the rest.

The whirlwind of lust and passion was as strange to him as to her.

The next morning she had rung his receptionist with entreaties to fit her in with a last-minute appointment that very day.

In between seeing patients he tried to work out what this meant. She had never altered or added an appointment before. She was also breaking her sacrosanct rules, coming at a time when she would normally be with her children.

Was it more news about the film that was worrying her? Or did she just want to see him again? He had come to no conclusion by the time he had succumbed to her request to join her on the couch again.

Even though he knew they were both single he knew it was wrong. But he was elated.

As he stretched himself alongside her she turned over onto her stomach, raised herself up on her elbows, and put her face close to his own and stroked his cheek.

"David, David," she breathed.

"Yesterday was wonderful."

He didn't dare move, passion and happiness imprisoned him.

"Then again, pretty much everything that has ever happened to me in this office"—she gazed round at the tall bookshelves, the low modern lamps on his desk—"has always been wonderful."

He smiled up at her and was about to raise his lips to hers when she continued.

"But I know the rules. There are always the rules," she intoned in a deeper voice.

"After you reminded me of them I had to check. You know me." She tipped her face to one side.

There was stillness between them, a waiting; a crossroad had been reached.

"You were right, as always," she said. "I can't keep seeing you for therapy if, well, if other stuff is going to happen.

"I read pages and pages about how it is vital that the therapist and the patient are not emotionally involved. Apparently it screws things up, excuse the pun."

"Well—" he began, but she interrupted.

"I hate to admit it but it does all seem very sensible, and David, you of all people know that it's too much of a risk, for both of us. You've done so well for yourself, come so far to get here."

He was still not sure where this was going and was desperate to interrupt, but she shushed him.

Speaking quickly, she continued. "I know that this will remain our secret, but let's just say, in my life, I have discovered that walls have ears."

He forced himself to look nonchalant but she wasn't fooled.

"Please don't be sad, I've thought of nothing else since I left here yesterday.

"I know what I need most is to talk to you. Here, in this room, I've found my release from hell and there's so much more straightening out that I need to do.

"So, if I have to find myself another therapist, who will I go to? Who will I be able to trust? Who else will I respect?"

"Well," he interrupted, "you know that whoever you go to, they are honor-bound to tell no one, absolutely no one, what you say, ever."

Even as he said it he knew he was lost.

"Yes, but they will never be you, who understands me, every single bit of me, as we now know?" She grinned. "Also, if you do find me a new therapist everyone will wonder why . . . not to mention the other shrinks, who will come to the obvious conclusion."

Gently she leaned over and kissed his forehead.

"Could we do it, have this"—her smile swept over the couch in a special reference to the application they had now found for it—"and still be able to have the other?"

"It has been known." He shrugged.

"Okay, I admit, you're a genius, so maybe it would work . . . for a little while. But we both know that in the end—"

"You think it wouldn't work?"

"We'll have become something else . . . won't we?"

He was now gazing firmly at the ceiling.

She could not guess what he was thinking. In her experience men who went quiet were upset or angry or both.

"Please don't be angry with me, I couldn't bear that. You know how much you've done for me, you know I could never trust someone else . . ."

"Yes, well no, I don't really." He still wouldn't look at her.

She knew that she had been right. Angry and upset.

Finally he turned to her. His expression, resignation tinged with lust, made her want to brush his lips with her own. They kissed again. Just before they began to undo each other's clothes he pulled back and whispered.

"Don't worry, I've got the message, I know that we must stop doing this."

Later, as once again he watched her while she readied herself to leave he realized how irritated he was with himself for thinking that there could have been any other outcome. The moment she had insisted on seeing him so soon, he should have known her well enough to have worked it out. Self-disciplined and determined to be finally at ease with herself, she knew that she still needed therapy. It was inevitable that she would not let sex, something she had done without for some time, remove her from his mental healing.

Making the best of it, he ascribed what had happened as a sensible addition to her treatment.

Before she left he told her: "Remember the discussions we've had about recrimination and revenge.

"As far as I know you haven't used this before but why not think of sex in this way. We've talked about how having conversations with someone who is not with us, whether they are dead or just elsewhere, can be a way of overcoming the pain they've caused."

She thought about the zillions of angry one-sided talks she had had with Jack since he had been shot.

"At least now every time you are in bed with someone you can think, 'Here's one in the eye for you, Jack.' After all, apart from you and the children, the thing he'll be missing most is sex!"

She laughed. "Oh, I hardly think that just because I've started again that I'll be doing it so regularly that it will be of major support, but I'll bear it in mind."

Then she made him solemnly promise that they would return, with as much certainty as they could, to their previous incarnations by Thursday afternoon. This made them both so sad, so they made love for the fourth and, as they both insisted, for the last time.

Two hours later, preparing for early-evening drinks with her mother, sister, and an old friend, a Russian diplomat whom she had got to know while living in the White House, she chose to dress in a more daring way. Choosing a simple Madame Grès dress in yellow silk, she left off the matching jacket and cinched the waist with a wide leather belt so that the hem became fashionably shorter. She then added higher heels.

Her sexual reawakening also made her feel less like behaving like a former First Lady and more like a real one. Instead of sticking to such asexual subjects as the subtleties of Hungarian wines and the relevance of foreign travel to the well-educated teenager, she managed to engage the man in a real conversation about his problems with a daughter who was hooked on sleeping pills, and while she had no intention of succumbing to his less than diplomatic overtures, she found that the last forty-eight hours had made it possible for her to launch herself back into the world of sexual nuance, flattery, and charm.

She was enjoying herself so much that she almost forgot that she was supposed to be trying to ease him out after just an hour. Guy was in town and had been unsuccessfully trying to visit her for nearly a week. He was due at eight P.M.

The last time he had visited she was still being reclusive. Now, as part of her determination to stop raking over the past, she had taken practical steps to fill her evenings. After Dallas she had been inundated with requests from many of the foreign diplomats, artists, and politicians that she and Jack had befriended. Most had visited Jack's grave but none had been given the chance to offer their personal condolences to his widow. Intellectually stimulating and knowledgeable, they were, she felt, a worthwhile alternative to going to New York events that brought back memories she wanted to avoid. She had vowed to do no more digging but she was still uncomfortable dealing with some of the old faces.

This low-key entertaining, usually no more than early-evening drinks at home, often including a member of the family because entertaining a man alone might give rise to gossip, gave her something to do at a time of the day when she was apt to feel low.

Since moving to New York she kept herself busy filling her day with routine; always sure to do regular sit-ups, since her riding and water-skiing needed suppleness, she also became a yoga fan. Apart from her regular meetings planning the JFK Presidential Library in Boston and involving herself with the children after school, which might mean a bike ride in Central Park or a trip to the movies, there were still some days when she might bury herself under the bedclothes. Wedding anniversaries, Jack's birthday, and the birth dates of their dead children would still bludgeon her to misery. But when she was feeling positive she would often paint or do some drawing at the tall, steel art desk she placed by the window in her study, visit the Fifth Avenue stores, Bonwit Teller and Bergdorf Goodman, or the antique shops on East Fifty-seventh Street. She enjoyed selecting the children's clothes at Cerrutti on Sixty-eighth and Madison who sold Florence Eisman's classic cotton outfits for boys and girls, with appliqué details like sailboats or daisies.

She would go for private consultations with Erno Lazslo, the Hungarian skin expert, and became dedicated to the rituals involved with his sea mud soap, dousing her face and then rinsing it many times. When she had been out of the sun for some time she would have the little dark hairs on her arms bleached. Weekends were filled with trips to the countryside where she supervised Caroline's and John's riding lessons and continued to go hunting. During the holidays, they traveled extensively but she knew she was just whiling away time and still longed to do something more serious. Reiterating their last conversation, she wrote to Guy to push this message home.

On his next trip he suggested, "Maybe it would help if we put our heads together. Analyze what sort of work you really want and what you think you'll have time for. After all, both Caroline and John are still very young."

"I don't know myself, but there must be something. Sometimes I wish that I hadn't turned down Lyndon's offer of an ambassadorship."

"Very smart of him," muttered Guy. "He could see that what you have is the status, stature, and knowledge for it. There's got to be a way we can harness all that."

She reminded him of when they had first met and her early attempts at spying and how she spoke several languages.

Over the next few weeks, buried deep in his Moscow office, Guy tried to formulate a plan. He knew that she had loved the intrigue of her snatched moments of espionage, but she could hardly join the agency's payroll.

He had come up with no hard-and-fast ideas by the time he next returned to the U.S.

This time "Her Elegance," as the fashion trade newspaper *Women's Wear Daily* was now calling her, had little free time. She made an exception for him and asked him to come and see her later than usual. She promised to telephone him after her predinner invitees had left. When, by eight, she had still not called, he decided to go over to her apartment and wait in the lobby for his cue to go upstairs. As he crossed Fifth Avenue he was surprised when he saw a highflier from Moscow, surrounded by his goonlike retinue, exiting her apartment building.

Guy had never taken much interest in Jackie's foreign contacts as she had assured him that all her connections were nowadays far less powerful than they had been when she and Jack had got to know them. But Guy, who had recognized the man, knew differently. He waited in the lobby and five minutes later watched as her mother left, before he was shown into Jackie's private elevator.

Having established that the Russian had been her visitor, Guy filled her in on the man's new role. True, he had been the number two at the Russian embassy in Washington but he had been promoted. He was now in charge of Soviet counterespionage.

With his CIA hat on, he asked if she would mind giving him some of the other names of her recent foreign visitors. All were men, and while many were has-beens, quite a few had become even more influential in the last few years, and some were from enemy Communist countries.

Again, on behalf of the agency, he asked if she would mind telling him about the conversation she had that evening with the Russian. Jackie, quite taken aback by the ruthless nature of her visitor's new role, was happy to oblige. Guy discovered that Jackie was a mine of information. Gently he grilled her about the chats that she'd had with some of her other foreign guests.

He was impressed with how much information she had garnered in such a short space of time. It only took one or two cocktails for some of the most unscrupulous men in the world to lower their defenses to such a beautiful woman.

In the middle of Manhattan she had been discovering the softer side of some of America's most powerful enemies, the type who would check that their mothers weren't miked up before visiting them for Christmas. In doing so she had accidentally discovered some factual tidbits that would be highly useful to the agency.

"Sometimes they ask me out for dinner," she confided.

"Where?" he asked.

"Oh, the usual places, Le Pavillon, La Grenouille, or La Caravelle. One or two of the better-looking ones have suggested that we eat in their suites," she said, chuckling.

"At their consulate?"

"No, silly, at their hotel!"

Guy was mystified. When he had last been working in the States, admittedly some years ago, senior politicians and diplomats from the Iron Curtain countries never had such freedom. In Washington they would have stayed at their embassy, in New York they would have either had to overnight at their consulate or with their ambassador to the United Nations.

Security was taken so seriously that when any senior personnel went to a reception where both Westerners and alcohol were present, they were obliged to eat a half a pound of butter, on bread or without it, it was up to them to choose, so that they would not get drunk and reveal any secrets.

At all times they were surrounded by an entourage, often swollen with some of the nastier members of their own security service.

Suddenly the role that she, and she alone, could perform for the agency was staring him in the face.

He desperately wanted to share his idea with her, but before he told her, or anyone else, he knew that he had to think it through.

It excited him so much that he was almost too impatient to tuck into the ratatouille, shepherd's pie, and salad that Jackie had ordered for them.

They chatted away easily but in the back of his mind Guy was beginning to work out how to use Jack's widow.

That night he put his idea down on paper. Within a week he and his immediate superior were talking to the director general of the agency. Between them they devoted their time to piecing together a scheme and finalizing a proposition.

Two weeks later, having received reports from the undercover men watching her Upper East Side apartment block, Guy had everything in order. The agency was aware that this plan would have to receive approval from the Oval Office. Not only would the president have to agree to using such an iconic figure as the former First Lady, he would also have to arrange for the CIA to operate in the domestic arena. As the situation stood the CIA was only supposed to run operations abroad; any spying or undercover work undertaken on American soil was in the bailiwick of the FBI.

The president himself made minor adjustments to the plan and decreed that nothing could be put into action until all the facts were made known to the person who was now at the top of the CIA hiring list.

"There is no way that you can begin this without giving Mrs. Kennedy all of the facts," he drawled.

"She has to know what will be happening behind her back, before we can go ahead.

"She must be informed that she may be putting herself in danger and that she may have to deal with more security around her, and so may her children.

"Remember, we are dealing with the most ruthless bastards in the world; if it ever gets out that she was involved, she and we need to be prepared. If she says yes, she will be agreeing to be used as the most glamorous decoy known to man."

The president wondered if he should be the one to persuade her to take on this task but was advised against it. He was reminded that she had turned him down before, doubtless because of her brother-in-law Bobby. Even though he was now junior senator for New York, he might still try to stifle any offer from Lyndon Johnson.

Magnanimously, the president thought the scheme was so vital that he insisted that Guy, its instigator, still based in Moscow, be especially recalled to put the suggestion to Jackie in person.

"As soon as he gets over here I want him to come and see me. I know Jackie well and I think I can give him some pointers. Jackie is very modern thinking. She transformed the White House in ways you don't know. Technically improved it, made the kitchens efficient, made it work. So show her our best bits, the cameras, the listening devices. Show her how they work. Explain how a man's bathroom cabinet can tell you so much about him. Draw her in. Make her part of the team."

Armed with the latest technology, a nervous Guy went to 1040 Fifth Avenue.

"Jackie, tonight I'm acting as the envoy of the president, who, I must tell you, will be very happy to take your call at any time this evening."

After her initial surprise he spilled his bag of tricks.

"These cameras can be hidden in all kinds of things, a cigarette case or a handbag. Behind the Iron Curtain it is hard to point a lens wherever you want to. These make it easier. The same with these tiny bugs.

"In the future all of these gadgets will get more accurate and even smaller.

"The notion of secrecy is so big behind the Iron Curtain, even things that could be public are kept hidden. Everything from the beet harvest to population growth is secret."

He filled her in on all the ways that the empire's system of guards, identity cards, and obsession with security made it almost impossible to spy on them at home. The CIA therefore wanted to take the opportunity to do so when they were traveling.

"When they come over here it's been hard to get anything out of them, but when you told me that they are being given this little window of freedom to talk to you, I had an idea. But before I tell you that, perhaps it's best if I explain how and why things have changed.

"It's all public relations," Guy explained. "In the old days they could act heavy but this is the sixties. They are never going to sell Communism to the young, always their best recruiting ground, if it looks like Big Brother is watching day and night. They want their system to appear as open as ours and for it to look so great that no one would ever want to leave it. They want to show that they are living as we do, with our freedom, our independence, and that their system, their culture, also gives them liberty.

"Nowadays they don't want people to think that it's the Berlin Wall, the armed guards, and the miles of barbed wire that keep people behind the Iron Curtain, but good old Communism. They are saying, see, our people can stay where they like and wander around at will.

"But of course, behind your charming diplomat there is a wife, a child, a mother, or a father who is acting as a hostage. They are not being kept in a cell, there's no need, but make no mistake, your charming guest knows that if he attempts to make a dash for freedom he puts someone he loves at risk.

"And if that is not enough, they have the bloodhounds—that is, KGB men—with them wherever they go, listening to what they say, watching who they talk to, and above all making sure they don't vanish. The Communists just couldn't stand to have another Nureyev seeking asylum over here so they simply won't take the risk of a politician or a diplomat going over the wall."

"All right," she interrupted, "but if this has been happening for some time what is so special about when they come here?"

"As I just said, they may be trying to look as free as a bird to the outside world but they are still petrified to leave their politicians alone, because it was the Eastern Europeans who virtually invented the honeypot entrapment scam. You know, where they use a beautiful girl, or sometimes a boy, to seduce one of our people and then blackmail them into revealing classified information.

"So even though they are pretending they are not standing guard over their own people, they are far too cautious to allow them to go anywhere solo, particularly if it is to see a beautiful woman. But the one place they are allowed to do so . . ." He paused.

"Is here," she said, finishing his sentence for him.

"So what could I do?"

To demonstrate how much she could help he showed her his homework.

"You may remember," he said, smiling, "that not that long ago I was asked if I could do some quiet investigating to trace every female visitor to the White House during the Kennedy presidency, and you may also recall that this request was viewed so sympathetically by the boss of the FBI that even though I worked for the opposition he handed me the complete records."

Jackie did have the grace to blush when she saw the endless sheets of paper covered with Guy's notes.

"What you and I didn't know when we asked for this information was that it would be so complete, so reliable. That there was someone other than White House security personnel who thought it essential that every guest should be monitored."

"He wasn't doing it to protect our safety?" asked Jackie.

"No. The little man who dominates the FBI has distrusted politicians for so long that many, many presidents ago, he convinced himself that the nation's security relied upon his spying on every supreme commander from the moment he was elected. So, you see, although it was always technically possible that someone like the president's secretary or some other members of his staff might have smuggled one or two others in, it is very unlikely. J. Edgar Hoover had made sure that he had his own methods of checking visitors in and out of 1600 Pennsylvania Avenue."

Guy stopped for a moment. Both he and President Johnson had discussed the fact that Jackie may have never grasped just how few secrets she had when she was married to the most powerful man on earth. The president had counseled him to let her have time to absorb this since in just a few minutes Guy would have to admit that over the last few weeks she had been spied upon once again, this time with the president's permission.

"I well remember the night when very sensibly you told me that you didn't want to know what was in that file. Well, the contents are very different now. I've edited it down to the people that you've met that we have an interest in. The ones we would like you to have a chat with."

Jackie was surprised by the lengthy list of senior politicians, diplomats, writers, and others, all men, that she had forgotten. As Guy pointed out their names and told her what they were now doing, she began to grasp how useful her role might be.

He impressed upon her that even if she had not seen some of them since her days as First Lady she was probably the only person capable of persuading them to pop round for a drink when next passing through New York. Not only that, she could do so without arousing any suspicion; her perfect excuse was to bring back good memories of her times with her late husband.

"We know it will work," muttered Guy. "As I said, if these guys wanted to visit any other woman with no guards present, warning bells would be ringing. But you aren't any other woman, you're unique."

He then admitted to her that the CIA had been watching her guests arrive and depart during the last fortnight.

"I apologize but it was the only way," said Guy.

"And what did you discover?" she said with an arch smile that told him he was forgiven.

"Curiously, when you invite one of these Eastern Europeans, all their watchers come with them. It took us a while to analyze why.

"First, it's your invitation, it's informal. You don't have a major-domo or anyone other than your secretary, so unlike most of the other functions that these guys attend, there is no printed list of do's and don'ts. In short, no etiquette is made available, no list of who will or will not be received.

"Second, you aren't some dull diplomat, they've all heard of you, they're all very keen to meet you, and they all want to come along on the off chance that they will. As it's a short gig—your guest is usually on his way to dinner—it's regarded as a risk worth taking."

Guy explained how unusual this was, that normally at least two of the bloodhounds remained behind to guard the hotel room.

"Of course we don't kid ourselves that high-level information will be left in an American hotel suite, but there is a lot we could discover if we could get some access."

Clearly, he set out the proposition.

First, the agency wanted to use her intelligence and intuition to dig out any information about her visitors that she thought they might find useful. The agency would occasionally suggest a line of questioning to her. If the visitor brought a briefcase, a coat, or anything else that could be searched while they were on her premises, the agency would like her permission to do so. A CIA man would be out of sight in the apartment.

"The president insisted that I tell you that we will want to take the chance to investigate your guests' hotel suites if we are able to ascertain that the room will be unguarded." Guy explained that to an expert just the contents of a closet could reveal a lot. The CIA might also be able to install a microphone somewhere.

"Assuming you agree to this, it is up to you to decide whether you want to tip us off as soon as your visitor leaves—that's just in case they're planning to return to their hotel—or if you prefer that we watch from the street?"

She told him she would think about it as well as the other subject that Guy had gingerly raised, the resumption of her formal dinners.

He also delivered a letter to her. She recognized the White House letterhead. It was from Lyndon Johnson, hoping that she would say yes without delay.

To convince her how important the work could be, Guy told her that without even knowing it, she had already discovered something of value. The information that she had given him about the Russian's worries about his ill daughter could be useful. With her permission, the agency, without revealing how they had found out, would like to do a deal whereby they gained some low-level information from him in return for drugs currently not available in the U.S.S.R. that would alleviate her symptoms.

Guy explained that simply by gauging these men's attitude she would give them a valuable insight into their current state of mind. Although it was acknowledged that it might well be a personal problem that pushed a man into being overargumentative or drinking or smoking too much, with these hard-boiled apparatchiks, the Eastern European dictatorships only allowed for the survival of the fittest. Any sign of nervous behavior was much more likely to result from their interpretation of the current political conditions at home and, more importantly, their position within it.

"Finally, Jackie, I feel I have to tell you, and I would have done so even without the president's instruction, helping us like this does have dangers. Obviously we will be very careful. Like all our sources we will protect you, as much for our sakes as for yours. If these foreigners ever became even slightly suspicious of you, they would stop coming. You also need to know that if we are ever, even in the slightest way, concerned about you, we would put more security around you and the children. We would, of course, warn you and explain why we were doing it."

She didn't hesitate. For the woman who had inspired her husband to write *Profiles in Courage* there could be only one answer.

"If you really think that I could make a difference I would love to help."

"Only you," replied Guy truthfully.

CHAPTER *Eleven*

On one of the last warm nights of summer, the evening of September 24, 1965, Mrs. Jacqueline Kennedy gave her first dinner party as a widow.

Secret Service men, three deep, kept watch as the guest of honor, the tall, craggy Harvard professor John K. Galbraith, who had worked as economic advisor to Jack Kennedy during his electoral campaign, and had been rewarded with the post of American ambassador to India, arrived with his wife. They were followed by family, her sister, Lee, and Bobby and Ethel Kennedy, old colleagues such as Defense Secretary Robert McNamara, Averell Harriman, and Arthur Schlesinger Jr., all with their wives. Limousines deposited the writer Truman Capote, the Italian industrialist Gianni Agnelli, and the rest of the twenty-one guests who were dispatched up to the raspberry dining room on the fifteenth floor. Among the diplomats were a Romanian and the Indian ambassador and his wife, invited especially because after dinner the entire group were scheduled to go to the opening of an exhibition of Indian paintings at the Asia House.

As news of this event spread the crowd in the street thickened. At ten-fifteen P.M. they were rewarded by the appearance of the hostess, regal in a pure white full-length crepe sheath beneath a cropped, sleeveless ermine jacket. Her stylish accessories, matching elbow-length gloves and satin high heels, were further emblems of her return to fun.

As her guests filled the waiting Cadillacs, America's newest spy was in business.

The party went on to the Sign of the Dove restaurant where Jackie danced well into the small hours, but before the night was out she would complete her report, a chore that she did as soon as she had left her guests and her mind was still full of what had just passed between them.

Under Guy's tutelage she had learned how to file a memo in agency style. It was essential that any information she gleaned was not only passed on swiftly but also blended in with the work of every other agent, incisive and anonymous.

At first the CIA was content for her simply to respond to those foreigners who wanted to maintain their friendship. As time went on and they came to respect her full and intelligent accounts and to rely on the data garnered by their covert snooping around her guests' hotel suites, they became more aggressive in their needs.

As soon as they flagged someone they wanted to put under the microscope they would first check against Guy's complete list of Kennedy White House guests. This had been completely refigured by the agency. For their own purposes it had been put into alphabetical order, but to help jog Jackie's memory the inventory remained in date sequence but was expanded to include anything that might act as an aide-mémoire. So a facsimile of the menu or a photograph of the table arrangement or the flower displays taken at the time was included. The agency painstakingly placed a photograph, preferably a head shot, next to every single name.

For more background Jackie also utilized specialists who had worked in foreign relations for her husband. Many of them had been stationed abroad for long periods so she had found it easier to remain close to them, untainted as they were by knowledge of Jack's "girling" activities at home. They prided themselves on their close and continuing relationships with contacts from their old stomping grounds. Often she only had to mention a name to get chapter and verse on someone, or at least enough to start a conversation.

These old friends were invaluable if she had no recall of the agency's intended prey. As soon as she was armed with enough facts to make her confident that any future meeting would be viable, she informed them. The agency then made it their business to find a mutual contact and work out a strategy whereby their next victim could be grafted on to her guest list in a perfectly natural way. With no relaxation of the Cold War, the CIA would occasionally, in desperation, infiltrate people that she had never met. She was aware that unsuspecting acquaintances were being used but she felt no guilt about putting America's needs first.

Her salon was rivaled by no other hostess. Her table was graced by excellence and genius, and her foreign guest would be grateful for his or her inclusion.

Once again she served her old French favorites, poulet chasseur and filet de boeuf Wellington, but was quite likely to provide a simple dish of the very best homemade chocolate ice cream as dessert.

Meanwhile in a hotel suite not far away, the CIA hunted through suitcase linings, inside toothbrushes and fountain pens. They photographed the contents of passports, notepads, and even checked the blotters on the desks and inserted microphones.

Some kind of normality finally slid into her life even though the Jackie-mania was unrelenting. The children thrived and her relationship with her in-laws settled into a mellow acceptance.

She went out with men, selecting those she had known for some time. Jackie asked John Carl Warnecke, an architect she had met when she was First Lady and with whom she had worked to save Washington's Lafayette Square, to create Jack's memorial at Arlington Cemetery. While he was working in Hawaii she took the children on holiday there. Aristotle Onassis, the Greek shipping mogul, slipped in and out of her life. They frequently were guests at the same parties. She enjoyed his company, he was an encyclopedia of ancient myths, he could recite Greek poetry in French as well as English. She enjoyed his relaxed attitude; he knew everyone, from kings to tin-pot despots, but totally lacked snobbishness. In his casual way he made her feel calm and secure. He kept asking her to visit Skorpios, his home in Greece, but the memory of all the publicity when she had done so five years ago kept her from saying yes. While crisscrossing the world he would phone her out of the blue. Not too proud to be accommodated anywhere in her crowded calendar, he had ended up at many Sunday lunches in the country where she had been surprised both by the depth of his knowledge of flowers and how attentive he had been to Caroline and John.

She also stayed close to two men who could assist her with her work; both had been close to Jack. The urbane British peer Lord Harlech was a former British ambassador to America and an expert on the political scene. So, too, was Roswell Gilpatrick. Unknowingly their knowledge often helped her CIA work.

She visited Buenos Aires, Rome, Madrid, and Seville, and cruised the Dalmatian, Adriatic, and Mediterranean coasts, but the international company she kept did more than just influence her travels, they also altered her view of what was sexy.

The discovery that some of the best-looking men had so much blood on their hands banished her trust in appearances. In the past she had always gone for classical good looks but now she found that they were not enough. The men she was now attracted to were the attentive and thoughtful types who valued women's minds. Meeting foreigners so frequently, she became accustomed to their voluble, if heavily accented, voices and to their championship of ideas, even if their arguments were overly emotional. She was enthralled by men who valued passionate debate with her.

But early in 1968 her carefully constructed new life ended.

It began with a dinner party in March. The guest list had expanded to twenty-eight.

They included the usual mix. Among them was an attractive

American author in the heavyweight league with a literary mistress who punched above her weight because of her ability to go for the jugular, an artist currently in vogue, who with his male muse tended to shock both on and off the canvas, a widower from the U.K., a senator and his wife whom she had known for years, all solid and reliable, an Italian contessa who was heavy going but had a cleavage that kept many men happy throughout all three courses, a financier and his model girlfriend, a former American ambassador and his wife, two of her own in-laws plus partners, and a sprinkling of socialites.

The man of interest to the agency was a Hungarian who had survived every putsch and was suspected of being the most senior Soviet spy in Budapest. He was clever and had a tendency toward self-deprecating humor, and she was not surprised when another guest, the former U.S. ambassador to Hungary, whispered that his reputation as a vicious infighter and longtime survivor was deserved.

She sat next to the charming Magyar but at the end of the meal she had still failed to ask the questions the agency had suggested. Forced to vie with the novelist pouring scorn on French poets, she was worried that she was never going to find time for a heart-to-heart. She succeeded after discomfiting the writer by expounding on her love for Baudelaire, and quoting him in French, at length. The author, beaten, returned to his Pétrus and she got her chance with the man from Budapest.

Now they had all left and she was alone. She stepped out of her Ferragamo satin shoes, hung up the Givenchy cocktail dress in crimson triple chiffon, slipped off the Schlumberger bangles, the Saint Laurent earrings, and her underwear. Dressed in nothing but a long, cool white cotton shift, she sipped a glass of water and sat at her desk mentally mapping out her report.

Over coffee, her Hungarian had been quite open about his country's frustrations with the slow-moving economy of the rest of the Eastern bloc. He also confided that his wife was keen to adopt, an idea that he would not countenance. Jackie wondered if this might prove useful to the agency.

The widow had said good night and thanked her small loyal staff, but the extra personnel that had been drafted to help were still cleaning up. Confident that the Secret Service detail would check around the fifteen-room apartment and ensure they were all off the premises, she ignored the sound of empty bottles being taken out of the kitchen. She was glad that the children were staying over with her mother. The temperature was high and humid and the windows were open so the noise of the street was louder than usual and might well have woken them. In the background she could hear the sound of someone counting the napkins. Somehow some of them always vanished. Jackie still didn't know whether people deliberately kept them, but now that she was left with just a handful of the original white linen ones that had been a wedding present she had stopped having her initials embroidered on their replacements.

As soon as she began to entertain on a larger scale she and her housekeeper noticed that other things had gone missing. Reluctantly, all personal effects, items recognizably belonging to her or the children, were removed from the public parts of the fifteen-room home.

Nonetheless the odd book still vanished, not to mention ashtrays.

She got up to close the door to deaden the din and took up her pen. As she did so she was aware of the last staff and the Secret Service men leaving.

She must have been writing for well over thirty minutes when she heard a small grating sound. She was accustomed to the city throwing up all sorts of clamor and continued. This report must be ready for collection tomorrow. She addressed it to a Mr. Collingwood, Collingwood Antiques, Oyster Bay. Since the Secret Service and the CIA were kept entirely separate, in the morning her maid would collect it from the hall table and deliver it to the doorman.

It was always picked up by nine A.M. Jackie had made it her business to check.

During her spy-craft lessons Jackie was given clear instructions to alter the address and the town on each envelope, and to ensure that the agency knew that the report was both urgent and from her, the word "antiques" was always included in the address.

On the off chance that the letter fell into the wrong hands, the former First Lady was taught not to mention anything that could link her with the contents and always to use the paper and pens that the agency provided because they revealed nothing about their origination. Also the agency gave her a list of code names to use which read like a global *Who's Who*. It included all the major leaders, their councils of ministers, senior military staff, royalty, financiers, and anyone else who had been of interest to the agency since the end of World War II.

If her visitor was too junior to have an alias the agency assigned a number to him.

Thus it was very simple to write about a person and his views on his peers in a way that no outsider would understand.

So engrossed was she that she didn't hear the subtle grating sound again or the quiet breathing of a slender young man sliding, forcing himself through the narrow opening of the back door, which led to the emergency stairwell and had not been completely shut and locked after the sacks of dirty table linen had been dragged through.

In fact it wasn't until she had finished her notes half an hour later, put them in an envelope, and left it on the large mahogany console in the hall that she realized that every light, except the Chinese lamp that she had just walked by, was off. At first it was just minor irritation that flummoxed her. The people who worked with her, her cook, the maid, and the special agents had all been with her for years. They knew that she hated the corridors of the apartment being in darkness. She assumed that one of the relief waiters had not known this and thought they were doing her a favor by turning the lights off on their way out.

She walked through the double doors into the library. She stopped to turn the orchid on the baby grand so it would catch the morning light. All the walls with their delicate paneling and elaborate cornices were painted her favorite greenish-yellow that she called citron. It was a neutral background with a twist for her collection of French and Italian Old Master drawings and watercolors. These, like the clusters of animal sketches, were hung away from the bright but damaging sunlight that poured in through the fourteen windows that looked out onto Central Park. Large beveled mirrors, framed in matching gilt or maple, reflected the capacious French fauteils and sofas, their cushions covered in heirloom fabrics picked up on her travels. On her way through the dining room Jackie smoothed the everyday chintz tablecloth that reached down to the ground and walked past the neatly piled little gilt chairs brought in for this evening. As she drifted through she switched more lights on and thought no more about the darkness until she entered her bedroom.

Jackie had always found it hard to sleep if any light crept in so her lavish bedroom curtains, a glazed cotton floral design by Scalamandré, lined with dense blackout material, were backed up with generously cut window blinds. When all of these were drawn, the bedroom was pitch-black so various side lamps were almost always lit.

She had no chance to be further irritated because the moment she opened the door a large hand gripped her neck and another grabbed her arm and forced it hard behind her back.

"Say nuzzing," a man with a guttural Foreign accent ordered her. "You are alone."

She thought of the men on night guard, fifteen floors below.

Guy and the president himself had warned her that the work she was doing might put her in danger and she knew there were madmen everywhere that made threats on her life.

Terrified, she tried to identify her assailant. He was powerful and was having no problem pushing her toward the floor.

He had grabbed her throat so tightly she couldn't scream.

To break his grip, as he pushed her down she tried to put him on the defensive by dragging him with her.

She kicked out but he was on top of her, holding her down.

"Not so fast, just tell me where money is?"

For a second the excruciating pain in her neck stopped.

"There is no money," she gasped.

Immediately the hand round her throat stopped her from saying more.

She began to thrash her head from side to side but the pressure on her throat increased.

"Money, money?" He released her for a second.

"My bag . . . over there." She nodded toward the round table at the end of the bedroom.

From his pocket he produced a piece of overstuffed fabric; she recognized a corner of her pillow and the fine cotton of her pillowcase that had been sliced off. He forced it into her mouth. When she resisted he pressed so hard on her larynx she thought she would stop breathing. The makeshift gag was embedded between her lips while her assailant knotted one of her scarves round her head to keep it there.

Jackie was strong and fit. She desperately tried to pull away but he hit her so hard with the flat of his hand that for a moment she couldn't breathe.

He used more scarves to tie her hands together so that any movement hurt her wrists.

Unable to shout or move her hands, she tried to stand, but he pulled her leg so hard that she fell. In seconds he lashed her legs together by her ankles.

He indicated that she should roll over and bury her face in the carpet. When she didn't move fast enough she felt the tip of something sharp against her cheek. Her eyes nervously flicked up. He had removed a ceremonial sword, a gift from the president of Pakistan, from a wall display in the hall.

While he scoured through her crocodile skin bag she tried again to see who he was.

She could only see black trousers and cheap shoes and large tanned hands.

He vented his anger at having found no more than thirty dollars in her wallet by hurling both across the room.

The bag pushed the bedroom door ajar, allowing a little more light in.

"You richi, richi. Where your safe is?" he asked to her back.

She could smell the remnants of tonight's sea bass on his breath.

He realized at this point that she could not speak or point. She tried to show him with her chin but he could not understand.

Roughly he dragged the pillow and the scarf from her mouth and face. She gagged on the carpet before speaking.

When she tried to look round she felt the pointed edge of the sword on the back of her neck.

"The safe is in the dressing room," she croaked.

Before she could add that there was nothing in it, he stuffed the wadding back into her mouth and retied the scarf.

With him in the dressing room, she attempted to roll over to reach the panic button that the Secret Service had installed. He raced back.

She lay prone, facedown on the floor.

"Number, quick, quick." The top of the sword in his hand rested on the carpet by her right eye.

He roughly pulled the wadding from her mouth for a second time. She gave him her father's birth date.

With the sword he made tiny slashes on the back of her legs. She felt her blood trickling out.

"Move, I will mark you. Shout, I will kill you."

He stood above her, out of view, and let the sword slowly trace up her arm.

Unsuccessfully she tried to wriggle while he clicked the four numbers into the safe.

The screech, quiet but malevolent, when he discovered that it held just three passports and a few papers, terrified her.

She was going to die, she thought. The thief was a madman.

She tried to think how she could placate him. Her furs were in cold storage and she had no real jewels at home, preferring fashionable costume jewelry by Chanel and Kenneth J. Lane. All her pearls were simulated so that they could be replaced when makeup and perfume discolored them, and she found that fake silver was less heavy than the real thing and could be changed according to fashion.

Her real stuff, the brooches and rings that Jack had given her, were in the bank vaults.

But maybe this man wouldn't know.

When he returned, looking crazed, she pointed her chin toward the cherrywood antique bureau whose drawers contained the small boxes that held her jewelry.

He understood, but when his hands were too clumsy to open the miniature drawers he swiftly cut the bindings from her legs and dragged her kneeling and crying toward them.

She couldn't move fast enough for him; the shift got caught beneath her knees and because her hands were still tied tight behind her she could not move it aside.

She felt the sword at her throat.

For a second she thought he had slashed her from collarbone to thigh but then she realized it was just the thin fabric of her nightdress that was torn.

He yanked it off her shoulders so it trailed behind her. Now her knees were like the rest of her body, uncovered.

"Open it."

She looked up at him and shrugged, trying to show her hands were still tied.

"You think I stupid and untie you. Open with mouth."

Her hauled the gag from her mouth.

Her knees aching from crossing the carpet so quickly, her tears falling, she attempted to open the bottom drawer with her teeth.

At first it didn't move. He put his hand next to her mouth and tugged but his fingers were too big to grip the tiny handle. With the sharp edge of the sword prodding the nape of her neck, he signaled that she should use her lips to tease one of them out.

Once the first one was opened, he removed the others by grabbing them from the inside.

He picked up the necklaces, there were about twenty, and began looking for silver hallmarks. Failing to find them, he hurled them one by one across the room. One or two hit and flailed her on their way.

In disgust he tossed them and the fake pearls aside. Some broke and exploded. He picked up her briefcase, and finding only papers inside, he hurled them and their container across the room, pushing the bedroom door open wider.

"You think I poor boy, new here, know nothing!"

He looked at her.

She was kneeling, her almost naked body outlined by the incoming light, wide-eyed at the torrential storm of luminous pearls.

Urgently he opened his trousers and signaled that he wished her to use her mouth again.

She tried to resist but he pulled her head toward him. She was reluctant to touch him and thought of biting him hard and racing to the panic button when again she felt the sharp sword stroke her neck.

When he had finished he insisted she continue licking and stroking him all over, and then in the manner of men who had never been able to afford contraception, he forced her to have sex in a way that could not procreate.

By then she had recognized him, a young good-looking waiter, Yugoslav, she thought, who had worked for her once before and who had supposedly been checked out by the Secret Service.

As he entered her for the second time he whispered in her ear, "You richi, richi, if you have money I no do this."

The whole thing had taken no more than an hour.

He left the way he came, via the staff exit at the back, so as to avoid the doorman.

When she was sure he had gone she staggered up and looked at herself in the mirror. The sides of her lips were bleeding and her insides ached. Her legs were covered with slashes. Blood was seeping through the worst of them and other places had smaller cuts where he had held the sword against her skin while forcing her to sexually respond to him at the end.

She felt so violated.

As she finally lurched toward the panic button she stopped.

Did she really want everyone to know about this?

As a rape victim she would be named, and if he was caught she would have to be a witness and live through this all over again, in public.

She guessed that he would look very handsome dressed up in a suit and tie. Despite the marks on her body it would be his word against hers.

It would be difficult for any jury to believe that her security was so lax that this could happen.

They might think that as she was alone and ten years older than him, this was a relationship that had gone wrong.

She started to cry.

Eventually she lowered herself into a warm bath and rubbed all the marks that she could reach with ointment. So that no one should know what had happened she crawled around for hours picking up every pearl, making a neat package of them. She would throw them away where her maid would not find them. It was far more than one necklace.

One by one she rescued the silver necklaces and returned them to their rightful place.

She stood in her bathroom and tried to work out how to eliminate the corner of the pillow and the pillow cover that had been wadded into her mouth. Carefully she sliced it into ribbons with her nail scissors and slowly let the fabric and the feathers flush away. As for the damaged pillow, she held it up and pushed a burning cigarette against the corner gash. When the slashed edge had been thoroughly singed she blew the small flame out.

Much better that the staff believed that she had accidentally burned it because she had fallen asleep while smoking, thought Jackie. She'd done it enough times before. Just as long as no one realized that a man had so crudely vandalized her and her home.

The only stains that remained were on the carpet; some of the blood would not come out, however hard she rubbed.

She would get some carpet cleaner, if only she knew where it was kept. Maybe it would come off when it dried. She would try brushing it before anyone came in tomorrow morning.

Once again she was glad that her first visitors would not be the waking children.

The next day she told her cook to use a different agency in future. She complained that they had been too surly. She insisted that they use older waiters in future and requested only Americans of long-standing should be hired.

"Let's show these foreign guests our very best," she told them.

She thought none of her own countrymen would have done this.

All she wanted to do now was to feel safe.

She was either going to have to get some live-in security, an idea she loathed because she would have no privacy at all, or she was going to have to escape.

She canceled everything except her appointments with David Goadshem. At least there she could be honest, but in the end she couldn't face even telling him.

"I need to get away. I'm fed up being watched, being talked about, being me!"

"There's nothing wrong with running away from time to time," he said, in an effort to calm her.

For the first time she canceled Guy.

"This place is too much. The pressure is impossible. I have to find somewhere that I can go where no one is allowed to photograph me or bother me in any way. I've had enough. It may mean that I do less for you, Guy, but to keep my sanity I'm going to have to find some way out. Live abroad. I've had enough."

Guy, disappointed he wasn't seeing her, tried to gently question her over the next few days. He was at a loss as to why she was so upset. A week later she was still adamant.

"I've had enough of it now. The years and years of being gawked at, having the children photographed all the time, having everything I do being misunderstood."

She was so decisive about it that he felt he should pass her views on to his boss when he went to see him at the CIA headquarters in Langley, unaware that there were some who were as keen for her to leave the country as she now was.

They had been so since the beginning of the year.

Desperate to save American lives and American pride, they had a very specific escape route that they wanted her to take.

They had never gone so far as to refer to what they wanted her to do as a plan.

It was far too Machiavellian.

In fact, so unsure were they about it, because of its very personal nature, that officially it had never even been discussed.

Unwittingly Guy's information arrived on the right day at the right time.

It was time to involve the president to see if he would agree to ask her for the biggest favor of all.

ven though the Oval Office contained both the veteran CIA man Harry Blackstone and the president, it was strangely quiet.

Under normal circumstances the two took loquaciousness to a competitive level, never missing a beat, let alone several seconds.

Harry had just finished making his recommendation.

Lyndon Johnson was in shock.

A few weeks ago, while thumbing through that day's top-secret memo from the CIA, he had been surprised when confronted with information about Jackie Kennedy's latest dalliance.

LBJ was more than content for the agency to have made special arrangements to keep watch over his predecessor's widow. Not only did he expect them to extend their protection to someone they now thought of as their own, he also knew that after she had undertaken a job abroad for him last year she had requested it. It was to be expected. She had never got over the fact that her husband had been murdered despite the presence of the Secret Service. As her children grew up and became more adventurous she became more nervous for their safety.

The task he had set her extended her remit far beyond her dinner table. Lyndon Johnson wanted to utilize her talents in order to try to charm the ruler of Cambodia, Prince Norodom Sihanouk, who had severed diplomatic relations because of America's role in the war in Vietnam.

Jackie had always longed to visit the ruins of Angkor Wat. The plan to combine this with a full-fledged state visit to repair the two-year split appealed to her. Like the old days, no expense had been spared. Airline seats were ripped out so that a full-sized bed could be installed to ensure that on her arrival she would wake refreshed. Schoolchildren showered jasmine petals at her feet, even the royal white elephants were brought to ululate at the royal palace.

The prince's comments that "a very great contribution to a moral and sentimental rapprochement had taken place," pleased Jackie, who told the agency how safe she had felt with them guarding her while she was abroad.

"When the children were young it was easier, but now that they are ten and seven, it is hard to find the right balance," she explained. "Some of the men tend to loom over them and almost end up becoming their servants, which is wrong. I want the children to have to deal with their own lives like every other child, have the little adventures that all children have, but when I ask the guys to stand farther afield, I don't feel sure they could defend them from any madman in the park."

Although she had asked for this extra security, Lyndon imagined that it was unlikely she had ever imagined it would lead to this. Based on information from those who watched over her, Harry, the agency's number three, would formally float the most extraordinary idea, the like of which he had never heard before, across his desk.

He understood why Harry had dreamed it up. Faced with the murder of three agents in as many weeks, the man was beside himself with worry.

An enlarged map of the area with three bloodred crosses marking the dates and the places where they had been found was spread across the desk in front of him.

It was because of the serious nature of this proposal that LBJ was still wrestling with the decision whether to take it seriously or to wonder if Harry, one of his closest advisors, had taken leave of his senses. It was such an outrageous proposition that it was hard to divine if it had any merit, or if it contained any resonance that might lead to the achievement of some foreign policy success.

The president's long fingers cupped his chin as one and then two minutes passed while he tried to decide whether to simply jettison the whole thing as being wildly improbable.

Then again, he thought because it was so over-the-top it deserved further appraisal.

Was this one of those strange and unexpected ideas that just might work?

How improper would it be to ask someone like her for such a sacrifice even though it could save lives?

Where, in the middle part of the twentieth century, were the moral boundaries to deal with a vicious unofficial war, crammed with covert battles being waged daily across the globe?

Despite his guilt at being so self-serving, if she was affronted, just how public might she, or those close to her who were his natural enemies, go? And if it did come out, what would the public think?

Would they see the proposal as an atrocity or as a sensible utilization of the one person in the world who just happened to be in the extraordinary position of being the only one able to offer the nation such assistance?

Did the country have that right?

It might not be the American way but hadn't her husband memorably once said, "Think not what your country can do for you but what you can do for your country?"

The president rose. All that seemed so long ago and certainly this idea was not what John F. Kennedy had had in mind.

"The trouble is that it's a woman and a civilian," he muttered.

"If this ever came out!" He decided that it just didn't bear thinking about.

Johnson took a quick glance at his guest in the Oval Office. He knew that the idea had only been born out of despair. But wasn't he, as supreme commander, the very person who should nip it in the bud? Why couldn't he decide simply to rule it out and forget about it forever?

Once again, as if hunting for the answer on the map, he looked at the three crimson crosses.

He glanced at his companion. The man had distress and embarrassment written all over his face.

"Look, Harry, you don't need to look like that," he said gently.

"I know that coming here today, being brave enough to tell me, this whole thing, this suggestion, is the last desperate roll of the dice. No one could blame you for that. It's what we do next that counts."

He hesitated: "I don't know why but I just can't make up my mind.

"It is obviously very extreme. After all, how would I feel if someone came and asked me to do this? That's what's so difficult. Yes, we know she sees Aristotle Onassis, we assume that he wants her, well, we think that he wants to win her, just like another prize.

"But maybe she likes that. The truth is we can bug, we can watch, but we can't see into their souls. And there are others involved in this, innocent children.

"He has a boy and girl too. The only difference being, his are old enough to object and put the kibosh on it. Imagine that, we get all that way and some poor little rich boy or girl has the power to stop it and humiliate her, this woman who has already suffered so much, just like that."

He stood and clicked his fingers.

In his usual Texan drawl he continued. "And, before we even get *that* far, just how were you gonna solve the problem of the senator for New York? Strikes me that brother Bobby is likely to have a highly antagonistic view of all this.

"Bobby will forbid it. He needs her to be just the way she is, the perfect, the iconic 'widow.'

"He uses her to remind people of the Camelot they lost, the

young, handsome president they lost. He doesn't want her to marry anyone, especially not someone he would regard as an oily, dangerous little foreigner.

"He doesn't want any of that tarnish to rub off on him. Onassis reeks of greed and money, boats and brilliantine. Of course, the Kennedys have dozens of friends who are as enthusiastic about these things as he is, but in places like Newport they hide it so much better. They are more practiced, they've had their money for a little longer—they know when to spend it and, more importantly, when to hide it.

"No, Bobby would stop her. If he needed to do so he'd call on the entire family to help him, especially if he thought that I was in any way involved."

From the sofa a hesitant voice emerged.

The younger man was nervously rubbing his horn-rimmed glasses.

Shorter than the president, he was usually fastidious about his appearance, over which he took some trouble, but today the black hair looked too curly, his button-down collar lacked its usual crispness. His full lips, usually a healthy pink, were as pale as his skin, except for the greige blush beneath his eyes.

"No, you're absolutely right, Mr. President," said Harry. "I should never have mentioned it.

"I don't know what I was thinking of. It was very good of you, sir, to see me. Let's just forget it forever. We'll just have to find another way, we always do."

The men separated, Harry Blackstone to return despondently to his controller's desk in the CIA offices in Langley, Virginia, the president off upstairs to the private quarters to seek out Lady Bird. Maybe his wife could give him a better steer on the idea?

He had always admired her intuition. Throughout the thirty-four years of their marriage, through his upward procession through the ranks on Capitol Hill, she had often surprised him with her clever insights on people, especially other women. He knew that although she had often felt sorry for her predecessor they had never been close; they had been too different.

He also knew that as the vice president's wife, Lady Bird had frequently and uncomplainingly stood in for Jackie and had some understanding about what made her tick.

Fascinated to know that Jackie had been covertly helping the CIA for some time and had spent New Year's with Onassis, Lady Bird surprised her husband by immediately reassuring him that a woman like Jackie would certainly not feel affronted but flattered by the suggestion that had been made earlier.

"She's a risk-taker, a high-wire, daredevil type, just look at the way she rides," said Lady Bird. "I know she misses some of the First Lady pomp even though Rose Kennedy, her mother, and I did a lot of it for her.

"Trust me, she would love to feel so wanted, so special. What woman wouldn't?"

She promised her husband that she would give the whole thing her undivided attention that afternoon.

After a charity lunch the fifty-five-year-old First Lady tried to put herself in the same position as the younger woman. Being naturally industrious, she found that her best ideas always emerged while doing something else, so she walked around the private part of the White House garden, hunting down the first flowers of spring and pulling and tugging at this bush or that branch.

She came to two conclusions.

The fact that Jackie, who could take her pick of the world's most attractive consorts and resorts, had chosen to spend New Year's Eve with Aristotle Onassis was a sure sign that she had already given him serious consideration.

It was Lady Bird's view that the last night of the year was an emotionally charged date for most women. That noisy, supposedly celebratory time was the outward sign of time passing, of aging, of all the dreams and hopes for the twelve months that had just passed being lost forever. She was sure that this would especially be the case for a sole parent, a survivor, a widow, like Jackie.

It meant that the woman was already quite involved, or certainly reliant on the man.

Lady Bird also knew that Bobby Kennedy's infinite ambition to step into his dead brother's role would mean that he would do anything to stop Jackie from spoiling his future political hopes by marrying the small Greek millionaire, a man so much less attractive and popular than the late president.

Lady Bird suspected that he would be ruthless and if necessary would plunder the Kennedy millions to keep Jackie as the asset she was and prevent Onassis taking ownership of a prized piece of the Kennedy mystique.

"And if, as you say, he knew you were in any way behind it, then he would redouble his efforts," she warned her husband.

Lyndon Johnson listened hard. He concentrated on the first piece of Lady Bird's assessment.

He had already been having private thoughts about how to deal with the second.

A week later, on March 12, the president only just beat the liberal, antiwar Eugene McCarthy in the New Hampshire presidential primary. Hardly surprising, as the Johnson name was not on the ballot; as the incumbent he had to be a write-in, and he did not campaign in the state. But the result was counted as a defeat for LBJ.

One way or another the voters were influenced by the Vietnam War. They were either against it so they didn't vote for him or they thought he was too timid in its pursuance, so once again he lost out.

Four days later McCarthy's weak showing brought Bobby Kennedy into the presidential race.

His statement, "I do not run for the presidency merely to oppose any man, but to propose new policies . . . to end the bloodshed in Vietnam and in our cities," irked Lyndon. America's thirty-sixth president felt that he had worked hard on what he had named the "Great Society" and had produced a hefty package of laws that helped the poor and promoted civil rights.

When Bobby continued to attack LBJ, the president decided that indulging in a little backstairs retaliation was irresistible.

At worst, at this critical juncture he reckoned it would slow Bobby Kennedy down and at best it just might help in the fight against the Russians.

To proceed, he invited his oldest and closest friend, General "Mo" Dodsworth, to the White House.

Mo, the president believed, was uniquely qualified to be his facilitator. The two men had been close since they first met in their twenties. Born within a few miles of each other in Stonewall, Texas, they both might have proceeded to have glittering political careers except Dodsworth, after a brilliant war career fighting in Italy and Greece, stayed on in the army until after Korea. By then he was his family's only surviving son, so he was forced to leave the capital to return to manage the family ranch in Texas.

Later when they both married and began raising children, the friendship deepened. Year after year they frequently entertained each other, at the Elms, the Johnsons' home in the capital and later at the White House. Equally, Lyndon and Lady Bird relished their trips back to their roots on Mo and Elizabeth's ranch.

They rarely went more than three months without seeing each other.

Johnson, always distrustful of the Washington elite, often tested out his ideas on his friend. He felt more comfortable with an idea when he had been able to chew it over with Mo, or the general, as he was often called. The man was wealthy but his opinions were down-to-earth and sensible. Lyndon felt lucky to have someone so reliable to use as a sounding board.

By coincidence part of the general's inheritance had been a stud farm. For generations the family had had a reputation for producing some of the most perfect horseflesh in the United States. In the fifties, attending a large Washington fund-raiser for the Democrats, Mo and his wife met the Kennedys and Jackie, who immediately recognized the Dodsworth name, and struck up a friendship with the couple based on equine excellence.

From then on Jackie and the general maintained an epistolary friendship. In their letters they discussed horse flesh. He was always sure to tell her if he was going to be visiting New Jersey during the hunt season. He liked seeing the many horses that had come from his stables. When Caroline needed to replace her first pony, Macaroni, Jackie had turned to the Dodworths.

As soon as he was summoned, the "general" dropped everything and came to Washington, but by the time he arrived the president was caught up in another Vietnam crisis.

LBJ was left with no option; he simply didn't have time to explain the whole darn mad, possibly ill-begotten scheme to his friend.

"Mo, you know I have always trusted you implicitly," said Lyndon.

Before there was time for a reply the president continued.

"I need you now to do something for me. You have special insights, ones which you will understand when it is explained to you, into something that I need handling, that for various reasons I should not be directly involved in. You'll realize why in due course.

"There's a proposal, a mad one, born out of real need that could help us score against the Russians in the Med, and possibly save many lives. It could also help stabilize the Greek government against the Communists. The genius behind this idea is a man called Harry Blackstone, a good man, a senior man in the CIA. I know that for years I have tried my ideas out on you, but now, admittedly at the last minute, out of the clear blue sky, I am asking you to do something for me.

"Do you think you could meet up with Blackstone in New York tomorrow, listen to his scheme, evaluate it, and let me know if you think it could work?"

The general was pleased to see the relief on his friend's face when he nodded vigorously.

"As importantly, if you feel that it has promise could you confirm that you will see it through on my behalf?"

Twenty-four hours later, the general strode across a wet and windy Park Avenue.

Even though he felt out of place entering the club at five in the afternoon the general figured that this was the least he could do for his leader.

He had been here before on his occasional visits to New York. It had an attractive air of calmness, never appearing too crowded, and its members were serious, decent sorts. The library was a good place to do some quiet work and the restaurant always served remarkably simple, wholesome food. He approved of its smoky masculinity, a perfect foil for the mildly raucous, successful, and often famous members. It could always be relied upon to entertain both eyes and stomach.

Before he reached the door it was opened and he was ushered into new territory, upstairs.

The large room was empty, refined yet windowless. All of the sounds of New York were blotted out, and although his briefcase was stuffed with papers that he needed to read, he couldn't bring himself to settle into one of the leather club chairs provided.

He simply paced and wondered just what it was that Lyndon had selected him for.

Minutes later he was grateful to see the door open.

Leonard Hobson or Hugh Mitchell, or Alain Lachaise as he was sometimes known, or alternatively Klaus Feldmann or possibly Lars Svensen (he had passports for them all), entered the room. The surprise that showed on his square, tanned face made it clear to the general that here was another who had no idea where this was going.

Covering up his surprise, the younger man introduced himself as Leonard Hobson, and as they shook hands the older man thought he saw a flicker of recognition hurtle across the newcomer's eyes.

They were just about to run out of meaningless things to say when the third member of their party came in.

Harry Blackstone had been working for the CIA for seventeen years. Unlike the general, who was six feet two inches of sleek grayness, hair, suit, and tie, Harry was in a regulatory navy suit, white shirt, and pale blue tie.

"Glad you could make it," he said as if the general had really had the choice.

He then stretched out his hand to "Leonard," whom he warmly addressed as Hugh.

At that moment the first two arrivals understood that there was going to be no further subterfuge.

Hugh apologized to the general and said he had just been following procedure.

Giving them no time to take stock, Blackstone explained that they had better begin, they had much to discuss. He also added that within this group there was no hierarchy, they were all equal and about to enter uncharted territory.

"You should both know that this meeting is unofficial," said Blackstone.

"As far as the rest of the world is concerned it never happened, ever. Not only would we have to deny that it had ever taken place, so would everyone else up to and including the president. Furthermore, President Johnson insists that none of what we three discuss should ever be annotated in any way or stored in any archive, so please put away your notepad, General, no notes at all.

"I apologize to you, General, for bringing you all the way to New York. Because our discussions are top secret it was agreed that we shouldn't use any of our safe houses, and General"—he bowed low—"we wanted you out of Washington where you just might be recognized. As Hugh flew here from Europe just a few hours ago it was thought New York was the best option.

"As for selecting this place, I chose it because, as you see, it has no windows, and I can arrange that it is swept for bugs; in fact our man left only about five minutes before you arrived.

"Thank you so much for being very punctual." He smiled and gave another little bow. "Using that entrance allowed you to remain unseen, and there are two completely secure exits.

"To be fair, even at this stage I do not know if we will ever need to meet again or if we will ever act on the suggestion that I have to admit was thought up by Hugh and initiated to the president by me. When I explain it later you'll understand that it isn't false modesty that makes us say that we have to admit that this was all our idea. We are still a tad shame-faced about it.

"If we do go ahead it is up to us to plan what the next part of the strategy should be."

While the general was given a swift résumé of Hugh's background, filling him in on Hugh's current role as the most senior man on the ground in the area, Hugh went to his briefcase and removed a large map of the Mediterranean. This was placed on the central mahogany table. He then invited the general to view the three crosses on it, marked in bloodred.

There was no need for the CIA staffer to describe the worldwide intelligence battle that the submarines of the American navy were having with their Soviet counterparts. Anyone with any interest in politics knew that there were constant reviews and discussions about the costs of constantly enlarging and updating the nuclear-armed submarine fleet, to leave no one in any doubt of the deadly Cold War games being calibrated out in the deep waters of the Black Sea, the North Atlantic, and the Mediterranean. It was a subject superceded only by the U.S.A.'s most pressing problem, the war in Vietnam.

Harry pointed to the crosses and explained that they marked the recovery places of three experienced CIA officers, murdered since the start of the year.

"We've done full inquiries on these men. All of them were working on separate, independent covert operations in the area. They were well trained and experienced, fluent in several languages."

Hugh, as he sat down by the table, counted them off on his fingers, Russian, Greek, Turkish, French, Italian, maybe even a bit of Albanian.

"We looked into their deaths. Two of them simply vanished without trace . . . only to reappear, drowned.

"Local fishermen found them. One, in mid-January off the coast of Greece, here"—his finger pointed to Levkas—"the other, just weeks later turned up closer to Athens."

Harry took up the narrative.

"One of them had assumed the job of assistant to the harbormaster in Piraeus, one other was working as a barman, fisherman, odd-job man on boats, in the ports.

"We quietly arranged to fly their bodies back. One of them had been tortured before he drowned.

"Two weeks later a third man was supposed to have died after he got into a drunken fight, apparently over a girl, in a small village on Corfu at Kassiopi." Harry moved the map round. "Right opposite Albania.

"Now, not only would our man have never let that happen, we could find no one who had seen the alleged fight.

"It was only after diligent questioning that we found a witness, the woman who helps the village doctor, who had not seen the fracas but said that he was dead when she and the local sawbones saw him.

"They gave him a pauper's burial. Our man was supposed to be a penniless idler, slightly mad and weak in the head. It gave him the cover to do little or no work and to vanish and return at leisure.

"You can't imagine how many people we had to bribe to dig him up and bring him home," interjected Harry, cost the U.S. taxpayer a fortune.

"Once again we carried out a full autopsy on the body and it was not helpful, one way or the other.

"So we went back to ask more questions and both the local doctor and our witness and their families have clammed up. The whole place has given us the silent treatment."

The Texan gave a heavy sigh.

Harry continued: "The agency has replaced the men but we cannot afford to lose anyone else. What we keep picking up is that the Russians, thinking our attention is totally focused on Southeast Asia, are not only more determined to keep us at bay in Europe, they are trying to extend their influence.

"The Russians think this area should be their preserve. Italy has always had a worrying interest in Communism and who knows what the Greeks really want?

"The Colonels are in power now but we all know that the Commies have their secret supporters right up at senior level among the politicians, the unions, and the civil service. Remember, unlike the rest of Europe, which settled down to some well-earned peace in forty-five, they started a four-year civil war. The Greek Communists didn't win in the end but the Russians would love to get control of Greece. From the geographical point of view it is perfectly positioned. President Truman knew it, which is why he poured in millions of dollars back in forty-seven, but the civil war split the nation so there are too many factions, too many political parties.

"The trouble is," Harry continued, "the right-wing military Junta has been very heavy-handed, and even while the average Greek in the street may be doing better, the ruling elite wouldn't win many popularity contests. Their argument is that they have no choice because the Commies are constantly stirring up trouble and that if we don't support them they'll be kaput. So we put more men and munitions in and the Commies fight back harder.

"Our thinking is that either the Russians have got something big planned in the Med so they are taking no chances and are determined to eliminate as many of our people as possible, or they have another secret, lying on the ocean floor."

With a sigh Harry pulled his spectacles off and looked straight at the man the president had told him he would trust with his life.

"I am bound to tell you, General, that this too is classified.

"Just recently, we discovered a Golf II missile-carrying Soviet submarine at the bottom of the ocean floor. The Russians have not admitted that they've lost it partly because they can't find it—so that makes us wonder what the sub was doing, she's in the Pacific not that far from Hawaii—and partly because she may have been carrying special equipment more advanced than their other subs and they don't want us to discover it.

"We don't want anyone to know that we've found it because our deep-diving submarines have been modified to contain special cameras capable of spotting debris on the ocean floor. They can locate the wreckage of Soviet long-range missile tests."

"Or a sub full of dead sailors," muttered Hugh.

"Because we want to extract every bit of data from that vessel, a joint CIA-Navy office is planned. We are working out a way that we can lift it out of the water."

The two CIA officers could see the general's surprise.

"Two of these men knew about this, so you can see, quite apart from our concern over the loss of life, we are very worried that we may have a spy in the camp. Because for the life of us none of us can figure how the Russians found these three very separate guys out," added Hugh.

"Since the beginning of the year, it is true, there has been an upswing in the number of violent deaths and drownings in the area—the world is getting to be that way—but the others, as far as we know, were locals. Maybe the Soviets just got lucky, but we have to put a stop to it."

The ex-military man kept his counsel and waited for Blackstone to continue.

"We need to keep tabs on what the Russians are up to, especially with their nuclear subs, and—again, it's classified—we've heard that another sub might be missing in Greek waters. We've picked up some radio chat about this. More urgently, we have also uncovered some of their plans to assassinate one or more of the Junta. We have warned the Colonels but it means that we have more men going in. This sort of work needs men who know the Med, so we are planning to draft some of our staff who have been based in Egypt, Jordan, Israel, and Turkey. We have to find a place where one or two can find safe haven."

"That's right," echoed the younger man, "we need somewhere to experiment with some new equipment of our own that is supposed to improve our ability to pick up more data on the movement of ships and subs. No point in spending millions of dollars and making technical progress if you can't put it to work."

"Needless to say, we are very worried about the safety of some of our other operatives too," said Blackstone.

Blackstone uncoiled himself, stretched briefly, and sat back.

"The odds against losing three would be high in a platoon or any other military group, but for our agency, the figures are astoundingly bad.

"Quite apart from the tragedy of their deaths"—there was a pause—"from the manner in which at least one of them died, it looks like the Russians suspected that they were working for us. Because of the possible torture we also have to worry about what else they told them.

"When an agent goes missing it is often very difficult to confirm how much of his network has been unmasked. It's hard to get a handle on it because they all know, if their agent goes quiet and they don't get their usual message, the spycraft is clear . . . go to ground," said Blackstone.

The general finally interrupted. "So you've got problems with the Junta, the new sonar equipment, and the possibility of another sunken Soviet sub. What kind of a plan can sort all this out?"

"There is a sort of an idea that has been raised, well, a long-shot idea that I put to the president," said Blackstone.

"I spoke to him briefly just this morning and I gather he hasn't yet decided whether to agree to it. I also gather that if it does go ahead, President Johnson wants you to be his representative," he said, looking at the general. "But as I say, I'm not sure he will agree to it."

The general was more bemused by the minute. This didn't sound anything like the Lyndon Johnson he knew or what he had always believed was the way the CIA behaved.

As if he could read his mind Hugh interrupted.

"There is this cautious feeling around because the idea is a very unusual one . . . abnormal, really, one that you will never, ever, see written about in the history books.

"But it could change everything."

The general repeated, "So what's the plan?"

Blackstone began.

"As I said before, we have this new listening equipment. If it does what the experts say, it will give us a much clearer picture of the

Soviet navy's activity in European and Middle Eastern seas. It is supposed to be able to work on dry land. In its infancy we tried to put this equipment into one of our embassies. First we tried Istanbul but we discovered that it is too far east. Athens was the next on the list." Immediately the general visualized the red crosses in his mind.

"Yes, we think that at least one of our men got fingered at this time.

"We have tried to work out somewhere else to put it and our search has taken us up and down the Ionian coast.

"We have inspected the mainland, the Aegean Sea, and the other Ionian islands.

"Ideally, it would be somewhere in the Ionian Sea, perhaps near the gateway to the Med from the Black Sea and the U.S.S.R. ports of Rostov, Odessa, Sevastopol, and Yalta."

The general began to understand why he had been chosen. He knew the area well from his war days.

"We contemplated asking the Greeks officially, paying them even, but they leak like a bucket full of holes. We realized that we would simply end up paying through the nose and the Russians might still 'find out' where our surveillance is based.

"We have thought of sneaking this equipment onto one of the islands, but the problem is that they are all small, and apart from the height of the summer season anyone new stands out, even when they have an excellent front as a Greek simpleton."

The three of them pored over the map for a few moments.

"Without doubt, the best conditions for it would be somewhere here."

The general looked carefully at the spot that Hugh was pointing to and then looked up from the page.

"Yes, I can see that it's ideal. Trouble is, am I right in thinking that it doesn't even belong to the Greeks?"

"Dead right. It belongs to Onassis, the shipping magnate," said Blackstone.

"A man I don't think we should trust," said the general.

"You're right; we've crossed swords with him before."

Blackstone revealed his expertise in all affairs Middle Eastern and Mediterranean by explaining that not long ago the CIA had acquired information about a potentially huge deal the Greek was hoping to do with the Saudis, supplying a fleet of tankers for the government to transport their oil under the Saudi flag.

Not only would the Greek's earnings soar into the stratosphere, the new Saudi tanker fleet would mean that the desert state could begin to be self-sufficient in the oil business, flagrantly violating long-term agreements the Saudis had with ARAMCO, the organization made up of the major U.S. oil companies, Standard Oil, Mobil, Exxon, and Texaco.

Harry continued. "Onassis, knowing that this contract would alienate the American government, had a draft contract drawn up by an ex-Nazi lawyer in Düsseldorf. It established SAMCO, the Saudi Arabian Maritime Company, and among other things gave the company priority rights on the shipment of Arabian oil with a guaranteed ten percent of the country's annual output.

"It became known as the Jiddah Agreement. Onassis was to pay for the fleet's sailors to be trained in that port.

"It was signed by the Saudi finance minister but Onassis knew that it would not be finalized until the king himself had signed it."

To collapse the deal Stavros Niarchos, Onassis's brother-in-law and bitter rival, leaked the details to the CIA.

The British, aware that if the deal went ahead the Greek might then persuade nations like Kuwait and Iran to do the same thing, began to worry about their oil supplies. Questions were raised in the House of Commons. To support American interests, Vice President Richard Nixon was drafted in.

"The Jiddah Agreement came to nothing," said Harry. "We had Onassis in our sights and some of the other deals we didn't like got spiked."

Blackstone with quiet confidence began to talk about his part in some of them when Hugh butted in.

"But like every man, he has his weaknesses."

Without drawing breath, Harry went on: "We know, let's not say how, that he spent New Year's Eve with the former First Lady . . . and her children."

The general was openmouthed with astonishment.

"With Jackie Kennedy?"

The younger CIA man laughed. "Our reaction entirely. I'm not yet married, in this job it's an impossibility, but I assume that you gentlemen have wives, so if either of you would like to explain women to me I could bottle it, become a millionaire, leave the agency, and settle down with one."

It was the first unserious note of the meeting.

Blackstone opened a large French armoire and produced drinks for them all. The general felt like he needed one. After a few gulps he started to realize that Jackie's involvement was another reason why Lyndon had pulled him into this.

Hugh continued. "We know Aristotle Onassis is a rascal with some unsavory ex-Nazi friends, but I am told he can be very charming, very generous.

"With his own airline, own shipping fleet, own yacht, own island, he is in an ideal position to make a woman feel safe and cocooned.

"He's not good-looking, in fact he's the absolute opposite of the man Jackie picked the first time, but with the sort of publicity JFK's been getting, 'adultery in excelcis,' that could well be part of his attraction."

The general was still dumbfounded.

"You mean you think there's a real romance there, that she might pair up with him, even marry him?" he asked querulously.

Hugh was about to continue when his boss interrupted.

"Sorry, I know here in this room I am no more senior than you but let me explain to the general.

"They are definitely dating, they saw the New Year in together. To be honest, we have no idea how close they are or how Mrs. Kennedy feels about him, but knowing Mr. Onassis, we are sure that he means business.

"After all, this is a man who just has to click his fingers and he can have anything, and probably anyone, he wants.

"To be with the former First Lady he left his world-famous opera star mistress to her own unhappy devices at one of the most special times of the year. He knows that there is absolutely no point in spending a great deal of time and money trying to seduce the most admired, most iconic woman in the world, unless everyone gets to know about it.

"He knows that Jackie will never publicize an affair or speak to him again if he does!

"For him success means that this must end in marriage.

"Remember, Aristotle Onassis is passionate about everything he does, he has come from nothing, he has no moral compass, no master plan, just very good instincts.

"He is an inveterate collector of famous people. He's entertained everyone on his boat from Winston Churchill to Greta Garbo, Cary Grant to Princess Grace. He may not care about being accepted but he wants to be respected. He knows that a brilliant dynastic marriage opens so many doors."

There was a moment of absolute quiet while the general tried to take it all in.

Hugh continued. "If, as we hope, as we wish, their relationship deepens, with their heavy social commitments it will be easy for us to get all sorts of strangers on the island, undercover agents, scientists, ballistic experts, and such will be able to come and go.

"No one will know if they are part of Jackie's extensive entourage, or a cook or a cleaner or any of the other staff they will need from time to time.

"It should be relatively simple to secrete whatever we need on the farthest tip of the island far away from Ari's home, which is actually two houses, the Hill House and the Pink House, where he does his entertaining."

"Ideally we can put it somewhere on the island where a small motorboat or dinghy can also be hidden."

Blackstone refilled their drinks and put down heavy glass bowls full of smooth cashews, rotund kalamata olives, and salty pretzels. "We fully acknowledge that Bobby Kennedy will try and do everything in his power to stop her," he said.

The general then understood the third reason why he was here.

Lyndon Johnson, his wily friend, who had never got along with Bobby, had come to the conclusion that this mad idea might help America in the Cold War in Europe. It had the added advantage of tying up Bobby Kennedy's time when he should be concentrating on the presidential primaries and his run for the Oval Office.

It was essential that Lyndon Baines Johnson was not to be found anywhere in the vicinity of this clandestine plan.

If RFK ever guessed that the president had suggested that Jackie marry Onassis, he would see it as a personal attack designed to dirty the Kennedy legend. The only way he could hit back would be to tell the public, who would also be horrified by such a union.

If LBJ ever emerged as matchmaker he would be in serious trouble with the voters.

The general smiled as he silently acknowledged how smart his friend Lyndon had been when the final reason that the president had selected him stared him in the face.

His old pal knew that lodged in Mo's memory bank were the bloodstock lines of virtually every American Olympic show jumper, not to mention most of Saratoga's best racehorses.

The general knew the genetic background of virtually every Thoroughbred dam and sire that amounted to anything in America.

He was a breeding expert.

Who on earth was better equipped to attempt to arrange a union between a social-climbing Greek millionaire and the most famous woman in the world?

CHAPTER *Thirteen*

After the meeting the general went straight to La Guardia and flew down to Washington. He telephoned Lady Bird in advance to ensure that he would not be in the way.

"Lovely," she replied, "that means there'll be just the three of us for dinner."

Over the meal he told them that so far he was without inspiration: "I have absolutely no idea what I might say to Mrs. K.

"Still, I've got a week until our next meeting and that will give me time to work on a strategy.

"Meanwhile, just so that I don't appear a total buffoon I was wondering, could you ask the CIA or someone to keep an eye out and find out if Jackie's still seeing Onassis or, just as importantly, dating someone else?

"If the whole thing was just a flash in the pan we might as well forget it . . . after all, my dears," he continued in a breathless Jackie-style voice, "it's been absolutely ages, at least ten weeks, since the beginning of January!"

Over dinner, constructed to take account of Lyndon's heart

condition—a cup of light soup, a simple chicken dish, and an optional dessert—he set out to entertain the tense, tired president by outlining the details of the New York meeting.

Ensconced in the second-floor dining room in the private quarters, the three of them gossiped about the likelihood of Jackie settling down with Onassis.

"Remember when I offered her a couple of ambassadorships?" recalled LBJ. "She told me she felt that she couldn't take the children away from Jack's family and her own relatives and educate them abroad.

"At the time I believed her," said the president.

"But times change," Lady Bird interjected.

"At the start, when Jackie was still living here in Washington, she used to visit Bobby and Ethel and Teddy and Joan and all the other Kennedys, but since she moved to New York she rarely comes down here for much longer than it takes to visit Arlington.

"It may well be because coming back here upsets her, and you know that she has always felt that she is not like her in-laws with their touch football and their sporty ways. I am sure she regularly takes the children to Hyannisport to see their grandparents, but she's always traveling to Europe and that doesn't give her much time. Then there's her own mother and stepfather to see, of course, and don't forget she still goes hunting. If there is any family that she is really close to it's her sister."

"True, but it's worth noting," her husband said, "that Lee did marry a foreigner, a prince yes, but a Polish one, and she seems quite content to live in London.

"The Kennedys, I mean the Bouviers, aren't like us. Just take the name, it's French, something that Jackie is mighty proud of. Do you remember when they went on that state visit to France and she chatted to de Gaulle in the lingo?

"She grew up traveling to Europe on a regular basis. Living abroad would be so much more natural for her than for most of us."

On the serious side the general reiterated his request for up-to-date intelligence and the president promised he could have it, on a daily basis.

As the dinner progressed the current First Lady made repeated attempts to discuss what she called the "Bobby Problem" but she failed to attract her husband's interest. He simply would not discuss it.

"Honey, I've spent all day worrying about how the Tet Offensive is going, the atom bomb treaty and the rest, can't a man have a break?"

The general, himself tired, remembered a time when these dinners went on late, but he could see that his old friend was exhausted. So could Lady Bird.

"I'd suggest a nightcap, Mo," she said, "it's just that we seem to be starting earlier and earlier."

The general took the hint and the convivial evening ended.

Back at his ranch the general awaited the special daily delivery that he had requested. It was far from conclusive.

He had been filled in on her CIA duties. All she did was to entertain or make occasional forays to the theater and the ballet, or to visit friends at home.

Onassis was harder to find. He would occasionally go to his office at Olympic Airlines but he didn't work the usual nine-to-five way.

He had a permanent suite at the Pierre Hotel and it was hard to keep tabs on him.

He would pop up in Paris, London, or Athens when the watchers thought he was tucked up on Fifth Avenue.

His constant movement convinced both the general and Blackstone that he probably feared some serious and dangerous enemies,

As a pair, the former First Lady and the Greek were not on the public or private radar.

Equally frustrating was that with the exception of the politicians of the New Frontier—Galbraith, Schlesinger, Lord Harlech, Gilpatrick, and the rest—they could locate no other man in her life.

Because of this, Blackstone was not sure that it was sensible to go ahead with the first meeting. He also didn't think it wise to drag Hugh back from Greece where an agent was still missing, and it was not fair to get the general to cross the country for what would probably be a fruitless discussion.

Carefully, mentioning no names, they talked on the telephone.

"Let's be absolutely clear," said the general, "I am not nervous about going to see her and having a friendly chat.

"I've thought about trying it this way and that. Finally I tried to put myself in her place.

"I decided that we aren't ever going to look like heroes to her. If I were in her shoes, the thing that would irritate me the least, and I can put it no higher than that, is if we are absolutely straightforward with her.

"The smartest thing would be to do to her exactly what you did to me, show her the map with the three red crosses on it, and take her through the tragedy of these talented, brave men cut down in their prime. Luckily for us, she is already nominally part of the agency. We should attempt to make her feel that it is because of her own splendid efforts that we have turned to her in our hour of need, that we are confident she can help us.

"Now, being absolutely logical, she could think, What the hell has all this got to do with me? But I think that we can move this along by what I call 'visualization.' Give people a picture and everything becomes clearer.

"I assume we can get close-up pictures of the island?" he asked Blackstone.

"Got 'em already," he replied instantly.

"As well as showing her the map, we can also mock up some drawings. Very lifelike. Detail how and where we would like to hide our technological equipment, our men, our boats, without anyone else catching on. The artist should make it all look very attractive. Ideally everything in the first sketch, all the surrounding area near the place we might choose to put the technology and the boat, should look just like Skorpios. The vegetation, the rocks, the shoreline, everything should be recognizable to her. Then we could indicate with some trees here, or a hill formation there, where on the island we would put them, i.e., far away from the main family home, the dock, and the staff quarters.

"Apart from this one maybe we could do one or two more, adding a little poetic license.

"Maybe there could be one that included a lively party on one side of the island, one of those high-octane occasions with lots of people, food, staff, drink, and noise, maybe a band, while on the other side of the island one or two guys could be sailing out to sea or arriving quietly.

"That should give her the idea. Fill them with some people that she is bound to have in her retinue, hairdresser, maid, a yoga teacher—good cover for CIA officials.

"On no account should we mention Onassis.

"When she raises it, and she's bound to, we should just say that we understand she knows that part of the world well.

"If she takes it further we will have to pretend that one of our men just happened to catch sight of her in a restaurant with the Greek.

"She'll probably recognize that this is code for our continual vigilance.

"If, as Lady Bird suggests, New Year's Eve is a big date in a woman's calendar, and we tell her that we saw them then, she'll suspect that we think that there is a hot romance going on.

"So we should be vague about any sighting. She's hardly going to like it if she thinks we are nosing around in her personal life even if she is keen to get as much security as possible for herself and her children. Of course, if there is nothing going on she probably won't make two and two become four, but if they are involved, well then . . . Anyway, that's my plan.

"The fact that we have no recent sighting of them together, and even I am not so old that I can't remember how things are at the beginning of a new relationship, seems to be bad news. I can see the whole thing falling apart before we start.

"Whatever we tell her, I'll have to ask her to promise that she will tell no one, absolutely *no one,* about this, ever. I gather she's very good at keeping secrets!

"Well, to go back to my plan, then we should probably remind her of the dead, her fellow CIA workers, and ask if she would kindly come back to us with some suggestions, help us with our dilemma."

When necessary Blackstone was a good listener, he knew when not to interrupt. He let the general pause before continuing.

"I have two more points.

"I've no idea what we'll do if she takes the perfectly sensible point of view that all this has nothing to do with her, or how we should react if she feels insulted, other than to apologize as gracefully as she will let us. But you can't plan for everything."

Blackstone, having based his success in life by spending his entire career meticulously doing just that, did not argue. The general's last thought was for the operative still missing in Greece.

"Has he been found safe and well?"

Blackstone replied: "Sadly, no."

"Well, let's hope he's come to no harm."

The line went quiet.

"We should tell her that too," added the general, returning to his theme. "As soon as we can, we finish, withdraw, and leave the map and the drawings with her. She should feel that there is no pressure, no pressure at all, and again we remind her that she is not to discuss a word of it with anyone, ever. Pity we can't mention the president."

"I'd just feel so much more confident if we thought she had seen the Greek at least once since we started watching them," said Blackstone.

"Me too," said the general. "Let me ask you, how far does she plan ahead? The Secret Service men must be warned of upcoming plans, I imagine. For example, where is she going for the spring vacation or for the summer?"

"Pray God it's to Greece," said Blackstone.

"Amen."

The two decided, come what may, their next meeting should go ahead seven days later.

Blackstone took the plane to New York on the evening before. It was Sunday night, March 31. As he got to his hotel he raced up to his room. The president was due to address the nation on television at nine P.M.

Stunned, Blackstone watched as LBJ dramatically announced that he was going to halt the bombing in Vietnam and would not stand for reelection in the fall.

The general, also watching alone in his hotel room, was depressed at the news.

The next day the two men met again. First they talked about the president's momentous decision. Without hiding their dejection, even though they were both relieved that the war would be coming to an end, they discussed how they would both miss LBJ sitting in the president's chair. The general talked of the president's high hopes for things he could do on the domestic front but had to acknowledge that the unwinnable war in Vietnam had left him no choice.

Blackstone admitted that since the Texan had become their leader he had received two promotions.

"All that, and total confidence in your ultimate boss. It doesn't get much better."

They wondered if yesterday's developments would herald the closing down of the Skorpios plan. The general had tried to get through to his old pal but found it impossible.

"We'd better continue until we hear otherwise," he said.

To try to brighten things up Harry feebly joked: "Well, up to a point that solves the 'Bobby Problem.'"

The general added: "Now I see why the president didn't want to discuss Bobby when I had dinner with him and Lady Bird. He knew he was quitting."

"Well," said Blackstone, "there's not much Bobby can do to Lyndon now."

"Mind you, he would still try to stop them marrying, wouldn't he?"

"What them?" the general riposted.

"I'm sorry, maybe I got our hopes up for nothing, but there is one last thing I would like to try before we give up.

"The agency does have one man. He brought her in, got her involved with a little light spying in the first place, and has known her since the fifties. He has a really good relationship with her.

"Under normal circumstances he would have probably been involved in this but he's been on special family leave in Florida, settling his wife and son into a new house and a new school. Seems she got fed up with living in Moscow, his current posting.

"His name is Guy Steavenson. I saw him early this morning.

"I decided to tell him nothing, not because I don't trust him, I do, with my life, but what with everything going on, I mean last night's bombshell, for all we know the president may shut this thing right down at any moment.

"No point in getting Guy involved at this stage. What he can do for us is find out her state of mind. I'm not saying he can walk right in and say 'so how's your love life,' but he always sees her when he is in town, in fact he told me he is seeing her on Friday. Jackie's always been quite open with him. If he can't find out what's going on in her life, no one can."

The general agreed and they arranged to meet at the same time and place next Monday.

Neither of them could have had any idea that two gunmen were going to make their job so much easier.

CHAPTER
*ourteen*

The news was bad, very bad.

Martin Luther King Jr. had been killed, shot while standing on the balcony of the Lorraine Motel in Memphis.

It was tragic and alarming.

Over and over again the TV was repeating excerpts from his Washington "I have a dream" speech. Guy saw people gathering around the windows of electrical shops to look at the screens.

The three TV network stations were putting out little else. The mood in the street was dour and nasty. Another good man's life snuffed out by an assassin's bullet. It didn't take a lot of imagination to see that Jackie would be very upset. Guy would have understood if she had called this evening off.

It would have been the second time she had done so; he would have been disappointed and Harry Blackstone's request for some answers to a short list of vague questions would have had to wait, but no call came.

As he left the sidewalk to cut across Central Park he began to wish that she had canceled.

Up until now these tête-à-têtes in her apartment had always been highly successful. Underpinned with a soupçon of flirtatiousness, the highly attractive pair would gossip and giggle well into the night. He knew that she was a bad sleeper and since he was someone who had been trained to get by with only five hours' rest, their evenings frequently spilled into the early hours. He was fascinated by her, a woman that he felt had never been and never would be understood by the outside world. Her gratitude to him for finding some worthwhile work with which to occupy herself had deepened their friendship. Although they probably only saw each other five or six times a year, combined with the occasional letters they exchanged via the agency, the relationship had developed into an important one for them both.

In their letters and face-to-face they would analyze mutual contacts, discuss their children, the war, American diplomatic initiatives, and places they knew around the world.

He was sure that there was no way this evening was likely to continue that tradition.

Added to the terrible news about the slaying of Martin Luther King was Guy's own unusually low mood. He had discovered that he could handle the day-to-day dramas of the Cold War, the depressing tasks of a secret life dealing with people who hated everything he stood for, the sudden deaths of old colleagues in the field. But when it came to his son, Guy realized how vulnerable he was.

Ever since he had left his wife, Marie-Helene, and Lucas in the new Florida house, the bells and whistles in his brain that attended all his planning, his dreaming, had slipped into a downturn, minuscule but determinative. To the external viewer Guy appeared exactly the same. He knew that he wasn't.

Strange that the first place he would have to test himself, assure himself that the sheen and glow of the persona that everyone expected was not dented, would be with Jackie.

His personal situation had upset him so much that he felt he no longer retained that automatic belief he had always had in everything he was doing. He had begun to question how effective his job was. From the moment he heard about the murder of Martin Luther King Jr., he started to wonder what good it was attempting to guard America from threats from abroad when the country was still capable of such uncivilized behavior at home.

Once again, it just took one man. One gun-toting loner. One madman.

Guy felt that it was a bad time to leave.

This was his last night in New York. Tomorrow he would go back to the office in Virginia, attend two conferences, dine with his mentor, Harry Blackstone, then head back to Europe, Moscow, and his job.

He had been imagining this evening for days. For a start he had been hoping that he could, for the first time, utilize Jackie's ability to understand children for his own personal reasons.

Perhaps she would have some inspirational ideas about how he could keep close to his ten-year-old, whom he would not see until the summer, and, as importantly, what he could do to make sure that his only child would not forget him.

Within the confines of a civilized evening at 1040 he had been hoping to receive some help.

After her move to New York a traditional pattern had been established for these occasions. They began with a drink while Jackie, who was an inveterate reader, unearthed some articles, usually related to someone they both knew, out of a foreign magazine, often *Paris Match* or sometimes the British *Spectator,* for discussion. Occasionally his gift of Beluga caviar would be presented with the usual accompaniments, onions, hard-boiled egg yolk, capers plus some vodka shots around it.

The following meal, taken at a small circular table in the dining room with its floor-length curtains in deep red and gold, would be simple. Favorites were soft-shell crabs with little red-skinned potatoes or medallions of veal with chive sauce and fresh peas.

The apartment reflected a cosmopolitan look of French and English eighteenth-century antiques enmeshed with long fringed rugs. The vintage appearance of the fine bone china in different colors,

pink for one course, palest green for the next, all added further lus-
ter. Good silverware, not just cutlery but sauceboats, saltcellars, and
oval platters, were utilized. Fresh flowers—sweet peas, hyacinths,
anemones, and tulips—as well as dried ones—blowsy bunches of
hydrangeas—filled vases and baskets. Candles, especially rectangu-
lar ones from Cape Cod, were everywhere. Wherever there was a
place to curl up and read, on a small love seat by a window, or a
chintzy upholstered settle in the corner, there would be attractively
arranged piles of books flanked by coffee tables with low lamps.

Depending on the weather, the fire was lit to pitch an even
golden glow on the paintings and small sculptures, some in terra-
cotta, some in bronze. For Jackie, fashion was for clothes. Houses
were to be reassuringly the same, sanctuaries of grace. When fabrics
wore out or antiques were damaged they were repaired or replaced
with the same.

As he walked across an eerily empty Fifth Avenue he knew that
the nation's mood was fear and anger. This concurred with the atmosphere at 1040.

Jackie was incredibly upset. As he entered, he heard her talking
in the library to her brother-in-law Bobby. Their telephone conversation centered on planning when she would go to Ebenezer to see
Mrs. King.

"I have just finished writing to her. I wrote, 'When will our nation learn that to live by the sword is to perish by the sword.' Bobby,
you should listen to that, this country has gone mad."

He could hear the conversation swiftly winding down.

In a minute she was by his side; there was a warmer hug between
them than normal.

Jackie was in straight black trousers and a charcoal gray turtleneck sweater. With her pearl and jet necklace, pearl stud earrings,
and Italian shoes, she could be the Jackie of the White House, the
most photographed woman in the world. She looked thinner but
just as stunning. Her bouffant hair was immaculate, unlike the desk
in the corner. She looked over toward it.

"Coretta King has four children, Guy. The eldest is just twelve, the little one is only five. What sort of country is this that any madman, any fool with a gun, can kill someone just like that? Why do we let this happen?

"He was a good man trying to make America a better, more equal place.

"Was anyone looking after him or watching over him? No, don't tell me—if it's the Secret Service I'll become even more petrified. You know I feel so much safer when we are abroad."

As soon as she stubbed one cigarette out, she lit another.

"You know I always stood up for the Reverend with Jack. I really thought he was working in the right way to sort out civil rights. Poor Coretta. Four fatherless children! What is it about America?"

As they talked on she started pacing.

She was getting into a state . . . "How do we get a drink around here?" she said, suddenly realizing that no one had come in to offer them one. Her cook arrived with a tray of bottles and cocktail biscuits. After she filled their glasses Jackie took hers over to one of the tall windows.

"There will be riots . . . we're lucky they don't burn Central Park down. I'm telling you now, and I know I've told you before, I'm getting out. I'm really worried. No one in the public eye is safe. I wish, oh, how I wish that Bobby wasn't running for president. Of course he ignores me. Talks about Jack, about his duty, and ignores the risk and the danger. The whole country seems to walk around with a gun in its hand. I'm almost thinking of getting one myself."

She didn't tell him, but this had been true ever since the rape. She had gone so far as to ask a friend for a gun catalog. Tomorrow she would ask one of her Secret Service detail if she could be taught to shoot.

For much of the rest of the evening they talked about assassinations. Her husband, Martin Luther King, Abraham Lincoln, and the attempted murder of Harry S. Truman.

She repeated that she was thinking of getting away from the U.S.

Yet, even though Guy, on Harry Blackstone's orders, asked several times where she thought she could go she was vague.

"Anywhere," she declared, "anywhere but here."

As Harry had asked him simply to ascertain Jackie's general mood, Guy didn't push it.

Her ire, anger, and fear would hardly surprise his boss. Most Americans felt that way tonight. The American dream seemed more like a nightmare.

On the way out he took a moment to tell her his family woes.

Furious with herself for not picking up the signs earlier, she made them return to their seats, poured them both another drink, and asked him to go through the whole thing from the very beginning.

"Maybe absence will make the heart grow fonder," she said, when he told her that his wife's move to Florida, in his eyes, signified the beginning of the end of their marriage.

"Have you ever found that silly edict to be true?" He gave her a hard look.

"I know that living in an embassy compound in a hostile foreign country isn't easy," he said. "But I've told her time and time again it wouldn't be for long. Lucas could start his new school at the beginning of the school year, the September after next. She says no."

Guy was trying hard to be fair. He wanted Jackie to see that he was hurt but not unreasonable.

"She wouldn't even consider moving near our head office in Langley.

"Let's be honest, I am bound to end up there. I can't keep up a fake front at the embassy and go crawling through the undergrowth forever. She wouldn't live near my grandfather in Connecticut; he is the only one left. She says that after Moscow and Prague, sunshine is all she wants.

"She does have friends down in Florida, she spent every Christmas and spring vacation there when her grandmother was alive. She also knows that I'll miss Lucas so much."

"When did all this moving-back-home stuff start?" asked Jackie.

"She came back for a college reunion about a year ago," he explained. "It wasn't immediate but I guess it all started a few months after that. I've repeatedly asked if there is any connection. I have to admit, and I'd only tell you, I've even had a little hunt around to see if there is anyone else involved. An old sweetheart, perhaps, but I can't find anyone and she swears there isn't.

"She does admit that she had a good talk with some of the women who were her contemporaries and she envies them their lifestyle. I did ask her to think again but I seem to be incapable of making her realize what damage she is doing, to all of us. And, before you ask, yes, I did compromise. I don't really want to give up my job but I told her that if she gave me just one more year, I would do whatever she wants."

"Well, my advice is to write to Lucas, write to her too," advised Jackie. "Write often. Receiving a few lines a day is better than waiting for a long screed, especially in the mind of a child. Say all the things that you find hard to say. Simple things, stories, draw pictures for him. Tell him you love him. And that goes for her. Most women never receive anything written, let alone passionate and loving, from their husbands."

"You sound like you know how this works," he said, laughing.

"I had many wonderful letters from my father but not from Jack," she said sadly.

"When he died I had just a few notes from him. Nothing really. I've always wished that I had something. It takes so little time. Do it, it's worth it. You might even persuade her to come back."

He shrugged. "I wouldn't dare hope for that."

"You know you can always call me and ask for advice," she said.

"Anytime, really. You've helped me so much, it's the least that I can do."

"Who knows, I might not be so far away from Moscow. Perhaps we could have more of these little evenings in the future?"

Then she started again about how she was going to escape, flee America.

"I am sure I can do a little work for the agency anywhere, London, maybe?

"There must be all kinds of people you would like me to meet over there. It could work as well as here, couldn't it?

"I promise you, Guy, this time next year, well . . . I won't be here so that any lunatic who wants their name to be in the history books can take potshots at me and my children."

As he left, very, very late, she repeated her offer. "Call me at any time. I'm always pleased to hear from you, Guy."

As Guy left the apartment he realized how much he admired and felt protective of her.

The next day Guy passed on what she had said. Over dinner he earnestly told Harry Blackstone: "Whoever is handling her next needs to know how unhappy she is. How raw her emotions are even though she tries to hide them under that cool exterior. Maybe there should be more protection for her and the children.

"Oh, by the way, although it is none of my business, is somebody guarding Bobby properly?"

After midnight when Blackstone returned home, as arranged, he phoned the general.

"If there was ever a good time to ask, this is it," said Blackstone.

"She does seem very upset," muttered the general. "Let me talk to the president in the morning."

The general did so, but not quite as early as he had intended.

Because of the heightened tension in the country the Secret Service and the CIA were working together like a dream.

When Harry Blackstone placed a second call to Texas, within nine hours of the first, all he said was: "We have been advised by the Secret Service that the lady has informed them that she has decided to go to Greece in June."

It was enough.

CHAPTER ifteen

The moment the plane soared above Dallas, Fort Worth, the general began to run through the Skorpios matter in his head. He had done so a hundred times since Harry Blackstone had suggested they meet at the usual place in New York. Just before he left home he put a call in to the White House.

Both of the Texans, Lyndon and Mo Dodsworth, had been in marriages of long-standing so they were fascinated by the dating pattern of Jackie and the Greek. Neither of them could work out what was happening between the pair.

The president said, "Must be the modern way. Maybe she just called Onassis up and invited herself over there. Or more likely they've been seeing each other all the time and we've missed it."

To Mo, his friend sounded tired and irritated.

Trying to cheer him up, the general continued: "Anyway, if you want to go ahead with this thing I am happy to do so. Let's face it, there couldn't be a better time."

The two of them went over everything again with Lyndon Johnson standing in for Jackie.

The general assured him that the map would now have a fourth crimson cross with a question mark beside it, marking the place where the missing agent was stationed, and the president said that he had been shown replicas of the drawings that the general was taking to show Jackie.

"They're brilliant, I can almost smell the Mediterranean. Very true to life. At first I couldn't make out our secret hideaway but I can see that making the hole in the rocks a little bigger works."

"Apparently they've discovered a place where a small motorboat can get inside," added the general.

"The listening apparatus works best there?"

"Who knows, but at least footprints show up less on the shale and pebbles while any other signs of human life can be buried at sea," replied the general.

"Please call me as soon as you've seen her and let me know how you got on."

The president then called Blackstone.

"Harry, I've had a healthy respect for Guy Steavenson ever since he and I inducted Jackie into the CIA. Isn't it time for him to be involved?"

Blackstone had also thought that when they reached this stage, Guy's inclusion would make sense. Now that the moment was at hand he counseled against it.

He couldn't tell the president that the Guy he had seen when the man had returned from New York had worried him. At dinner he had been different in some indefinable way. It was not simply his depression about his wife's decision to return home. Blackstone noted that the only time the younger man became enthusiastic was when he talked about Jackie. Admittedly, Guy's report of the evening that he had shared with the CIA's most famous, most secret spy was correct in every way, but there was something about it that made Harry suspect that getting Guy to persuade Jackie to marry Onassis might not be his strong suit.

He wasn't going to tell the president of his presentiment. Instead he relied on simple psychology; he would play on the man's understandable nervousness.

"Sir, I feel that we don't need him with us at this time, it would be overkill, he would be wasted. The place we need him is in the fallback position. Realistically, even though we have always found her to be good at keeping secrets, this is different, it's very personal.

"Of course, we will say that it is vital that she does not discuss the problems we have in the Med with anyone but us, but the whole suggestion is so off-the-wall. You remember, sir, your first reaction to it? She is quite likely to want to discuss parts of it with someone."

"That's true," said the president, "so your thinking is . . . who would we rather she discussed this with?"

"Do we want her to ask her brother-in-law? Or her sister, who, it is said, had her own hopes in that area?" continued Blackstone.

"No, we want it to be one of us, someone who will encourage her, who will tell her that this is the perfect solution to keep her family safe. Someone we can guide her toward, someone whom she can take totally into her confidence, because he is one of us."

"Exactly," said the president. "You'll brief Guy; that's if she doesn't throw you and the whole idea out . . ." he continued.

Blackstone, still worried about his young colleague, comforted himself with the thought that when he did talk to Guy he would take the precaution of making the whole thing highly official. The charming Mr. Steavenson would have no option. He would be under orders to back them up.

Twenty-four hours later the general and Blackstone were doing their spiel, for real.

Jackie had been delighted to hear from the general. As usual she arranged to meet him at the New Jersey house, right after the hunt. Assuming that he was also seeing other customers of the Dodsworth stud in the vicinity, she suggested that he come by for predinner drinks.

Exhausted but exhilarated by the jumps and spills of the day, she found that some of her depression had lifted. After watching the two children show off their latest horseback skills, she bathed, fluffed up her hair, slipped into a pair of cyclamen-pink tapered trousers and a dyed-to-match cashmere crewneck.

The general barely had time to introduce Harry Blackstone before Jackie vanished upstairs to bid her children good night. The wait made them doubly edgy. When she returned, Mo broached the difficult subject.

He explained who Harry Blackstone really was and Harry took the moment to put into words his admiration for her work for the agency. The general could see that her surprise had turned to pleasure with Harry's paean of praise. Keen to retain this atmosphere, he began explaining that he was not in New Jersey on four-legged business.

By nonchalantly expressing the view that as all three of them were, he was sure, fully conversant with the Cold War struggle between submarines of the U.S.S.R. and the United States, he gently drew the former First Lady in. He began with a thumbnail sketch of the new U.S. sonar equipment and continued with the problems of installing it. At this stage he produced the map of Greece and the three moved into the adjoining dining room to see it better. Pointing to the crosses and the dates beside them, he itemized just how deadly this technology had been for three, possibly four, of their agents.

Harry Blackstone progressed to America's need for a safe place for some new oceanic listening paraphernalia and for the scientists and others involved with its utilization. He also mentioned the sunken Russian sub in the Pacific and the possibility that there was another in the Med. Interested and flattered to have been included in such a heavyweight discussion about the wider role of the CIA, Jackie much enjoyed his performance.

There was some further talk about the covert activities of the Russians in the area, the discovery of a plot to assassinate some of the Colonels. This took them back to the map and the various spots that the Americans had scoped since the loss of their spies.

Then the drawings were produced. Immediately she recognized the landscape; it was Ari's island, Skorpios. She had loved it when she had been his guest nearly five years ago when she'd been convalescing after little Patrick's death.

The artist had made the place look perfect.

At first she failed to see the narrow harbor that had been gouged from rocks by the seashore but after a minute or two she found it.

Within no time she assumed that all this was leading toward a request for her to ask Ari if the agency could make temporary use of his island. The next two drawings blew that notion apart.

In the first there was a full-scale party down one side of the island while on the dark, uninhabited side two men in a small motorboat were headed for the mooring inside the rocks.

The final sketch was a close-up view of the celebrations. She could see, among the white-gloved waiters, the decorated marquee, and the many well-dressed dinner tables, figures looking much like her cook, her hairdresser, various relatives and their children, her own two children, and Ari himself, all of them much older than they were now.

With a shock she realized that the agency didn't want the island for just a few weeks to deal with current difficulties, they wanted to use it for months, for years.

In that moment the conversation slipped from the political to the personal.

The general and his accomplice were quiet, keeping their eyes on the sketches as if their lives depended on it.

Slowly Jackie looked at all of the drawings again. The silence seemed endless to her, but she did not fill it, especially as she wasn't sure of her response.

She was thinking how alluring Ari's island was without realizing that the general and Harry Blackstone had silently got to their feet and were preparing to leave.

Harry Blackstone was murmuring what a pleasure it had all been.

At the door the general turned to look at her.

"Just take your time, there's no pressure, Harry and I are here for you, whenever you want us.

"Please keep all this to yourself, please talk to no one, absolutely no one, about it."

"Except Guy," Blackstone interjected. "Naturally he knows about it, you could always talk to him."

Once again she was alone.

Only the map and the drawings reminded her that the meeting had been real, that she hadn't imagined it.

Slowly she replayed it in her mind.

The dead men, the Colonels, the lost sub, the rig that could find Russian ships and submarines, and the scientists who wanted to operate it.

Could it be, that in their acute need, the general, and who knows who else, were attempting to make her mistress of Skorpios?

That night she dreamed of bougainvillea and eucalyptus, of cypresses and olive trees.

Was this perhaps the escape she dreamed of?

Harry and the general drove back to New York. Full of nervous relief, the general asked Harry when he would call and warn Guy.

The senior CIA man told him that he had taken the precaution of finding out how the former First Lady usually contacted the man. Apparently, using trade craft Guy had taught her, she always left a prearranged message via a switchboard that was only available to the CIA.

She never called him at home. Blackstone told the general that every agent was trained to keep their families and friends as much in the dark as possible about their secret life.

Harry knew he had time; nine P.M. Eastern Standard Time would mean that in Moscow it was still early morning.

"If it was another agent I wouldn't have to worry about him being in the office on a Sunday," Blackstone told the general. "But now that he's alone at home, I imagine it might be likely that he goes in. I checked. He did two hours' work in there today."

"Do you think she will call him?"

"Don't know, she was so calm, even when she got the message about Skorpios."

The general rhetorically asked: "You don't think she will do anything silly?"

"No, I don't. She was enjoying our talk, she liked being included. I guess, once you've lived in the White House, there is an excitement, a buzz that, however detached you are from current events, you miss," said Harry.

"I never thought she was that disinterested anyway," drawled the general. "Jack Kennedy encouraged her to be that way so as to give himself some space."

Harry set his alarm. He must speak to Guy at dawn.

Guy's response needed virtually no help from the telephone company. He erupted: "That is the most preposterous thing I have ever heard! How could you do this without talking to me? He's a crook, a liar, a bastard, and heaven knows what else. Does the president know about this?"

Guy, normally so careful, so clipped, so in control, could not stop. Mentally Harry Blackstone congratulated himself. His instincts about Guy had been correct.

Putting on his most authoritarian voice, Harry interrupted Guy's flow.

"Guy, I want you to keep away from the embassy today. That's an order. It's Sunday, you don't have to go in, and I can hear from your tone that it is not advisable that you speak to Mrs. Kennedy yet. I also forbid you to call her. I want you to calm down and think of all the plusses of a relationship like this for her, and I want you to leave your own feelings out of it.

"When she does call you, I want you to be supportive to the idea. That's another order."

Guy's foul-tempered farewell left his boss in no doubt that he thought the idea was a bad one.

On Monday Guy was ready for the call but Jackie was on the move, she was traveling to pay her respects to Coretta King. By the time Martin Luther King's funeral took place on April 9 there had been riots in more than one hundred American cities and the president had declared that from now on the civil rights leader would have his own national holiday, an annual memorial to the man's work for equality.

Jackie, once again feeling isolated and nervous, returned to the city from the South.

She left a message for Guy and he returned her call within minutes.

He suggested that she begin by describing the meeting in New Jersey. He was interested to hear how this ticklish subject had been dealt with from her point of view.

When she finished she put it to him bluntly: "Well, Guy, first, do you think the island really is so important?"

"I imagine they would not have made this suggestion lightly," he quite fairly replied. "One of the guys who was killed, the one living in Corfu, he was a great friend of mine."

"And what do you think of Aristotle Onassis?"

He waited a moment and when he spoke his voice was distant, dull. "You must do what you believe is right for you."

When she tried to push him on the subject he became even less animated.

"Never met the man, but I suppose chatting to you, of all people, I should not be influenced by what I've read in the newspapers."

He then changed the subject and talked about his family and his progress without them. When she attempted to return to the subject of Skorpios he would not be drawn any further.

After he put the telephone down he couldn't help feeling that he had obeyed orders, just barely.

And, of course, the jealousy growing inside him.

Over the next few days, when thinking about the meeting in New Jersey, she felt intrigued, rather than affronted. Her knowledge of European history made her feel that the proposition, made she thought with subtlety and taste, had a meaningful significance about it.

The whole event put her in mind of the role of women who had been in a position of great influence and power in the past. Of queens like Britain's Elizabeth I and Scotland's Mary plus French, Spanish, and other noblewomen who according to the history books did or did not marry in order to secure alliances between warring nations or to make peace.

These women hadn't simply responded to their own needs or hormonal yearnings but had behaved in a way that was judged to be for the common good or for the benefit of their family.

Jackie wondered, Was it so stupid to think of the union of two people in this way? Was it too cynical a view to see it like any other contract, a deal, one designed to achieve greater security for her country? If she proceeded, it could only work effectively if they were married. Not only would it be *unthinkable* for a woman in her position to settle for the role of mistress, her family and the nation would be horrified. For the relationship to be any use to the agency it would have to be public, be open. Her seniority, her dominion over Onassis-owned land, would have to be unquestioned. Only then could the CIA utilize the island for its own purposes.

Amid these thoughts she derived great satisfaction from knowing that a project as substantial as this would, at the very least, have needed approval from the top. It was entirely possible that the president, having been one of the earliest to see her potential, might have thought it up himself.

For a day or two she daydreamed about life in Greece, life with Onassis, but all this stopped when soon after Dr. King's funeral, the newspapers began running stories about the slain man's private life. Various reports claimed that he was frequently unfaithful. These were followed up by more articles about his infidelities, including information that some of his adulterous behavior had been recorded by bugs planted by the FBI.

As she penned further sympathetic letters to Coretta King, Jackie felt that history was repeating itself.

She upped the number of therapy sessions with David Goad-shem when newspaper stories about the infidelities of one assassinated leader began to openly refer to the identical conduct of an earlier one.

America was disinterring its leaders in the nastiest way.

Jackie started to avoid crowds. She didn't want to place herself within sight of their knowing looks. It didn't matter whether they were the gawkers who based themselves outside her home, the photographers, stalkers equipped with telephoto lenses, the audience at the ballet or the clientele at Le Pavillon. Stuck inside her luxurious prison she felt even more isolated than she had three and a half years ago when the Marilyn stories emerged.

She felt bitter.

Murderers and thieves worked their sentences, paid their dues, and were free. Not her, she would never feel secure or safe again.

For the spring vacation she had arranged to go and see her in-laws in Hyannisport. As she watched her children enjoy their Easter egg hunt, she relaxed a little. This at least was one place where no word against her late husband would be heard.

In the private world of the Kennedy compound they walked, picnicked, and bicycled free of attention. This was what she now needed, to be part of a family of her own and to have somewhere safe and secure where she would be under no scrutiny. The most photographed woman in the world wanted to be out of the picture.

She thought, Why not do my patriotic duty?

Why not make life easy? Well, at least, why not give it a chance?

Onassis, whom she had seen at several private parties since the New Year, had been away on business in Europe for most of the time that he had been under CIA surveillance.

He had been excited when she called and mentioned that she had often told her children what a wonderful time she had had on his boat. Without demur he asked if it would be possible for the three of them to come to visit him in Greece.

She told him they would travel as soon as the summer vacation began in June.

Busy on deals in Saudi and Paris, he nonetheless threw himself into planning for the visit.

Toys were ordered for the children, an easel, fresh watercolor and oil paints, and an artistic tutor were acquired for Jackie, not to mention the most proficient yoga teacher from Bombay and a new Swedish masseuse.

Knowing that the family liked Italian food, he ordered a wooden pizza oven to be built and asked his chefs to work on their Italian recipes. More snapdragons and mature jasmine plants, both of which would blossom at the correct time, were planted near the house.

In his enthusiasm he cut a business trip to South America short and flew up to New York to attend a dinner with mutual friends, but Jackie refused to allow him to accompany her to 1040.

Onassis was at first nonplussed. Having begun his charm offensive when Jackie first came to Skorpios while she was recuperating after baby Patrick's death, he had been well satisfied with his progress over the New Year. Then he realized that he had been behaving like a simpleton. A connoisseur of women, he knew that they were most impressed by time and attention. Foolishly he realized that he had lavished neither on Jackie. In four weeks' time, during the second week of June, Jackie would be on his boat. Now was the time to apply his full concentration to the subject.

With no idea that the CIA was bent on matchmaking, he set out to woo her. Amid groups of friends they went to the ballet, the opera, charity events at the Metropolitan Museum, the Natural History Museum, and the restaurants and nightclubs of the Upper East Side.

But one place they never got to was bed.

She had to admit that Ari, with his constant tan and dark mischievous eyes, had a Continental charm that reminded her of her father. Earthy and frank, he was glamorously dominating, imposingly clever, an expert on the paucity of style in modern life and the lore of the ancient Greeks and the early gods. He could even make her laugh.

But, could she love him? Could she live with him?

They enjoyed flirting. When he confided that his full name was

Aristotelis, she called him "Telis" for short. In front of other people he would whisper sexy endearments in French. She began to request hostesses whom she trusted to seat him next to her. Until she knew how she felt this was as far as she would go. She watched as film stars, models, and actresses threw themselves at him. She would make him wait. She was going to be no pushover.

The CIA agents, covertly watching, reported every date faithfully and, insofar as they could, in full. Harry Blackstone passed their reports on to the president and the general.

Whenever these appeared there would be instant telephonic communication between Washington, Texas, and Langley. At the beginning the three of them acted as if they were the nervous mother of an old maid, but as May progressed they became disheartened.

As the president said, "Plato was a Greek, but a platonic relationship is not what a guy like Onassis is looking for."

Onassis himself was on the point of giving up. The situation was impossible. Three times he had tried to come upstairs with her at the end of the evening. He had been charming but direct.

"Jackie, how can we get to know each other if there is always a dinosaur"—they had just been to the Natural History Museum—"or a mummy between us?" The evening before they had been to a charitable debutante cotillion.

Each time she had sweetly turned him down.

She had tried to assure him that it was not personal, that she was just being consistent with her rules of widowhood in the Jackie fishbowl. Because reporters and fans patrolled outside her front door seven days a week, often watching her go out and then waiting for her return, she was very careful about whom she entertained. Any well-known man, especially if he was alone, seen entering and leaving at night would lead to speculation, even if he was visiting someone else in the building.

She tried to explain to him that there was already too much gossip surrounding her, her every move, her every purchase. She was nervous of fueling more.

"The children don't need to see any more Kennedy headlines. So

I very rarely entertain a man on his own, especially a famous one like you," she said, smiling.

There was silence for a minute.

Ever the gambler, the Greek stretched his arms wide and said, "Okay, I guess I am not such an egotist that I can't take a hint. You don't know how rare this is for me. Jackie, I think you are fabulous, but I give up."

She didn't believe he would. She knew that he had been attracted to her ever since her first cruise on the *Christina*.

Three days went by without a phone call and she realized that he was serious and that, surprisingly, she was missing him.

It must be feasible to arrange things so that they could have some privacy in her hometown. Without telling him, she arranged to meet a friend, a woman, for drinks at the Pierre Hotel, where he had a permanent suite.

Would it be possible for her to slip into his suite from time to time?

Ten seconds in the lobby and she realized that the Jackie syndrome would make this impossible. The white noise of recognition crackled around her; couples checking in, other guests walking through to dinner or the bar, were transfixed.

Grabbing her pal, she fled to an uptown restaurant that could handle her.

It was a regular visit to the psychoanalyst that gave her the inspiration.

She telephoned Onassis. She was relieved when his office told her to hang on even if it might take a long time. She deduced from this that they had orders to put her through to their boss wherever he was and whenever she rang. He was definitely still interested.

He was on his boat. "At peace in the harbor at Hydra, right in the middle of a smooth, sun-filled sea," he told her.

Wasn't this what she had thought she wanted when she had been at her in-laws' at Easter?

Breathlessly she asked him, "Telis, do you still want me?"

The silence of surprise and then the whoop at the other end told her everything. She continued. "Rent us something in Midtown. Something in an anonymous block, small and simple, just for us." Quickly, her voice got breathier. "Soon."

Within days he found a place on East Sixty-fourth Street. Antiques, lamps, mirrors, and a miniature indoor garden were installed.

His men, working quietly so as not to annoy the neighbors, labored for forty-eight hours. There were paintings by Picasso and Rousseau, drawings by da Vinci and Michelangelo.

Flowers were flown in from all over the world, calla lilies, stephanotis, roses, and mimosa.

In the middle of Manhattan he created an arbor in which he was going to seduce the biggest prize America had to offer.

On the drive downtown Jackie thought about how to deal with Ari. He might think that sex was inevitable tonight but until she decided exactly what she wanted from this relationship she must continue to keep him waiting. At sixty-two he was a man in a hurry; it would have been years since he had bothered to spend time with a woman he desired, instead of just showering her with money. To do what the general wanted she had to ensure that the Greek proposed to her.

"Sorry, Telis," she breathed to herself, "I'm going to have to continue to be difficult."

Meanwhile Ari was also expending thought on his seduction technique.

I don't want this to take forever, he thought, so whatever happens tonight must be different, special. He looked in the mirror and was glad his time on the boat had given him a tan. He practiced one or two of his stories.

Ari decided they would speak French in their love nest. Wrapped tightly around a French word, the slight rasp in his voice sounded sexier to him. Jackie had told him she liked the way foreigners spoke; she found so many of her guests had enticing accents. But he also knew that women responded to sound like men reacted to sight. He was betting that his intonation of a language that needed the *r*'s to roll and the vowels to growl could penetrate the few walls that her brain might have erected against foreigners. Also, he knew that his English was not perfect. Remove her mother tongue, he thought, and I will be on a level playing field with all of her other suitors.

Under her trench coat she wore her newest, most enticing cocktail dress. Beneath the boned bodice in aquamarine silk there was room for little underneath. She must not get carried away. This wasn't as simple as just having some fun. Onassis might want her publicly on his arm but for how long? He had enjoyed a long affair with Maria Callas, the opera star, yet they had never married. He already had a family. Why would he want her as anything more than another conquest to brag about?

So far she had only taken a first, timorous step toward becoming the Greek's secret mistress. If they were ever discovered, her family and the nation would not understand.

She would gaze at the drawings of Skorpios and wonder, Could she marry him? Could she live with him? In their jet-set world they would probably have to spend no more than six months a year with one another, but could she cope with that?

She had always been a brilliant flirt. Tonight she would learn how to tease.


When he was in town she spent every night with him. If they needed to attend long prearranged events alone, they would meet up afterward. If he was at the apartment first she would find him practicing the tango or marveling at the latest consignment of flowers.

Work was never allowed to interfere. No papers, no phone calls, no telegrams. Every time they met he would have something for her.

If he had flown in from Athens it would be chokers of gold and matching rings and bangles from the Greek jeweler Lalaounis. If he had arrived from Paris it might be an Art Deco diamond brooch from Cartier that he picked up on his way to Orly Airport. If he had flown in from Turkey he would produce necklaces embellished with coins of such antiquity they were barely legible. Sometimes he would simply pop into Harry Winston's for something beautiful.

At first, he simply handed all these to her in their magnificent boxes. But as their heavy petting roused him to the heights of sexual frustration, he cunningly placed the items she loved in his trouser pockets or up his shirtsleeve. He enjoyed the hunt, and so did she.

He felt like a teenager in love and the more she denied him full sex, the more he wanted her.

They laughed a lot in that apartment. He always had the best gossip. Opening a bottle of champagne, he told her, "Churchill told me when he went to stay with Ike at the White House, he took four cases of bubbly in case they didn't have any!"

He told her about Peter Sellers falling for Princess Margaret when they were all holidaying in Sardinia. He knew everything about everybody.

He read poetry to her, reminisced about his childhood in Turkey and Greece. She appreciated his knowledgeable comments on how she looked. He explained that this was how a Continental behaved. It was normal to be interested in how women put themselves together. She was spellbound by his slightly old-fashioned, courtly airs, his demonstrative touch. He was always kissing her hand, holding her arm.

She recalled her life with Jack, how many times she had entered the room and he hadn't even looked up. How out of the public eye, boarding *Air Force One* or arriving at the White House, he would leave her to soldier on with the children while he made himself comfortable. There were times she excused this because of his bad health but then it became the norm.

How he only touched her in bed, rarely in public. She could not recall him tucking her arm into his, or stroking her hair.

Onassis could not have been more different.

No servants, no family. No friends to comment on his brilliantined hair or to fret about the five-inch height difference between them.

No mild disdain when he sang noisily.

No judgments.

It took the agency some time to discover whom she was visiting in the prewar apartment building. The president and the general were kept up-to-date by Blackstone.

Guy, buried in work in Moscow and still under orders not to call her, hoped that her silence meant that she had decided to take umbrage at the proposed plan or at the very least she had realized that it would not, *could not,* work.

Doubtless she thought that he had been part of the Skorpios conspiracy. Well, some time in the future, when it had all gone away, he would set her right about that.

In between their exciting evenings Ari spent hours on the telephone making sure everything was perfect for Jackie and the children's forthcoming arrival in Skorpios.

He was enjoying their relationship very much and was looking forward to getting close to Caroline and John. Even though they had not slept together he felt success might be in his grasp, culminating perhaps in an announcement on her birthday in a few weeks' time. This marriage was going to open so many doors for him. Before he left town he ordered a flawless forty-carat diamond ring to be delivered aboard his yacht, the *Christina.*

After another wonderful evening at Sixty-fourth Street he returned to his suite at the Pierre Hotel when he heard the news of the shooting of Bobby Kennedy at the Ambassador Hotel in Los Angeles. The presidential hopeful had just finished a speech to the party faithful. As he and his wife left the ballroom and walked toward their exit via the hotel kitchen, gunfire rang out, and in seconds he was lying on the floor, badly wounded.

Ari and Bobby Kennedy had never gotten along. The Greek was convinced that when Bobby was attorney general he had stopped his plans for expansion in the States. The president's brother had not appreciated the Greek's willingness to deal with both the Americans' friends and their foes. After the initial shock Ari knew that this was a moment when he could show Jackie how different life would be if she were with him. Suddenly galvanized, he saw this as an opportunity.

All three networks were showing the scenes in the hotel. They reported that the senator, who had just won the California Democratic presidential primary, was still alive.

Ari called Jackie. Even though it was very late he could give her a plane to whisk her from New York to Los Angeles, right now. In tears, she thanked him and was relieved to reach Los Angeles Good Samaritan Hospital before Bobby died.

Later, there were those who said that Jackie made the decision to marry Onassis when she stood, once again, at a burial at Arlington National Cemetery. This time, in the heat of June, a black lace mantilla covering her head, white short gloves hiding her hands, she gazed forlornly at the many fatherless Kennedy children gathered around the casket, ten of Bobby's, eleven if the child as yet unborn was counted, plus her own two.

But they were wrong.

Upset, desperately unhappy to think that the tragedy she had so dreaded had happened to Bobby, and worried that now anyone with the Kennedy name, whether large or small, had become a target, it was the offer of a plane, of the cocoon of utter privacy, of the ability to respond so fast, that affected her greatly.

If there was any moment that made up her mind she should marry Aristotle Socrates Onassis, that it was not only her patriotic duty but that only he could look after her and keep her and her family safe, it was as she climbed the steps of his plane on that fateful night of June 5. She prayed for Bobby to pull through but she also decided, Now was the time to get out.

## CHAPTER Seventeen

From the moment the decision was made Jackie was aware that she would have to tell the Kennedy family in advance so that they would be prepared. It was not fair to allow a situation where her in-laws could be upset further. In another family she could just get on the phone. Tempting but disastrous. She would have to arrange to see one of them.

She decided that she would wait until a few days before the wedding scheduled for October, before letting them in on her secret. It had to be a talk-and-run situation.

The entire family was still in shock. She knew all of them would invoke her children, her late husband's memory, anything for this marriage not to go ahead. She couldn't have this conversation anywhere public.

Apart from never wanting to be seen arguing in public, she had promised Harry Blackstone that no one other than the Kennedys would know anything about the forthcoming marriage until her mother made an announcement shortly before the actual event. This gave him and the agency a little time to set things up. Just this morning he had called to say that the boat with the new equipment and two scientists had already sailed.

She decided that the only person she could speak to was her mother-in-law. Jackie knew that Rose was in New York for a few days on an autumn shopping expedition. As a dutiful mother, Jackie always made sure that her children saw a great deal of their grandmother when she was in town.

Nervously she paced and smoked, smoked and paced. In one way it would be easiest to handle this at home, but as Jackie had always been most fearful of being trapped in a situation that she couldn't get out of, she discounted it. If things went badly she knew it would be just too rude for her to leave.

She remembered that the Kennedys still had an office in the city. Because she and Jack had always been based in Washington, Jackie had never been there. By the time she moved to New York her father-in-law was too unwell to travel so she always saw her in-laws up on the Cape. This would be the best place for this confrontation.

In her usual disguise of sunglasses and headscarf, Jackie traveled downtown. She was shown upstairs to a suite of high-ceilinged, well-furnished rooms. The largest overlooked the Hudson River, in the distance the Statue of Liberty was clearly visible. There was an expansive partners' desk, two sofas, and an antique bookcase. The walls painted in severe gray were completely covered in photographs, all in matching frames. There was a small one of the old Fitzgerald clan in Boston, a portrait of Rose with her husband and their children when young. The rest, many of which she had never seen before, were pictures of her dead husband and his mother sailing, playing touch football, going to church in Washington, in Hyannisport, in Boston, in Palm Beach, in the Vatican. On the beach, on the hustings, at the White House, in the Rose Garden, in the Oval Office, in the Senate, at two Democratic conventions, in the embassy garden by London's Regent's Park. The largest photograph, covering virtually a whole wall, was of her dead husband gazing out to sea, flanked by the Stars and Stripes.

Despite the light coming through the windows, the whole room seemed like a bleak chapel dedicated to the late president. Jackie was perturbed and upset. Could it be that while the rest of them had moved on no one had acknowledged the depth of loss felt by her mother-in-law? To have lost so many of your children, now four of them, including Jack's elder brother and sister and Bobby, must be so hard, particularly when one of those, an infant that you had cradled, had been taken away from you at the pinnacle of his success.

Jackie thought that there would be nothing worse, nothing more impossible to be borne, than the untimely, early death of a child. To lose four was unbearable.

She walked around, touched her almost life-sized dead husband's face. It was only eight-thirty A.M. Her instinct told her that this was not the place to be talking of new marriages, of new lives, of love, of hope. She could sneak away. She would have to talk to her mother-in-law somewhere else.

She was getting up when the obliging secretary, thrilled to be in on this little secret, returned with coffee specially made the way she had been assured the former First Lady liked it. Putting down a small tray, she chattered on, oblivious to the desperate need of her guest to escape.

"How long has this office been like this?" the widow asked quietly.

"Lovely, isn't it?" said the secretary, placing the white lilies, which she had read in the *National Enquirer* were the former First Lady's favorites, on the low table.

"Whenever Mrs. Kennedy finds a picture of her and the president together we get it framed by the same place. The framer won't charge, he loves the whole family so much. Sometimes we just hear of a picture and we get someone to track it down. One or two of them have arrived in a real mess and they have to phone the paper or the photographer for a new print. I guess we'll run out of wall eventually."

Then, embarrassed at what she had said, the secretary made to leave but turned around when she realized she was being followed out of the door. One look and she sensed that the visitor wanted to exit fast.

"I guess this room must be upsetting, I should have taken you to another part of the office," she started. Then her voice trailed away when she saw Jackie give a resigned sigh as the outer door began to open. They watched as it opened fully. It was the post delivery.

The postman was so taken aback at the sight of the former First Lady that he dropped several small parcels and letters right in front of the door. By the time he had cleared them it was too late. She could hear her mother-in-law saying her cheery hellos as she walked down the corridor.

Jackie took a deep breath and returned to the inner sanctum.

"For God's sake, why?" Rose had cried when she told her.

It was as Jackie had expected.

"Wouldn't it be best to go to your grave as a great man's widow? Wouldn't history judge you better?"

"Wouldn't your children judge you better?" Rose smiled sadly.

When Jackie tried to say that she was in love the older woman turned on her.

"You, you are loved by this entire nation, by the whole world. You don't need love.

"It's money, isn't it? More money! You were left enough, then the family gave you more, I fixed that for you. But it's not enough, never enough for you, is it?"

Jackie whispered: "It would just be good to have someone care about me, really care," she said as she bent to pick up her bag.

"Yes, I know things weren't perfect. But he loved you in his way, like Joe loved me," said her mother-in-law.

They had never discussed this before. Never. Not during her marriage when he had taken holidays without her, after his death on the days that the dreadful stories about his affairs had appeared in the press, nor even later during the family holidays at Hyannisport.

Jackie was poised to flee but she felt that she had to say something in her own defense.

"I never, ever raised this with you or any of your family."

The tears behind the words threatened to gush out. "None of you, not one of you, I may add, ever rang me up to ask me how I was feeling about those stories, or suggested how best to hide them from the children or how to stop the newspapers from printing any more of them. But let's face it, this is what the men in this family do as a hobby, as a sideline.

"So don't tell me you didn't know."

Rose held her hand up.

"You know it meant nothing," she replied quietly. "The boys saw it like getting a cup of coffee, not even that much, a coffee warms you at least. He loved you." Saying this, she came toward Jackie and pointed at the wall with its life-sized portrait.

"Look at him, he was beautiful. How can you face *him* after him?"

Jackie turned to face her mother-in-law, a woman she had known for more than sixteen years, but still didn't know at all.

"You don't understand. I don't feel safe here anymore, I feel under threat in New York, in this country." Jackie sobbed and for the very first time began to tell someone about the robbery and the rape.

"I have never felt so low, so used, so belittled." Her sobs filled the room. At the end of it both women were in tears. Rose gently reiterated that she would rather Jackie did not marry but she understood her pain and her fears.

Then Rose gave Jackie something her own mother had withheld, her blessing.

Three days later Jackie was on a boat traveling from Athens to Skorpios.

She was the first to see it. The island looked like a green and gray opal on the smooth Ionian Sea.

Private, guarded, safe.

Someone handed her some binoculars. She was pointing things out and explaining to the others.

There was the big house with its entry lined with silk the color of walnuts visible through the open collonaded porch. Around the walls lit by mirrored sconces were long linen-covered tables littered with elegant hurricane lamps. Through the airy hall was the glass-covered orangerie with its twin lap pools beyond. One was tiled the same shade as stonewashed jeans, the other in pure indigo. The Greek always explained that he had chosen them so that his casually dressed visitors in jeans would feel at home.

The pale pink building was wide and spare. Its twelve bedrooms all had balconies overlooking the sea. Joined to it by a tributary of paths were wisteria-covered pergolas, bottle-green tennis courts, and several exquisite summer houses painted in shades of melon, fig, and strawberry, each tiny home accessorized with everything matching from steamer chairs, recliners, hammocks, and awnings down to table linen and china.

"Keeps the place tidy," her brand-new fiancé had said. "No one gets their things mixed up. The children like feeling independent, away from the servants, probably away from me, you know . . ."

He shrugged with a minimal smile.

They had spent many hours discussing his two children, who still blamed him for their parents' divorce. She wondered if they had been told about the wedding, if they would be there.

At least their intransigence meant that the whole place with its simple miniature houses was in perfect taste, unlike the boat she stood on or for that matter the plane she had just left.

Still, taste wasn't everything. She laughed to herself. If only the outside world knew that her priorities had so changed.

Harry had explained in detail to her that there was another side to the island when the sea looked bad-tempered and the trees sullen. "It can get cold and choppy," he said. "This is why we need to get to work. The weather will be too bad for you to hang around in winter. When you are not there we can't do much either."

She told him that she would be on the island for at least six weeks during the summer holidays while secretly preparing for the wedding.

"We won't be doing any entertaining. We don't want to tip anyone off until just beforehand," explained Jackie.

"That's fine. Just by being here we can have people around on
the island that are not expected. It means the Russians can't work
out who is working for you or who is working for us."

Now at last the preparations were over. Almost against her will,
Jackie's mother came to the island and brought her stepfather, Uncle
Hughdie.

Needless to say Janet was unhappy about the engagement but had
made the announcement because it was correct form.

From her vantage point at the front of the yacht Jackie thought
the island, named after the scorpion because of its shape, looked
perfect today. Even in October the sea was almost purple, the shade
often mentioned in Greek mythology as wine-colored. Jackie remembered how in the heat of the summer the flowers and plants
had released their fragrance for the pleasure of the butterflies.

Apart from the jetty the whole place looked empty.

It was just what she had dreamed of.

She looked behind her at the rest of the adults on the ship. How
brilliant of Rose to ensure that several Kennedys came to the wedding.

"We want to look united," explained her mother-in-law. "That
has always been our strength. I'll see that you are not alone."

They both knew that public opinion would be against her, that
they would hate the idea that she would be taking a divorced foreigner, who lacked Prince Charming looks, to her bed, not to mention relinquishing her role as a widow, still mourning the slain
presidential prince.

Jackie had discussed this with Harry too. His advice had been,
"A baby, Jackie, just something as simple as that, as quickly as possible. It would have the public eating out of your hand."

Jackie knew that Rose would not have liked this idea, but Ari
was enthusiastic.

Her mother-in-law had not only persuaded two of her daughters
and their families to go to Greece as part of the wedding party, she

had already made it known to the family that she thought Jackie was entitled to any happiness that she could find. She also promised her daughter-in-law that after the wedding was announced she would repeat this to the news media.

The whole group was becoming excited now that they could see ten sailors standing on the dock in a navy and white line. Their broad shoulders were accentuated by the gold braid and buttons that adorned the epaulettes of neat navy cable-stitched sweaters. Crisp white shorts meant that twenty tanned muscular legs were also on parade. Each of them had sworn loyalty only to the Greek.

From Saturday they would extend that allegiance to her and her children. She told herself that whatever happened, whatever people said, this was what she had needed. This was the best she could have done.

Reassured, she turned to look at the faces crowding the ship's rail. Her children and their cousins watching as the crew worked at bringing the boat into harbor. Her sisters-in-law, tall and angular, their pale faces slightly pink, already hyped up by the flight to Athens on the private plane. Their husbands in determinedly happy mode, lips creased into smiles that didn't quite reach their eyes. Her mother and stepfather doing the best that they could.

Thank heaven her own sister supported her. She and her family had arrived yesterday.

Jackie knew that Ari was watching them from the privacy of the boathouse.

The couple had decided that they would meet inside.

It would be the start of their life together. So far their love had been hidden. She and Telis had decided that only their families would see their greeting. There would be no photographs of them at the airport in Athens or taken by some trippers out on the sea.

His son was at the jetty. He was cool toward her.

Luckily, she had never believed that anything about this wedding was going to be easy.

CHAPTER *Eighteen*

The honeymoon had been better than either of them had expected.

The sex had been exciting. Jackie was enthused by Ari's zest for lovemaking and the extraordinary nights of their courtship had taught them both a great deal about what pleased the other. But the moment they returned to New York as man and wife their idyll was over. The East Coast gave them as lukewarm a welcome as it dared. There were more rebuffs than receptions. Manhattan and Washington acted in unison; from the White House to the Russian Tea Room, it was the same. Few wanted to see or be seen with them.

Jackie was not surprised. The hideous response worldwide to their nuptials—SHE WENT FROM A GREEK GOD TO A GODDAMN GREEK—ran the headlines, was a clear warning that there would be scant acceptance. While still honeymooning she had warned Ari that this was how it would be, but he had absolutely refused to believe her.

He was confident that once everyone had recovered from the shock, they would soon become used to the idea. He told Jackie that he had overcome bigger obstacles making his millions. This he could handle. It was simply a question of dealing with the American suspicion of all things European.

He blamed the press. Those cartoons showing him as a toad or a warthog straddling his American beauty still rankled. He assured his new wife that after he had entertained a few editors and journalists at lunch, one or two papers would separate from the herd. Cynically he was convinced that it was in the nature of the beast for the press to disagree with one another. Once some of them would begin to be more favorable to the marriage, the whole drama would be over.

She, however, did not believe it would be that simple but she lacked the heart to disagree with him. Throughout their honeymoon, he had made it clear with much pleasure that he was looking forward to returning to the States with his bride, his prize.

"Now they will have no choice," he said, "those rich old-moneyed families will have to let me in. Now I shall be able to take my proper place."

He would laugh while cooking up plans on how to run into this friend or that acquaintance. He would gleefully discuss with her how "these poor sops" would react. The ways in which they would have to hide their chagrin because he, not they, had walked off with the biggest deal the West could offer. He would turn with gusto to the imagined fury of his compatriots and competitors, the other Greek billionaires.

On the shakiest of gossip and no real evidence, he had convinced himself that all of them would have had no hesitation in dumping their wives if they could have won her.

Then he would think of her countrymen, enumerating those who he was sure would have been thrilled to be in his place and who, he was certain, would feel doubly thwarted that a foreigner had carried off this beautiful American trophy.

If she tried to remonstrate that many of these men were happily married or would frankly have been too terrified to have taken her on, he would hear none of it. He would respond that she was far too modest and unworldly.

In the end it was he who ended up not understanding.

Universally it had been made clear that by marrying the Greek she had not only blemished the ex-president's memory but had tarnished herself forever.

She had understood this before agreeing to marry him because she knew what her friends and the public didn't. In her eyes security was more important than reputation, although she had never imagined that they would be so reviled.

As they looked forward to their first Christmas together, she covertly watched him read the papers every morning. On the island he had always turned first to the financial pages; now he hunted through the gossip columns for stories of parties that they had been excluded from. Once she overheard him phone his secretary to ask whether the invitation to that season's grandest affair had not been sent to his office in Athens by mistake.

He would never reveal to her how hurt he was. Although this had been going on since their return to the States in early November his pride forbade him to say a word.

Her family had done its best.

At Christmas her mother had organized a dinner for about sixty at Merrywood. The number of guests should have been nearer a hundred, but her old family, her ex-in-laws, or as she now called them, the outlaws, sent regrets. The same applied to old political friends when her sister held a party for them in Washington.

As Easter came round she herself tried to arrange a large picnic, "so that the children shouldn't lose contact."

The ensuing conversations made it very clear that the children were more than welcome at the Kennedy compound near Cape Cod or to stay with their cousins in Palm Beach, Boston, or Beverly Hills, but apart from the ever-faithful nanny it was made perfectly clear that adults were not invited.

Of course it had all been done with the most glacial politesse. One couple said that they had building going on while another used the excuse that the children had invited so many friends to stay that making any new arrangements was impossible. Another explained that the house was being turned into a tennis camp and only the children would enjoy the daily round of serves and volleys.

It was obvious to Jackie that her in-laws' attendance at her wedding had been strictly for public consumption and for pleasing Greek-American voters. From now on she was history.

Ari, surprised by the coolness of many of his own friends in New York, refused to be defeated. He decided that he would buy their way back into society. He bought tables at charity events and vacuumed up raffle tickets as if they were confetti. His donations were record-breaking but even this failed to get any of the real movers and shakers to invite them to dinner. Socially, politicians, U.N. diplomats, Manhattan moguls, Oscar winners, and other creative megastars cold-shouldered them.

It took just one evening, with the Greek-American community to sadden them completely. Here at last was a loving, warm, effusive welcome. The contrast with the way they had been treated by everyone else could not have been greater.

She knew that the CIA in the shape of Harry Blackstone was keen that they return to the island. They were missing the busy comings and goings that their arrival entailed. Without much difficulty Jackie induced her husband to return to their own piece of paradise. But once there, try as they might, they could not re-create the happiness they had experienced before.

She found it impossible to console her husband because he refused to talk about the subject. Every time she tried to raise it she found that he had surrounded himself with his cronies. His right-hand man, Nikos Dervizoglou, a distant relative, had virtually moved in. Jackie did what she could to charm him but knew that she would never be able to win this man's approval. Everything Nikos said, even his slightly arrogant gestures, suggested that when it came to relationships he was an archconservative. As far as he was concerned, she was too independent, too opinionated; he believed a good wife should walk in her husband's shadow.

Soon just being alone together seemed to upset Ari as if he blamed her for bringing this curse on him. As communication between them worsened, he made a frenzied return to work. His office, a pale green edifice in the garden, filled with extra staff. Seven days a week they came and went. It became usual for his most senior employees to join them for lunch where the main items under discussion were deals, contracts, contacts, and friends that Jackie knew nothing about. Often Ari, in his disgust at America, seemed to encourage these conversations in Greek. The only Greek words she knew were the naughty ones he had taught her, words only uttered by a lover.

Soon she started to lunch alone, or when they were there, with the children.

Ari decided the only way to show the world what he was really made of was to be ever more successful. He would only return to the States when he had done the greatest deal of all time.

Only the sex was not in short supply.

As if he were fighting to obliterate the world's resentment, he demanded to be given more caresses, more kisses, more sensual thrills and excitement. He was insatiable and made love to her frequently and often roughly.

She was desperate. Now not only did the whole world think she had married a monster, on occasion she was starting to agree with them. She had to make this work. She needed to. There was no going back for her. Those weeks in New York had made that very clear. The people they knew despised her and loathed her husband. As she thought calmly about it, she realized, What did they know? They just thought that he was low in the looks and high in the wallet departments. How amazed they would be if they knew that even now she thought her second husband was as funny, knowledgeable, and exciting to live with as her first and so much, much better in bed.

After the assassination she had been counseled by everyone to move on but in reality they wanted her to be stuck in a time warp, staying loyal to a flame that had never really burned for her.

Her bitterness deepened, knowing that the New Yorkers with the biggest pursed lips had such double standards. Those most resolutely against the new Mr. and Mrs. Onassis were such hypocrites, many of them with secrets far more shameful than her marriage.

Another six weeks went by. Her family came to visit but only briefly. When her mother started to apologize to her son-in-law on behalf of her country he immediately held up his hand and insisted she stop. "As your daughter must have told you," he said in a slow, deep monotone, "we do not discuss that in this house. It is a temporary situation. We'll get over it." He then withdrew to his office with a wintry smile.

Once her mother had gone, Jackie was left to her own devices and she explored the island.

Everywhere she went she took her basket of Greek conversation tapes and a copy of the Greek alphabet. She tried to absorb herself in Greek songs and the poems of Cavafy.

She was bored and she was lonely so although she knew it was risky her walks took her to new beaches. After several visits when she had failed to see evidence of anyone else being there, she found a secluded spot that was perfect for nude sunbathing. Ari had told her that all the strippers in Paris did this. He described how much sexier an all-over tan looked by comparison to a body patterned with white skin.

Lulled into the certainty that she was alone she became confident enough to try it, and since her breasts and bottom had never before been exposed to the sun she took great care not to burn them, only baring herself toward the end of the afternoon when the sun was gentler. To ensure that her lithe body roasted to an even coffee shade she did this every day without fail.

It was the housekeeper who showed her the down-market weekly magazine. Nervously, as she left the veranda after going through the day's menu, she signaled that she had left the tabloid for her employer on Jackie's favorite sun lounger.

Jackie had discovered that reading rubbish in Greek, especially the lurid weeklies, was a really easy way to understand the language, peppered as it was with names she recognized. It was so much simpler to understand with just a few new words to grapple with.

As she picked up the tabloid she was amazed to see herself in the full-sized, full-on nude photographs on the front page. The snaps left nothing to the imagination. Her skin gleaming with sun oil from her forehead to her toes revealed that she was a regular nudist. The only items that were not chocolate brown were her shaggy black hair, both on her head and lower down.

Tears welled up in her eyes. This was shameful. Now she and Ari would never be able to hold up their heads in polite society again. Her children would become objects of satire and ridicule, as she had been.

Everything, the marriage, Ari's lack of communication and total involvement in his work, had gone so wrong, so quickly. All they shared was sex.

Before she had time to be depressed any further she saw her husband barge through the half-open French windows of his office and come running out, loudly shouting her name again and again. In his hand, the magazine.

This was terrible, how could she have been so stupid, so naive, she thought.

His face was contorted and there were tears on his cheeks. For a second she thought he might have been crying but then as he grew closer she could see that he was laughing.

"That's done it," he yelled. "They can put that in their bloody sanctimonious pipes and smoke it." He pointed at the picture with his cigar. "You look fabulous, fabulous." He bent to kiss her. He looked straight into her eyes. A hard, sensual look.

He was proud of her, but she knew he was also so proud of himself.

"You look sensational. The perfect woman, a goddess. Who cares about those numbskulls, they are not living, they are simply existing in their laced-up shoes, with their laced-up wives thinking that a round of golf is an exciting adventure. They are barely tasting life. It is us, we are living." He reached his arms out and did a yelp and a few steps of the Greek village dance he enjoyed so much.

And he laughed.

"We are living and we are leaving. Yes, darling, we are going back to the States and to hell with them all. Only this time, we will be clever. When we go out you will enter and exit on your own. You are the Venus of Botticelli, you should stand alone. This unknown photographer has done us a favor. Yes, there may be a few silly sermons on Sunday that might be a little nasty about you. But every red-blooded male in the world will know that you are the very best of womankind."

He looked at the picture again and pulled her close to him.

"Be honest, it is me they object to! Not you, my darling."

She tried to argue and say that the universal feeling was that she should never have married, but he shushed her.

"We will always be together but not in front of the camera, it will offend everyone less. As I said to your mother, they will get over it, but I never thought a picture of you naked as the day you were born would be the answer. We will be patient. I'll be patient, well, I'll try."

A week later they were back in the Big Apple.

Following his suggestion, they arranged their lives so that they would not often be photographed together.

He was right. Public opinion mellowed when the magazines showed her going out alone, and though the powerful and mighty knew they were very much together, the fact that the pair now took great pains not to give that impression pleased them. It confirmed that their concerted action on the pair's posthoneymoon exclusion had been correct. Slowly the invitations began to roll in.

There was another spin-off that pleased Onassis even more. Privately he thought that many of the photographs published by the newspapers and magazines had been carefully selected so that next to his willowy wife he looked like a small gray slug.

Now the only photographs taken of them together were when

they were seated at dinner. Sitting down, they were of equal height.

Unfortunately the fewer pictures of the newlyweds appearing gave quite a different message to the one woman who would never accept the marriage of Aristotle Onassis and Jacqueline Kennedy.

In her dressing room, whether at the Royal Opera House in London's Covent Garden or at the Paris opera house in the place de l'Opéra, Maria Callas scoured the international press. Whatever her New York friends told her, this lack of togetherness suggested one thing to her, the relationship was already in difficulties.

She thought to herself, He had wanted a trophy, but not any longer.

The opera singer, no stranger to drama, relished the chance of using her artistry to win back her lover.

Her first ruse, summoning him to Paris to discuss her financial affairs, had started well but was over too soon. Disappointingly he had deposited her outside her apartment with nothing more than a chaste kiss on the cheek and three days later took his wife to the selfsame table at Maxim's.

"Give it time, the man will soon become bored," was the advice she received from Nikos and Ari's other Greek friends who also felt uncomfortable around Jackie.

The diva listened and waited.

The CIA kept in touch with Jackie but made only one major request during her first year as Jackie O. They wanted Jackie to ask for a gazebo to be built on a promontory overlooking the ocean, a fifteen-minute walk from the house.

Swiftly an elegant, white-painted folly with double glass doors was erected. Apart from the wrought-iron wall lights, heavy white cotton curtains, her easel and a few shelves it was bare.

One week later, the agency telephoned (using the same code, "Lace," her original codename when she was First Lady) and asked her to have the oak floorboards painted black and to request a very large built-in cupboard in the corner. She made no comment when a few days later she saw the fine outline of a circle had been cut inside its floor. For safety's sake she scribbled away at some sheets of paper and piled these above it.

As soon as the studio was complete, two men arrived to chisel away at the narrow sliver between the rocks directly underneath. Working steadily, they enlarged the natural chamber to become a minicave with an entrance big enough to take a small motorboat. The mooring, just two iron rings and an incline down to sea level, was added. Two bunks were fitted into the cavern. The installation of the listening device was simple but it was not yet serviceable. The two scientists that accompanied the machinery had failed to make it work so far.

Early in 1970 the CIA, who had assumed that their fourth agent was dead, had received a photograph of a man resembling their missing operative. It included no details; only a recent newspaper was also in the picture. Langley had implored all their informants in the area to see if they could check if anyone knew of the agent's whereabouts.

Although convinced that their missing man could no longer be alive, Harry Blackstone knew that he had to take action, if for nothing else then for the morale of the service. Any leads that could help them locate the lost man must be investigated. It would need someone experienced who was fluent in the local languages, Turkish, Greek, and Russian.

Guy Steavenson had no inkling of this when he reported for his first day's duty at CIA headquarters in Langley.

In the end he had not needed to negotiate himself out of Moscow. He had the prescience to know that the Russians would accomplish this for him. It was only a matter of time before they became too suspicious about just why the handsome, successful senior press attaché seemed to be languishing in the same post for so long.

The agency was expecting this but had delayed taking any action because they were facing a dilemma. They could take the next natural step and promote Guy. Yet a new post would keep him so busy on proper ambassadorial duties that he would have no time for the far more important job of monitoring Soviet infiltration of Europe and the Middle East. They also knew that giving Guy a new job would not necessarily be enough to stop the KGB sniffing around. In the diplomatic corps, the norm was that a new position meant a move to another embassy in another country.

Putting this decision off resulted in two nights of terror for Guy when he was nearly caught with one of the agents he was handling. The agency had to admit defeat and pull him out.

His arrival in America revealed that he had been right all along about the demise of his marriage. Marie-Helene's new life had proved even more attractive than she had imagined. Not only had she fallen in love with Florida but also with the local well-to-do garage owner.

He was upset, not so much for the loss of his wife (if he was honest they had been growing apart even before she left Moscow) but for the breakup of the family unit and his injured pride. All of it was rendered more bearable by the joyous reunion that he always had with his ten-year-old. Lucas continued to behave as if they had never been apart, and in Guy's view, the more important relationship had been maintained. As soon as they could, father and son went off to join Guy's maternal grandfather for two weeks of fishing and riding in Connecticut.

Moscow was no longer part of his day-to-day responsibilities but Harry had kept close contact with Guy throughout and felt highly sympathetic to him. His own marriage had not survived the long days and nights spent in his last posting.

In his office the two began to discuss Guy's next assignment.

"As you know, at one stage I just wanted to come back to the States. But now that I know Lucas is fine, I don't know if I am ready to come here and sit behind a desk yet."

"Well," said Harry, "sorting out Lucas was the most important thing."

His eyes slid to the photograph of his twin daughters, whom he still had difficulty accessing, no matter what the court ordered.

He could not have been more delighted when Guy continued. "I'm forty now and I think I have one or two more foreign jobs in me yet."

Harry fished a photograph out of his desk.

"Take a look at this."

It was a fuzzy shot of a man who looked like the missing CIA officer.

"It could be George," replied Guy after a long, hard look at it.

"We don't know how real or how old this picture is yet," Harry continued. "The original is under examination now but we have to check it out. We can't just do nothing.

"If it is him, we want him back and we want to know what the hell he has been doing all this time. If the experts say that the photo is a fake we could ignore it, but it could be useful for us to find out exactly who, after all this time, is setting a trap, and more importantly, why?"

Guy, keen to take this assignment, asked, "What do you think they want?"

"It's possible that we have a turncoat on our hands, but either way, the whole thing shouldn't take long. You'll meet him and you'll know."

Guy agreed on the condition that while he was abroad Harry would work out a career structure for him. He wanted to know what his future role would be; he hated being in limbo.

Last on the agenda Harry mentioned Skorpios.

Harry told him that the listening equipment was still faulty but that the man-made harbor was functional, especially as it had two escape routes, the sea or a narrow stone staircase that led up to a studio above.

"Operating on the notion that these stories and this photograph just might be a trap, the island is quite far from Patras, but if worst comes to worst you could go there for sanctuary."

Later that evening, with Guy already on the plane to New York to catch the connection to Europe, Harry recalled that the words "Jackie" or "Onassis" had not been uttered once.

Guy looked forward to landing in New York but there was always that pang. No more evenings at "1040." He had been at one with the rest of the world in his horror at Jackie's marriage. But he recognized that his disgust was personal.

Consumed by self-pity, he realized that somewhere along the line he had fallen for her. Guiltily he wondered if his wife had sensed it before he had. Had he mentioned Jackie's name too often or stayed away for a night too long in order to see her? Had it triggered his wife's wish to leave Moscow?

Again and again he had cursed Harry for banning him from calling Jackie before she had taken that final step.

Immediately after the wedding Guy could not stop himself going through agonies thinking of her on her honeymoon. Time after time he would logically tell himself that even though he would be very well off one day, he was the sole heir to his grandfather's wealth, he would not be in the same league as Onassis.

Nonetheless her smile haunted him. Their evenings alone together had been very special. His anguish was spiked with resentment, knowing that it was because of her trust in him that she had become embroiled in the agency in the first place.

During long weekends alone in Moscow, he would constantly recall that last night when she had taken so much time over his problems, over him. He suspected that she felt something too. Hoping that she had married Onassis solely because she felt it was her patriotic duty, he could not condemn her but admire her more.

Raised to behave properly, he had sent her a congratulatory note after the wedding to which she had replied with a very gracious, handwritten thank-you letter. And there it had ended.

Understandably, the intelligence role that she had previously carried out on the agency's behalf was over. Her new focus was to find reasons for undercover agents to keep coming to the island. For this, gardens were dug up and replanted, rooms redesigned, outdoor seawater swimming pools created, and patios repaved.

Ari was fascinated by her enthusiasm at first but when the budgets started to reach the stratosphere he grew impatient. He asked Nikos Dervizgolou to keep him abreast of the rising costs. As time went on the new Mr. and Mrs. Onassis grew quite content with their separate-but-together lives.

He continued to travel the world on business. When she was free she would join him but his life was too peripatetic to make a base elsewhere, and Jackie was against uprooting the children from their

American schools. Luxuriating in Ari's wealth, she added more staff to make her feel safer.

For tax purposes Ari maintained his suite at the Pierre Hotel but spent time with her at the apartment.

Gradually everyone could see that behind her perennial sunglasses, Jackie was happy again and the couple began to be feted in the U.S. Everywhere they went they were serenaded with the theme tune from *Zorba the Greek*. The Americans were trying to make him feel at home; it signified their acceptance. Ari often told her that she had brought him everything he had wanted from the marriage.

He only moaned to Nikos about two things, her expensive redecorating and shopping habit and her fascination with reading. Frequently he was abashed that she would prefer to spend the evening quietly at home with the children and an undisturbed hour or two in front of the fire with a new book, rather than go out on the town with him.

But he loved that she loved his island so much. Mindful of the agency's needs, unless it was deepest midwinter, she was always suggesting they go there. Once again she invited friends and family down to catch the first rays of the summer sun during the spring vacation.

Even though an influx of the superrich created a great deal of welcome work for the locals, Nikos was unhappy. As he sat in his Athenian office and surveyed the latest round of expenses, he was shocked by the figures that were leaping up by hundreds and thousands of dollars. He knew that soon he would have to tell his boss and when he did it usually led to a row. Instead of hollering at his wife, however, Ari took his irritation with the constant refiguring of Skorpios out on him.

Nikos sighed. How much easier his life had been without her.

Although they were distantly related and old, close friends, he worried that during one of these shouting matches Ari would discard him. It was so unfair and so unlike him. If Ari couldn't stop her, how on earth was he supposed to do so?

The costs, the worry about having everything done in time, the constant demands of this landscape artist or yet another interior designer, were ruining his life. They made mistakes, they blamed the local artisans, it caused bad blood, and then it all started again.

Just handling their travel arrangements needed an army of staff. They wanted to go to Athens, *now,* they wanted to go to New York, *now.* The motorboat and the *Christina* were kept busy ferrying them to and fro. They took up many first-class seats on Ari's airline, Olympic Airways, and all of this had to be done through interpreters and Nikos had long run out of local ones.

Nikos wasn't greedy or lazy. About to hit fifty-five, he was worried for his future and nostalgic about the past, for the life he had led until just a couple of years ago. He remembered the old times, the good ones when, whoever they had had on board, whether it be Sir Winston Churchill, Greta Garbo, or Prince Rainier and Princess Grace of Monaco, the two of them, himself and his boss, had gone carousing around the ports of the Med. Wherever they stopped, once they had the VIP tucked in for the night, they would please themselves and hop off for an ouzo or a glass of retsina at any taverna they fancied.

They'd bedded women in Piraeus and Paros, Sparta and Spetsai. Not to mention Monte Carlo, Cannes, Italy, and Spain. They had got in and out of trouble with irate boyfriends, angry mothers, and barking dogs.

And always he and Ari had laughed. The older man would bounce his more crazy ideas off him. Or he would talk honestly about what was worrying him, his son and daughter with whom he was not close, his ex-wife Tina, his latest deal, the advantages or the complications of a particular situation. He would enjoy talking through all the angles.

For Nikos this was the time he could fix things for friends and family. With Ari in this mood Nikos could organize a new job here, some medical bills paid there, and he could do all this with a good heart. Not only did it help everyone in the Onassis empire, it contributed to Ari''s happy life. It meant that his boss was genuinely beloved, often for things he had forgotten about, that Nikos had done in his name. Nikos thought of this as creative work. It was as important as his role of guardian of the Onassis coffers.

Now, since the arrival of Jackie, there was never time. And with his distant cousin looking older every time he saw him, Nikos was beginning to wonder if they would ever besport themselves or even be alone together like this again.

Happy that Ari had secured his trophy wife, at first Nikos had given "the widow" the benefit of the doubt. He knew that his grasp of English was not so good, that he could not follow everything she said, not the jokes, the little asides. But very soon he found that he could not understand her. To him the relationship seemed far too modern. Among Greek men it was understood that a man could continue to have all kinds of friends when he married, as long as it was done discreetly. But the wife, never!

There were men calling Jackie all the time. Nikos knew that many were not the sort of men Ari would count as rivals; they would leave messages about lace this and lace that. Why didn't she see that the island was perfect as it was? Why did she have to keep changing everything?

Sometimes she talked to them for hours.

And she telephoned America all the time as if it were next door!

Callas, for all her fame, was always grateful for very little. Some attention, some financial advice, a few furs, a few jewels. In every way she was a woman who barely interfered. She was as she should be, under Ari's control.

Like most of Ari's Greek friends, Nikos far preferred her. Ever since she had been ejected from Onassis-land they spoke often on the telephone. Callas knew her old lover's every move through contacts like him.

Callas was a realist. She knew that like most men Onassis had created very clear classifications of infidelity for himself. Over the years, in her quest for honesty both ex-lovers and male confidants had admitted their adherence to similar rigid codes that covered all aspects of being unfaithful.

It seemed that if the male did not undertake or initiate sexual activity, if he was simply on the receiving end of sexual attention, it didn't count. In their eyes, taking responsibility for passive acquiescence, however enjoyable, seemed ludicrous.

The diva reasoned since he had not wanted to trust himself alone with her in her flat in Paris, the only sex with her that would appeal to him would have to be guilt free. She needed some regular contact with his office in America. Ever since "the widow" had lured him to her side he spent more time there than anywhere else.

A year after their split she telephoned him and told him that she still missed him and his ardent lovemaking.

She also revealed her heartbreak and made him swear that from now on he would never, ever come and see her perform. Fighting the most famous woman in the world with the only thing she had, the voice that she knew he loved, she hoped that if she banned him from hearing her sing, he might come looking for her.

"If I look out at the audience, any audience who I will cry with or smile with . . . well . . . if I ever thought you might be out there, my voice would stop working. I would not be able to carry on," she had sobbed to him.

When he was silent she raised her game.

"In fact, I don't think I could bear it if I simply saw you by accident in the street," she had continued in a theatrical way. "Supposing it was the day of a performance or even the day before. I would be so tense, so unhappy, that I would not be able to sing. My voice would die. My career would be over."

In his haste to get off the phone Ari promised that in addition to the million dollars he had given her the year before, he would throw in a quarter of a million and keep out of her way. He agreed that if she let his office know her schedule in advance he would see to it that they were never in the same town.

Every month she would handwrite a letter to him. Each missive followed the same form. She would ensure that the letterhead was as impressive as possible. Then she would begin with a description of the men she had been seeing in the hope of making him jealous.

She would go on to include this or that snippet to try to impress him either intellectually or with her business acumen. Finally, she would spend at least a page inquiring into his health, suggesting various tisanes and infusions. Attached would be a list of her engagements.

After the first one arrived he arranged for his personal secretary to telephone her each time to confirm that the message had been received. The secretary, although totally discreet, felt she could not be rude to the famous former girlfriend so that often these chats went on for some time. Unintentionally, this gave the songbird encouragement. Callas had no idea that Onassis did not see the letters, which was why he never felt he needed to tell his wife about them.

In the late spring of 1970 the songbird had her most successful season in New York. Hailed as the best soprano in the world, Callas attributed it to her even slimmer figure.

She had found no one to replace the Greek. What was the point of applause when she lacked the man she wished to share it with?

Quite deliberately, the diva decided to remain in the city until she knew her old lover was back.

Part of the pattern of the former First Lady's life in New York was to go to the house in New Jersey to ride every Friday. It was no secret that Onassis would leave the city later to join her.

Callas decided that this would have to be the way that she would insert herself into his world again. Her success had been based on discipline and patience. She put her trust in them once again. Like every other woman, she had learned to make herself look different in "Jackie O" style, using big sunglasses and a headscarf. Wearing these, she hid, sitting low in the back seat of her limousine behind her driver, as she watched for Ari outside his office.

Three Fridays went by with no appearance from Ari. In desperation, the next Friday morning she rang his friendly secretary and explained that she had a crisis, that her driver was sick and she needed a lift to stay with friends out in the countryside right near the Onassis home in New Jersey this afternoon.

The soprano trilled that she was hoping and praying that the

Greek ("her Greek," as she still privately thought of him) was going that same way.

Onassis didn't stand a chance; as he exited the building he discovered the songbird in the corner of his car. From below her long eyelashes she gazed up at him and with a tiny gesture raised her cashmere wrap as if to envelop him in its warmth.

The journey to the country took little more than an hour and a half.

After she raised the privacy board between themselves and the chauffeur, Onassis was treated to an incredible crescendo of passion. His old flame had learned more extraordinary tricks with her lips than the ticket-paying customers at La Scala had any idea about.

After dropping the opera star off, he felt a tiny stab of guilt when he saw Jackie, but later that week, when he confided the story to Nikos, he explained, "I'm in the hands of a professional. What can I do?"

Urged on by one or two intimates in Ari's coterie, Callas continued her seduction. As the weeks went by and the opera star repeatedly turned up for her "lift," he started to look forward to it. After all, he reckoned as he eyed the soprano, making little moans while on her knees, he exchanged no telephone conversations with the songbird, engaged in no plots to meet her, never discussed love or emotion with her.

Truth to tell, he was doing nothing. The active partner was Callas.

With her teeth, her tongue, the tips of her fingers and tendrils of her hair, she nuzzled up to those erogenous zones he knew about, and some he didn't.

When Jackie occasionally suggested spending the weekend in the city, his insistence on spending Friday night in the country thrilled her. Naively she thought that after all the wonderful places he had introduced her to, she had been able to reciprocate with one at least.

But as suddenly as Callas had appeared, she vanished.

Onassis had become an addict. He missed his little treat too much. Casually he asked his secretary for the latest letter from the diva. She was at the opera in Paris. By the next night so too was Jackie's second husband.

After her week's performance, both on the stage and in Ari's bed, the diva telephoned her ally, Nikos.

"So where do you think your boss has been all week?" she asked him.

"Paris, I'm sure Paris," was the answer.

"Yes, but what you didn't know was that he works at Olympic by day and has been gold–medal–sporting in my bed every night," she purred.

Nikos was delighted. Now how to let "the widow" know.

Callas told him it was too early.

She was about to vanish again. She wanted to make sure that her hold over this man was as strong as ever.

CHAPTER *Twenty*

Guy was depressed because he had found nothing.

While the Mediterranean sweltered he had hunted around Patras but could find no one who looked like George. He tried some taverna owners near where the man had last been spotted but only one admitted to remembering him. Guy knew that spies used all sorts of guises to go about their business. Perhaps George had favored keeping himself to himself. The local who did recall the man explained that he hadn't been around for at least a year.

Worse, he couldn't even find Dimitri, the agency's long-term collaborator. All the usual methods had failed. Both his home and boatyard had the look of longtime stagnation.

Dressed as if he were a visiting American university professor, Guy had thought his deliberately well-heeled appearance would have been enough for someone to cough up some information.

His story, that he was looking for the man because he was a friend of a long-lost relative, was supposed to act as an additional incentive. Guy knew that family members in the Old Country loved finding out that they had some access to those in the New World.

Guy was sure that Dimitri himself would have been very happy to reward someone who brought him this good news.

So Guy had flashed around Dimitri's picture too. The agency had smudged it up to look like a local, amateur job. The Greeks near his home recognized him but they all said that while he had been around until recently, they believed that he had gone to see a girl near Athens.

After several days of getting nowhere Guy telephoned Harry.

"This thing gets stranger by the minute," he confessed to the older man.

"You bet," said Harry. "We're still receiving stuff from Dimitri, nothing to write home about but solid background stuff. He's been sending it as always, on a monthly basis. Maybe he has chased off after some woman, but why didn't he tell us? After all, we can't insist he stay in Patras," he continued.

"Do you have any other leads?" asked Guy.

"I've discovered that we don't send the payments to him at his home or the boatyard. We send it to general delivery in the next village. If I give you the address why don't you go there?"

Retaining his cover, Guy headed there in a taxi.

He had used this ruse many times. Often a cab driver would tell you more than other locals. Before his journey Guy made sure he had plenty of packs of cigarettes and a few Greek beers stashed in his professorial carryall.

All he could find out from the driver was that Dimitri was a very good mender of boats. He was not married and he did not get on well with his two older brothers who had been enthusiastic fighters in the civil war.

"Big Communisti, big, big," was how the driver described them.

After their father died last spring and left the boatyard and the family home entirely to Dimitri, they had vanished.

Guy wasn't sure that he wanted everyone in the village to connect him with the man looking for Dimitri and George, so after he bade farewell to his driver he went into the cubicle of a bar's toilet and speedily changed his appearance. A floppy, dirty white hat with long stringy brown curls attached covered his naturally pale blond hair. The specs were removed and hard brown contact lenses inserted to hide his vivid blue eyes. The smart shirt was whipped off and a T-shirt, very worn and ever so slightly dirty, replaced it. To make doubly sure he watched out of the toilet window until the taxi moved off with his next fare.

In this instance general delivery was a very junior version of a post office, no more than a large broom closet at the back of the mayor's office. Guy decided to try it straight and ask for Dimitri Papas, but the bearded, bad-tempered man looking after the place irritably waved him away. Guy ignored his behavior and spoke up louder. "When he next comes in to collect his post tell him his uncle Yannis from Chicago called and said he has a lot of stuff from the *Queen Mary* to show him."

Guy then wrote out the same message in Greek and left it in an envelope.

He was not disappointed. Within minutes the man had closed up and moved swiftly up the road, away from the village. His dark hair was spliced with gray but for a man of his age he moved fast.

From a distance Guy watched as the man entered a house on the edge of a small vineyard.

With the foresight of an experienced observer Guy had stuffed a bottle of water and a hunk of bread and cheese into his pockets. He settled down out of sight to wait.

Over an hour later, when the man returned to his work, Guy approached the farmhouse and looked through a ground-floor window. On a makeshift bed in the small front room lay a figure. He looked very like Dimitri.

Waiting for some time to check that no one else was in the house, Guy could not decide whether to knock on the door or creep in. Old habits die hard. Eventually he hauled himself up through a window in the back and climbed in.

Approaching the sick man, Guy could see fear in his eyes. Quickly he explained who he was and asked the man what he knew about George.

"Look in my back pocket. I thought even if I am killed the pictures in the back of my trousers will explain."

Turning slowly as if in great pain, he shifted enough for Guy to fish out two photographs. After extricating them from multiple layers of protective plastic, he found they were both of George. The first was a copy of the one that Harry had given Guy; the other, in exactly the same pose, was the same shot, but it was obvious in the second picture that George was dead.

"They fixed it," explained Dimitri.

"My father died this year and left the boatyard to me alone. He didn't get along with my brothers and so he chose to give it to me. There was no dissuading him. My brothers threatened me that if I didn't give them the profits, they would simply put me out of service, injure me, and take it over by force."

He winced in pain and continued. "I ignored them, tried to talk them out of it. The boatyard makes very little.

"They both want to be in politics, they are always trying to stir up trouble. I thought as long as I gave them food they would be satisfied. But they got impatient when I said that there was no money, we had to enlarge the boatyard, to do repairs to motorboats, speedboats. They saw that I had some money—money I had earned through working with you. But they became enraged and thought that my father had left me money as well.

"So they planned to give me a going-over, but unfortunately on the night they did I had arranged a meeting with George. George was bringing a new man over to meet me, a new CIA officer for me to work with.

"My brothers are big believers in Communism. They listened to us and became furious when they realized that I'd been helping the Americans. There was a fight; I am left like this and they killed George. My middle brother has always been very strong. I think he meant to break his neck. He's an animal.

"It all happened so quickly, we were taken by surprise. Philippos took as much of the money as he could before Costas, the eldest, stopped him.

"My oldest brother is much smarter. I didn't know but he is still very close with Communists. He thought he could get more money out of the Americans if we pretended that George was still alive and I continued sending intelligence. He knew someone would eventually come for George if he arranged a picture of him to look alive. His 'comrades'—Russian educated"—Guy noticed Dimitri's curled lip—"took two weeks to make it. When it was finished, see, the eyes look as if he is smiling, the lips too. They sent the picture anonymously to Athens, to the U.S. embassy. When someone did come looking for George, Costas knew he would be senior, he would be a handler, he would have money. He would extract as much as he could from him and then . . ." Guy did not need Dimitri to paint a picture. He thought for a moment; the Soviets were brilliant at doctoring photographs. They had been doing it ever since Lenin had taken power. Even now, when their leaders stood watching their annual march on November 7 they would move any of the leaders out of the photograph if their face no longer fit.

"Tell me, how did you find me?" asked Dimitri.

When Guy explained about going to general delivery Dimitri became really nervous.

"That bearded man is my cousin Andreas. He took the job because he and my brothers want to know everything that is going on in the villages around here. He tries to read everyone's letters."

"What did you say to him this morning?"

When Guy told him, Dimitri suggested that he leave immediately.

"He will know that you have come looking for George. He knows about code, about big boats. He made me tell him," said Dimitri sadly, "I had no choice. I have tried to walk, tried to move, they have seriously harmed my back, I think."

"Don't worry, I understand. I'll get you out of here. I'll do everything I can to help you," Guy promised.

As he went back he kept checking that he wasn't being watched.

When he returned to the room he had taken in a guesthouse, Guy changed out of his sloppy appearance. He did not want to bump into Andreas looking the way he had this morning.

As he ate his lunch he tried to think. He had to help Dimitri, but how? He needed more manpower. It would be too difficult to get the injured man out alone.

"The trouble is Dimitri is a brave man but in a lot of pain and can't walk," Guy told Harry at Langley over the phone. "His brother won't let a doctor near but just gives him painkillers bought over the counter. What help can you get me and how soon?" asked Guy.

"Give us twenty-four hours," said Harry reassuringly.

The CIA response was instantaneous. Another CIA officer based in the capital was on his way, but in a small motorboat that had to hug the coast. A small U.S. Navy vessel was also making full speed toward the area.

"If you can get Dimitri to the boat, it will all be smooth sailing," Harry said confidently.

"Just watch out for yourself."

Early next morning Guy returned to Dimitri's home to assure him that help was on its way.

He waited until Andreas had gone. Guy was worried that there would be someone on the lookout for him now that Andreas knew that he knew the code and was looking for Dimitri. He spent some time checking out the vineyard until finally he crept in.

The couch was empty. The young Greek was on the floor. Guy looked for signs of life, but Dimitri was dead.

He turned the body over and extricated the two photos of George from the dead man's pockets. Andreas would know that he, or someone else, had taken them, but now that they were both dead it was too late to worry about that. He was about to leave when he sensed breathing from behind.

Guy was quick but there were three of them. Strong arms grabbed him and pushed him to the floor. Swiftly and expertly, he was tied to a chair.

Recalling Dimitri's story about their keen interest in money, Guy decided to gamble on their greed and ignorance. He told his attackers that if they let him walk he could get them a lot of money from the Americans. Except for one of them, an ardent anti-American who would have liked to string him up there and then, he sensed that the others were swayed by the promise of wealth.

To Andreas he said: "If you come with me to the local bank I will give you more money than you will ever possess."

The three had guns, old revolvers that they now used mainly to shoot small animals and birds. They assured Guy that if he ran they would shoot to kill.

They looked like they were no strangers to exercise. Guy guessed that although they were probably very fit, all of them were about ten years older than Dimitri.

If he got the chance Guy knew that he could outrun and out-swim them.

His jailers began to argue. They disagreed about what to do with him. By nightfall, still disagreeing, they put him in the cellar.

The rough twine, tightly drawn around his wrists and his ankles, chafed and dug into his skin, making sleep impossible. As he listened to them bellowing upstairs he tried to work out how he could escape.

Jackie too wanted to make a getaway from Skorpios. Her problem was she didn't know where.

In yesterday's newspaper, delivered that morning, there was an item about Ari seeing Maria Callas in Paris.

The piece was short, just a paragraph referring to her husband and the diva being at a party at Maxim's abutting a picture of them walking out of the restaurant with others. In the piece there was no inference that they were attending as a couple but Jackie's high-strung instincts yelled *cheat, cheat* in her ear.

This was insupportable.

It was not the first time since she married Ari that he and Callas had been mentioned together, but she knew that before the stories had not been true. Now there were ugly rumors about her private life. Not again.

Without stopping to think, she took the offending newspaper to her room and flew to the phone.

Being told that "Mr. Onassis is in a very important meeting and cannot be disturbed" did nothing to calm her.

"Tell Mr. Onassis this is urgent," she snapped.

Even though stressed and angry, Jackie was not going to be too hysterical or reveal anything to his staff. She knew that her demands had already made her unpopular with some of them.

She began to pack some things in an overnight bag. She would travel light, shop when she got there. If he was not on the telephone in ten minutes she would fly to Paris and disturb him in person.

Angrily, as she hunted for a new lightweight Courrèges coat, she thought, I will not put up with these stories about him and Callas, not after Jack, not after the last time. She repeated this like a mantra as she located a necklace and asked for her passport to be brought to her. She was ready. As she was about to order the boat and the plane to be prepared for her immediate departure, he rang.

"My darling," he began.

"I am not your darling," she shouted.

"What is wrong, I am so looking forward to seeing you—"

"Have you seen the papers this morning? The London papers. There are pictures of you and that woman, the one you told me you never see. How could you? How could you!" she screamed.

"What papers? What have I done?"

"You've been with that scheming cow Callas, that bovine bitch."

"Jackie, Jackie, do not insult yourself by this. Yes, I saw her, across a crowded room. We were in the same restaurant, at the same party."

"Oh, come on! It says here that you left with her—"

"I haven't seen it," he lied. "It's a rag, made-up rubbish. I am sure if you read it closely it does not say that I am with her. I may have walked out at the same time, but that was the extent of it. Why would I be with her when I love you?"

Refusing to be sidetracked, Jackie shouted, "Swear you weren't with her. Swear it."

"Why would I want anyone else but you? Come to Paris, come now. I can't wait to have you in my arms. Come now and you will be here by lunchtime. I will make love to you all afternoon and then we can go to Maxim's."

"I can't take this again. You must not do this to me," she wailed.

"I would never do anything to hurt you. Come here and I will persuade you of how much I love you, how much I want you."

She threw the phone down, unconvinced. It was useless. She had everything but a faithful partner. She would see him and have it out with him once and for all. She was not going to put up with this. She was not going to be fooled anymore.


Meanwhile the same newspaper article was being discussed at KGB headquarters in Moscow. Addressing the chairman of the small group whose special area of influence was the Mediterranean, Vladimir Zerev, distinguished-looking Muscovite, was on his feet.

"Remember, Alexander, all those years ago when I suspected Mrs. Kennedy of working for the CIA in Geneva and everybody laughed at me? Now I think they will not be so amused.

"In this folder I have a selection of photographs, all taken by Greeks loyal to our cause, of the many, many people who are coming and going to Skorpios."

Vladimir prised them out, one by one.

"Look at him. He is supposed to be an interior designer. Looks far too big and bulky, more like a boxer. Look at those shoulders, look at those hands. I am suspicious. What about this one? He was supposed to be a sous-chef cooking American specialties. Apparently on his first day in the kitchen he was regarded as so useless

Madame had to intercede and say it was her mistake. And was he sent back? No, he was given a job in the garden.

"And this one and this one." A shoal of slightly out-of-focus photographs of various men, most in caps, hats, sunglasses, and spectacles that helped hide their faces, were laid out.

"And this one, this is my favorite. Simon Brunton, recently arrived from Cairo, hidden to look like a beekeeper. Unfortunately, however keen he is that Mrs. Onassis gets her honey, the beekeeper's hat is so uncomfortable it has to come off sometime, to reveal, lo and behold, our CIA friend. The man has been a thorough nuisance to us wherever he has worked. What is he doing there?

"Let us look at the evidence. Onassis has been married for less than two years to the so-called most glamorous woman in the world, but he does what he likes and is still sleeping with Callas. Jackie puts up with it. Clearly the situation is what she is used to." A titter went round the table. "But why?

"Yes, she comes and goes when she wants and spends his money, but more and more of it is lavished on his tiny island, which she clings to far more ferociously than him. Why? Perhaps after the assassination of her husband and her brother-in-law she feels safer there. But she and her husband are so rarely together, we have to ask, why did they marry?"

"Meanwhile we are nowhere nearer overthrowing the Greek Colonels, we may have lost another submarine in this area, and now we have at least one known CIA man, and a senior one at that, working in disguise on Skorpios."

"I have never believed she was a spy." The sonorous voice of the chairman interrupted.

"I am convinced of it," said Vladimir.

"I haven't finished," the chairman droned on. "What I do think is that the Americans have bribed her to use her as an umbrella, to let her be a cover for their people to use the island.

"We need to discover exactly what they are doing. Vladimir, you are convinced of Mrs. Kennedy's—Mrs. Onassis's—guilt already.

You will work hardest to prove it. Talk to special operations and come up with a plan. I shall make sure you get all the help you need. I suggest the only way to find out is to get yourself out there, fast."

It was still warm when Aristotle Onassis left the Paris office so he decided to stroll to his apartment on the Avenue Foch. As he walked, his chauffeured car following behind him, he couldn't believe his good fortune. He was on the brink of concluding one of the biggest deals of his life and it had come out of nowhere. He had been approached by a Swiss group that had won several new contracts with countries in Africa and the Far East. They needed to buy and rent container ships and oil tankers. Their urgency was reflected in some of the higher prices they were prepared to pay. Their chairman had been insistent: "We are keen to negotiate for as long as it takes to reach a suitable agreement."

Ari had picked up hints that the Swiss had been involved in negotiations with some of his rivals, but the Onassis organization seemed to be the favorite to win the order.

As he grew older, the Greek had become more cautious in his business life. He knew many Swiss bankers, but the men involved with this outstanding offer were strangers to him. In the normal way, he requested his offices in London, New York, and Greece to investigate both the background of the company and its chairman and senior board members.

Everything seemed to be in order. He made a few judicious calls himself and discovered the business was fairly new but no one had a bad word to say about them.

Their paperwork came up trumps every time.

He was still not convinced. For the second night in a row he had decided not to see Callas. She was furious with him. Last week Jackie had come to town and now he was wrapped up in business affairs. He would send his mistress something to placate her.

Tonight, like last night, he would have dinner à deux, with the Swiss chairman, Pierre Harnier. Last night had proved inconclusive.

The restaurant the man had selected was so crowded Ari had not felt comfortable asking the questions he still had about the Swiss company's finances and budgetary constraints.

Tonight he had organized dinner in a private dining room he occasionally used at the Hôtel Georges V. Before he got into bed with this man he wanted to put him under a microscope.

When Jackie woke on Friday in her bedroom in Skorpios an exquisitely wrapped gift lay on the breakfast tray, next to her plate of sliced grapefruit. The double bow and shiny purple box had the expensive sheen of Paris about it. Of course it was from Ari; he'd been very attentive over the last week or so, since her quick trip to Paris. As she tugged at the lilac grosgrain ribbon, she fondly thought that underneath his bluster and bravado her husband was quite insecure. No one would guess that his usual gambit of sending a present a few hours before his arrival was done to bolster his confidence. It was a charming habit though she knew he did it as much for himself as for her. It was his fail-safe method to ensure that not only would he be in the good graces of the grateful recipient, it would also enhance the excitement of his visit.

As she uncovered a Fabergé picture frame enameled in translucent apple green and gold, nestling inside its matching case, she breathed out loud, "What a gift." It must have cost a fortune. She examined it, back and front. It was extraordinarily perfect. Without bothering to look at the outside of the miniature envelope, she fished the small card out. As she read the short but loving message she realized with horror that it was addressed to another woman, Maria Callas.

Appalled and hurt, Jackie did not know what to do. Her instinctive reaction was to bury the present and the note in one of her drawers and run off to the ocean.

As she ran she felt her chest and lungs ache with suppressed tears.

How *dare* he? How long had this been going on?

All the newspaper stories, all his denials. Every time she had asked him if there was still something between him and his old flame, he had sworn there was nothing.

When they had argued about Callas in Paris he had admitted there was only one connection between them: occasionally her accountant asked him to look over some of her financial papers.

Obviously he was lying.

A terrible thought occurred to her. Had he and Callas been lovers throughout their marriage?

How could this be happening to her again? What was wrong with her? Why couldn't she keep a man happy?

As she walked from the beach into the sea she hurled herself into the waves, her salty tears mixing with them.

Suppose this got out? How could she face the world if they knew that her second husband had gone looking for happiness in another woman's bed?

Was this Ari's fiendishly weird way of telling her that despite his protestations of love, she was second-best? If so, what did he expect her to do? Did he want a showdown tonight when he returned from Paris? Surely not in front of their houseguests; it would be too embarrassing.

She stopped her backstroke for a minute.

In Paris he had been so genuinely upset on her behalf, so warm and romantic. He had sounded so loving on the phone yesterday and the day before, and the day before. What could have possessed him to cause a riot right now?

It seemed so incongruous, so ironic that she, hailed as the world's most glamorous woman, whose picture alone had sold millions of magazines and newspapers, could not keep a man interested enough to stay faithful.

How they would laugh at her, the critics who had ridiculed her wedding.

Jackie knew that anything by Fabergé had to be very expensive. If Ari had sent it to Maria, it was much more than a birthday or saint's day gift. It could only be a thank-you for services rendered and she was in no doubt about what those services were.

For an hour she swam and swam.

Soon the children would be off to visit her mother in Newport. Ideally she could wait. Ultraprotective as a sole parent, she did not want them to see her upset or quarreling with their stepfather. A further complication was Rose Kennedy's imminent arrival. The woman, whom she still thought of as her mother-in-law, had finally agreed to come to stay. Ari had decreed they should have a huge party for her.

Jackie decided that she could not postpone the matriarch's visit. For now she would have to play the game and be the accomplished hostess.

She decided that when Ari arrived she would flaunt the gift to gauge his reaction. If he wanted to raise the subject, she was ready. She dried herself, rubbing the towel hard against her skin.

When she returned to the Pink House the place was in an uproar. Ari's office had called. There was a possibility that there might be four extra guests for the party next week. Some businessmen were coming to Athens to complete a deal. If he deemed it necessary, Ari might invite them and their wives to the island.

Jackie could see the maids opening up the cottages. At least two of them would be dusty as they were normally left undisturbed in case the Onassis children deigned to put in an appearance. One in a dark blue ripe fig shade was designated for Alexander, the melon-colored one for Christina. If four more guests came these would be needed.

She saw Caroline and John happily running in and out of them, taking advantage of exploring these miniature homes. Next week some of their cousins would be joining them.

When Ari appeared he was in the very best of moods. He was sure this Swiss deal was going well. His mistress had telephoned to forgive him for deserting her. She would be even more well disposed toward him when she received the gift by Fabergé he had arranged to be delivered to her this morning. One that was equally as valuable as the one that he believed he had given his wife.

Callas meant more and more to him. Approaching his seventies, Ari was thrilled that her eroticism made him feel so sexy, so alive. She had ensured that there was no weakness in that area. She had done him a service. He was as vibrant and sexually powerful as any man half his age.

Jackie too was working out well. Luckily this independence of hers that Nikos so complained of suited him well. How dull it would be to come home to the old-style wife who had done nothing exciting while you were away and had simply been staying at home, guarding her virtue. With Jackie he always knew that she would have uncovered some interesting information in a book, invited guests who would be entertaining, and doubtless had prepared an enthralling list of new projects to improve the island. She wasn't cheap but she wasn't boring!

As his glorious yacht swooped upon the Ionian Sea, Ari looked forward to the weekend. Two days of relaxation and then next week both the chairman and the managing director in the Swiss business were coming to Athens to continue their talks.

She avoided being alone with him when the *Christina* first docked, and at the beginning of dinner she could hardly bring herself to look at him, but when she produced the expensive gift she noted that he seemed perfectly at ease.

Aware of every nuance at the table, Jackie realized that it was not Ari but Nikos who was the jumpy one tonight. He had noisily examined the frame several times, frequently asking Ari if this was one of the better Fabergé frames and where and when had he found it? Were there many of them and how did they compare?

He was not a very subtle man so when he started to shadow her every move, Jackie began to wonder why. They had never got on. Their endless arguments about money had made it obvious that he was irritated by her presence as Ari's wife. Like many of Ari's cronies, he clearly preferred the opera singer. Callas was of Greek extraction and probably conformed more to his taste. She began to wonder if he had, in some way, been responsible for this morning's shock.

When it came to bedtime Jackie was still unsure of what she should do. Seeing Nikos continue to monitor her, she decided there could be no half measures.

On the one hand there was her pride, her pain, both private. On the other there was her fear of public ridicule, of being alone, not to mention giving up the island that the agency needed and that only a few days ago they had told her they were finally getting some benefit from.

There was something about her husband's right-hand man tonight that seemed to make it more important to spite him, rather than her husband.

She would make love to a husband who she was sure had betrayed her. She had done it before.

When she woke on Saturday there had been an early telephone call from the agency. The message, given to her by the butler at the breakfast table, included their code, the mention of lace.

Nikos was there; he had dawdled over the meal, waiting for Jackie, agog to see how things were between the couple. He had Maria calling him at noon for an update.

As Jackie went inside to return the call, Nikos nonchalantly picked up the crumpled piece of paper she had left by her plate of fruit.

He had so little to tell Callas. There had been no visible histrionics, both Mr. and Mrs. Onassis seemed happy and at one with the world. Instead he began to moan about the frequent phone calls from the States.

"It must be the middle of the night there," he told Callas. "Who would be calling now about curtains and whether she wants them sewn with Queen Anne's lace?" he complained, looking at the note.

"But Niko, are you sure?" asked the diva, very disappointed with the day's events so far. "Queen Anne's lace is not a fabric, it is a flower."

"So what is she up to then?" asked Nikos. "These lace and curtain messages have come for her ever since she first arrived."

"I have no idea. You worry about that. Meanwhile I will have to think of another way to boot out 'the widow.' All we do know is that obviously she has not confronted her husband."

"And maybe she never will," added Nikos. "After all, who else would give her this money, this freedom?"

"Perhaps someone should watch more closely what she gets up to?" suggested Callas.

"If the situation changes I will call you," he promised.

Nikos was not up to watching Jackie as well as doing his job so he delegated observation duties to the only person in the world, other than his boss, that he trusted. His son.

Three nights later the eighteen-year-old had some news.

"I wait outside the house. Their bedroom light goes out and I think I will turn in myself when I go and get some ice cream from the kitchen. As I come back I hear a noise, it is Madame. She is coming out of the house in the dark and she is going round to her studio, but she is creeping. She goes inside for a long while and then watches the sea, just sits and looks out. After many hours she goes back to the house."

Jackie's nighttime activity was no great surprise to him. The whole island knew that she was a bad sleeper. As soon as she became Mrs. Onassis she ordered deep wooden shutters and extra thick blackout curtains for their bedroom suite.

Nikos knew that sometimes Ari, a bad snorer, slept on his beloved boat so as not to wake her.

The staff was under orders not to clean or work near their suite until ten in the morning. He imagined that since seeing that note addressed to Callas yesterday, she obviously had a lot on her mind.

Nikos wondered if his crafty boss had somehow managed to wriggle out of it. He had no idea what Ari's note to Maria had said.

He had had only a moment to swap the parcels last week while waiting to go into a meeting with his boss.

But now his son had told him that Jackie was making secret visits to her studio at night. Nikos thought when it was safe he would take a much closer look.

The Queen Anne's lace message had also alerted Jackie. So far she had received calls about Honiton lace, Valenciennes lace, guipure lace, Alençon lace, Nottingham lace. Someone, in the middle of the night, had made a mistake.

Didn't they know at Langley that Queen Anne's lace was not a fabric at all?

Down a crackling phone line, Harry apologized: "We were in a panic.

"A few days ago we sent Guy Steavenson to Greece because we received a photo of one of our men who worked for us over there who vanished some time ago. Guy is checking out if he's alive."

How well Jackie remembered the fourth red cross on the map of the Mediterranean in the dining room in New Jersey.

"Sunday night, we get this message from Guy. He has found our man. This fellow has worked for us for years. The trouble is that he's been badly injured by some local Communists. Not only has he been loyal to us, he knows about our methods, our other under-cover agents. So far he has told them very little. It would be a disaster if he were tortured and forced to reveal everything.

"We are sending a CIA officer to help him but he'll take a while to get there. We have also sent a small naval cruiser from the Sixth Fleet that can sit in the area for as long as it takes; it just depends how soon Guy can get this fellow, Dimitri, off the mainland.

"We sent you the message because in a situation like this we al-ways warn everyone in the vicinity in case they can give aid. I apol-ogize, the call was automatic. Frankly you were the only one to point out that the lace thing was wrong. Thank you, it's the sort of stupid mistake that could be dangerous. I'll tell our people. Anyway, you probably can't help.

"But you ought to know that before he left I told Guy about your tiny mooring and its two exits and said that if worst came to worst he might be able to find sanctuary with you on Skorpios. But I doubt he will; when I spoke to him he was in Patras."

Jackie was stunned.

Guy. She remembered him very fondly. Then she recalled that it was Guy who had got her into this mess. So very attractive, so very amusing, so very polished, and so very well trained.

Had she agreed to do many of the things she had done for the CIA because he had charmed her into it and she wanted to impress him?

Looking back now, she realized that she had entered into this marriage to escape, yes, but also because she had wanted to be able to do something extraordinary with the rest of her life. Being just a mother in Manhattan would not have been satisfying.

Was Guy the man who had really trapped her? And that call for aid worried her. Was he now in trouble himself?

That night, as a sexually satisfied Ari slept and snored, Jackie found sleep more elusive than ever. As she continued to debate how she should deal with her husband she tossed and turned.

She was going to make him pay but hadn't yet worked out how to do so without damaging her own reputation. She wondered how long she could keep up the pretense.

Now that she knew Guy was possibly not that far away she had to stop herself from going to watch for him.

The next day Ari rose very early to go to Athens to prepare everything for the Swiss deal.

As soon as he left she walked to the studio. This time, her observer told his father, she had stayed inside for three hours.


As he walked with his captors toward the village Guy was reviewing every conduit where he might find aid.

The Greek civil war had done much worse damage to the country than World War II. More than one hundred thousand had died and seven hundred thousand people had been displaced.

The different factions had never truly reconciled. It had taken a mixture of the British army and millions of dollars from President Harry Truman to halt the fighting.

Like all civil wars, it had divided families and friends. Guy knew there were still bad feelings on both sides. As he listened to Dimitri's family, he could not deny the disapproval they felt for their brother's empathy with America. He could feel it in their attitude toward him. When the brothers took Dimitri's body to the undertakers, Andreas had stared at him as if he were the devil incarnate. At one stage he thought Andreas would kill him, but eventually he had given him a small hunk of bread and water.

Guy's brain was whirling with thoughts of escape. He assumed that the locals knew who the brothers supported. Surely if he could provoke them to attack him in public, the authorities, who were now very anti-Communist, would come to his defense?

While pretending to sleep he eavesdropped. After some argument he ascertained that his jailers had finally succumbed to greed. They decided that first they would take him to the bank to get his money. They hadn't bothered to discuss what they would do to him later.

As they marched toward the square, Andreas stopped, and marched Guy into a dark alley.

He pushed his revolver hard into his ribs. In fractured English he whispered, "I am coming in bank with you. Others wait outside door. You run, you dead."

As they arrived at the bank Guy noted the taxi stand at the front, close to tavernas full of vacationers having lunch. As planned, he and Andreas went inside.

Guy told the bank teller that he wanted to cash all of his traveler's checks and made a great fuss of signing each one, taking his time.

Holding the gun he had hidden in his trouser pocket, Andreas stood close and watched everything he did.

The bank teller began counting. He apologized and told Guy that he had to go downstairs to the safe to get more dollars.

Guy immediately sighed loudly, drummed his fingers on the counter, and looked at him with an impatient expression.

"Do I have to wait out here for my money? Has the bank taught you nothing about looking after your customers' security? I'll be robbed the minute I leave."

In an instant the bank teller moved along, opened the mahogany counter for Guy to pass through, alone.

Guy didn't hesitate. Instead of sitting down in the chair provided, he raced into the manager's office, opened the window, jumped out, and ran.

Fitter and faster than the others, he knew there was nowhere for him to go but the shore. Running onto the jetty, he leaped into a small dinghy moored to it. Pulling at the outboard engine, he threw himself to the floor and lay flat in case his would-be kidnappers decided to use their weapons. He concentrated on putting as much sea between himself and his captors as possible.

He was in no doubt about what they would do to him. They had already killed two men, possibly three. Raised during two wars, these men would have no scruples about finishing him off too.

Fearful, he headed out to the open sea. Soon his fuel ran out, and exhausted, thirsty, and hungry, he could not keep up his rowing and it slowed down to an ineffectual paddle. His damaged wrists ached so much he fainted. For a while he simply floated with the current. When he awoke he forced himself to push closer to the shore.

Guy blessed his obsession with Jackie. He had spent hours poring over the map during his time alone in Moscow. At first he was examining whether the island did have any worth to the agency, and then after the marriage, wondering just how the arrangement was working and what the agency had built there.

Feverish, hollow-eyed and in pain, he took nearly two days to reach Skorpios. His survival instincts made him wait out at sea until it was dark. Only then did he dare to limp into the tiny mooring.

He had just strength enough to climb onto the slipway before he collapsed on the floor.

A few feet away a scientist slept soundly in his bunk. Guy had been so quiet the man didn't find him until morning. Immediately an urgent message was sent to Harry by radio transmitter that Guy was alive.

Not wanting to alert the Onassis household, the CIA official called Jackie on the dot of ten in the morning, at his time of four A.M.

"Anything you can do to help would be gratefully received. Guy's in a bad way. Luckily our scientist, Lenny Fleckerl, has some medicine and food down there.

"Now Mrs. Kennedy, I mean Mrs. Onassis, how can I say this without sounding forward? Your natural reaction will be to rush over there and check that all is well. Please don't, please be careful. He is very weak right now but Guy is going to be fine. Please do nothing that will attract any attention. Behave normally and only go over to your studio in the way and at the time you usually do. We don't want anyone to discover that there's anything there, do we?"

Jackie seldom did any painting until the sun made long shadows in the late afternoon, so she forced herself to wait. Finally, just before five, she got ready. Making herself as small and as dark as possible for a late-night return, she slipped on nothing but a black cotton T-shirt and matching tight trousers.

She got the children off to bed and told the chef that she would prefer to eat alone in her bedroom and asked for an early dinner of bread and pâté on a tray. Once it was delivered she turned it into a sandwich and wrapped it in a scarf. Carefully hiding it under a large hat, she ambled to the studio just in case she bumped into anyone. She was completely unaware that she was being secretly observed.

The shock and then delight at seeing Guy almost overwhelmed her.

She spent three hours with him and Lenny. She and the scientist both listened as Guy whispered his story of the dead men, George and Dimitri. They tried to console him for the loss of Dimitri's life, which he blamed on himself. Both of them applied cool creams to help repair his cracked, burned skin and his blistered hands. Jackie, who brought medication from the States and always kept a cache for emergencies, gave him antibiotics to get his fever down.

The next day Lenny was due to leave. Once they were alone, Jackie and Guy, who was feeling much better but still not able to speak in much more than a whisper, talked over everything: her marriage to Ari, his marriage breakup, the CIA. When they stopped, Guy took her hands in his and said, "Jackie, I want you to know that I've loved you for a long time. I couldn't tell you before, I didn't dare," he said. "Not very brave of me, was it?" Encouraged by the look in her eyes, which glistened with unshed tears, he continued. "I just couldn't imagine you would be interested in me. I just couldn't see how it would work." He felt her fingers shaking.

"So I was dumb. Then when I wanted to say something, Harry stopped me, absolutely banned me from trying to dissuade you from marrying Ari. He actually ordered me not to call you. Too well trained, I just couldn't disobey him. You can't imagine how many hours of misery I spent when I heard about your wedding."

"Oh, Guy, if only you had." Jackie sighed. "That last night at 1040, that night when you told me your wife was moving back to the States, I can't tell you how pleased I was. I thought to myself that it would never work and soon you would be free. We would both be free. I wanted to tell you how I felt, to shout it from the rooftops, but something held me back too. I thought, suppose, just suppose this marriage works out fine? How can I, who so despised those women who moved in on Jack, do the same?

"But then, I thought if you said something . . . well, I was a mess. I kept hoping that you would. That's why I stopped you from going and we had that long, long chat about Lucas, remember?"

"Remember?" The word tore out of him. "Jackie, I can recall every single thing about that night. For months I thought about nothing else. I can remember what we ate, what you wore, what we drank, and every word that was said. I felt you were warmer to me, kinder to me, than ever before. But as I said, I didn't even dare think you would be interested in me. I thought you were just being sympathetic. I thought it was because of your horror of divorce. You'd told me all about that before, remember, when we were talking about your childhood and you and the president."

"That's partly true. I did feel sorry for you, but secretly I was glad. I thought, he's going to be free! He's going to be free! But I was too scared to make the first move, *I* was too well trained by my father," she said.

"Oh, Guy." Before she said another word he wrapped her tight in his arms. He ignored the pain in his hands as he caressed her back.

"Can we forget all about that now, make up for lost time?"

Later she told him her suspicions about Callas and her husband.

"Don't tell me that you love me, Guy, I'm no good for love," said Jackie. "There's something I do, or don't do, that means that no man ever finds that I am enough for them.

"My view is that relationships between men and women are always faulty and I always seem to be the one who gets hurt. My marriage to Jack, my marriage to Ari, externally they work, internally they are damaged things."

By this time she was in tears. Lying on the narrow bed, built as bunks for the scientists, he held out his arms to her. "I'm going to show you that I am different," he whispered. "It's not your fault. Up until now you just made the wrong choices. No one need know about us; we won't have an external life until you are absolutely convinced that I will be faithful to you for the rest of my life."

Between kisses he repeated that this time things would be different. Unlike her other men, he wanted, needed nothing from her. With their bodies they comforted each other, worshipped each other, enthralled each other.

Then he talked to her about practical things, their children, his possible desk job with the agency, his future inheritance.

The next day she could not resist going earlier to the studio.

~∞ ❧ ∞~

Nikos decided that since the place seemed to have such a hold over her, he would take more than a cursory glance. The morning after, as soon as he saw her deep in conversation with the housekeeper, he went over the place, literally on his hands and knees. It took just ten minutes to discover the carefully concealed trapdoor in the cupboard and the stairs going down below.

Puzzled, Ari's aide went no further.

Perhaps his boss knew about this. Maybe these cold stone steps led to a cellar or some other strange room; maybe it was part of their relationship and Ari might be mortified if he knew.

On Ari's return he would very lightly and carefully allude to it and take it from there.

The next day, with Ari still locked in meetings with the Swiss in Athens, Jackie could not resist going down the stone staircase when the sun was still high in the sky.

Guy looked so much better.

"Bad news, I'm afraid. I've been on the radio transmitter. Harry says thanks, but wants me back pronto. I tried to talk him out of it but he's insistent."

He held out his arms to her. "I am so sorry, darling."

Seeing her sad face, he tried to lighten her mood.

"Remember everything we have been to each other these last few days and keep them in your mind. This is just the beginning.

"Tonight while you're asleep I will somehow have to swim out to a small motorboat that is waiting to take me to Piraeus. There is a navy ship on its way but Harry won't let me wait a day more for it. He wants me on a plane by tonight.

"I am so sorry I have to go," he said as he kissed first one and then the other of her tear-filled eyes.

"We'll meet again the minute you get to New York. How soon will you be back in the States?"

She stroked his cheek. "After Rose goes home so will I."

"That's in two weeks, isn't it? By then I'll have found us a little hidey-hole"—he smiled—"a bit more comfortable than this."

He held her to him.

"Harry also asked me to tell you that because they feel that this place has been so useful, they hope that you will continue to let us use this island for some time to come."

"I knew that there had to be a catch," she said resignedly.

Guy pulled her to him again, and looking down on her upturned face, he said: "It doesn't have to be. Everything that we've been planning will take a little time. Getting a divorce from Ari without anyone ever getting a sniff of the Callas thing will need careful planning."

"You're right. I would hate to go through all that again, especially now that the children are old enough to understand."

"And we'll have to be very careful. If he suspects that you have been unfaithful I imagine he will behave badly. I don't believe Ari believes in equality," said Guy, raising his eyebrows.

"So let's tell Harry we'll give him six months," she said as she snuggled into his arms.

"Tell Harry nothing," said Guy. "If he falls in love with this experimental sonar equipment he'll think of something to keep us apart. We can see each other here or in New York, anywhere you please. You told me yourself your husband is only around fifty percent of the time."

Their farewell was tender rather than passionate; Guy had not regained all his strength.

He hid his concern about Harry's order that he get off the island as fast as possible.

"Whatever the time, find a telephone and call me the minute you hit the mainland," were his boss's final words.


Jackie slipped into dream mode when her husband returned. That night as the candles flickered and bouzouki music played, she laughed and even danced with him.

Nikos wondered at the woman's sangfroid. She didn't seem to be bothered about Callas at all.

Early the next morning, while Jackie was still in bed and Ari was inspecting the condition of his olive trees, Nikos caught up with him.

"Niko, I thought only activities in the counting house got you out this early," Ari said, laughing.

"To what do I owe this pleasure?"

Trying to hide his nerves, Nikos took the plunge. "It is nothing. I just wanted to ask you whom you had ordered to put the trapdoor in your wife's studio floor. I haven't opened it but as we are thinking of putting one in the storeroom, I wondered who had built it because it looks like a very good job."

"Don't be ridiculous, not in the studio. As far as I know there isn't one," said Ari.

They looked at one another and began to walk in that direction.

Within moments they were both inside. Jackie's drawing papers were roughly moved aside and the small manhole cover lifted. Both men looked at the narrow steps and then gingerly walked down them through the rocks and out to the secret mooring at sea level. Some of the machinery was quietly clacking away. In the hollowed-out chamber were the two bunks, one just recently vacated.

Ari, nostrils slightly twitching, raised his head and inhaled deeply. He followed the slight scent. He said nothing but was sure that he could smell Joy, his wife's perfume, on the pillow.

Beneath the beds, they found the packing cases that the machinery had arrived in.

"American," Ari said quietly.

Nikos felt he had to say something. "Did you know that she had invited Yankee spies in here?"

Onassis exploded.

"Know, of course I didn't know! Do you think I'm mad? Here, on my island!

"Niko, think about it, I have always tried to remain politically neutral. If some of my business associates found this out, it would be the end. How dare she? After everything I have given her!" he boomed.

"Niko, I have always been impartial. Unaligned. That even applies to this island. I am allowed to come and go if I keep my nose clean. Currently our rulers, the Colonels in Athens, are friendly with the Americans, but who knows in the future? That's why I have always stayed out of politics, away from the whole grubby business. We have to dismantle all this—soon. Let us think who we can trust, trust with our lives, to do it."

Guy was surprised how weak he still felt. He was gasping for breath when he reached the boat. He had no strength to haul himself up so he was grateful there were two men to haul him onboard.

It seemed ages until he disembarked. Although he was longing for sleep, his first action was to look for a phone.

"You remember Vladimir Zerev, KGB smoothie and thug?" asked Harry, sounding worried.

"We've found out that he's been pretending to be a high-powered Swiss businessman in Paris for the last week or so, a man with a very sweet deal for Ari Onassis. He's been working on the Greek, producing the best forgeries in the way of bank statements and foreign contracts you've ever seen. We have no idea where Onassis stands in all this; for all we know, he might be quite happy to be doing some undercover deal with the KGB. Anyway Vladimir has got so friendly with Ari that he's on his way to Skorpios right now. That's why I wanted you off the island. It is vital he doesn't see you, or know that we are on to him. I've got Brunton to keep an eye on him to find out what he's up to."

"You're worried that he will discover the mooring and the equipment?" asked Guy anxiously.

"We wouldn't want the Russians to get their hands on the technology. It's supposed to be far more advanced than anything they've got. But let's be honest, so far, out of the lab, the stuff hasn't worked properly. It's people I want to protect.

"There's no way that he would physically harm Jackie. But think of the propaganda if he could find the stuff and prove she was in on it. I want her out of there. We are busy concocting some story that will make her leave, that will get her back home as soon as possible."

"There's no way," said Guy. "The children are with her. Rose Kennedy is turning up tomorrow, it's her first visit to Skorpios. There's a big party, even Jackie's mother will be there."

"*Shit.*" Harry sounded very nervous. "You know she doesn't have the children's Secret Service guys on the island. She says she doesn't need them."

"Under normal circumstances that's probably quite true," replied Guy.

"I'm sending them over but it will take all day for them to get there."

"Harry, you've got to let me go back," said Guy tersely. "Don't worry, I will arrange things so that Vladimir has no idea that I'm keeping an eye on him. Is he on his own?"

"No, he has a man called Mikhail Ryblov as a sidekick. He is KGB as well, quite senior. They also have two women who are supposed to be their wives, probably part of the organization too."

"That worries me. A woman would not seem threatening to Jackie, Caroline, or John."

"I know. I'll have to wait until a civilized hour but then I am going to speak to her myself. First I will tell her she must not go anywhere near the secret harbor. I don't want the Russians to get the chance to take a photograph of her there. In case they try to expose her, it's important that she can plead complete ignorance of the place.

"I'll also warn her about these four and tell her not to trust them, or anyone else. You never know, they may have allies among some of the other guests. Who knows what types have been invited? She's got be on her guard and make sure that, other than her husband"— Guy heard the sneer in Harry's voice—"she's not on her own with anyone. And she's also got to make sure that there is always someone safe, like the nanny, with the children."

There was a moment of silence. The former First Lady's exposure to possible danger was all too real. Harry was worried about Rose and the other Kennedys too.

"The trouble is, I am tempted to give in to my fear and haul them all off the island, but there would be a terrible political stink. The Junta would be furious because the world would think that they knew about our little base on Skorpios, which they don't, and the Russians would denounce us from the rooftops.

"Guy, I'm going to keep the motorboat positioned in exactly the same place as last night in case you feel you need to get out. That includes anyone else you are worried about. I don't want to terrify her but I feel that I should advise Mrs. Onassis of its existence too. It won't come to that, of course, but just in case.

"If only we could warn her husband," muttered Harry.

"Well, we can't, the man's only allegiance is to himself." Guy's words tumbled out before he could stop them. "Please let her know that even though she won't recognize or even see me, I'm coming back," said Guy.

"Sure, Sir Lancelot."

Harry had lost none of his intuition, Guy thought.

Just a few hours later, looking old and gray, he was hunched by the water's edge watching his old Moscow adversary, dressed in sophisticated traveling clothes, an elegant trench coat and blazer, with his suitably attired "wife," boarding the *Christina*. His colleague looked equally smart and self-assured. The only one who looked a little out of place was his much younger "wife," who looked like a honeypot trap in the making.

As soon as the large yacht left port Guy reboarded the motorboat that had collected him the night before. He did not need to tell the local Greek steering it to head straight for Skorpios while remaining a suitable distance behind Ari's boat and its evil cargo.

By late morning Ari and Nikos had come to the conclusion that there was no one they dared trust with their new information.

Nikos, ever the problem solver, said, "I will deal with it. My son and I will bring the American machinery up here, bit by bit."

"But it will take you days and where will we put it?"

"What about a fire?" suggested Nikos.

"Just our luck, the whole island will come and put it out." Ari gave a cryptic smile. "Let's wait until everyone leaves, then we can load it all onto a boat and bury it out at sea."

"But shouldn't we make sure that no one finds it for now?" asked Nikos.

"Good point. I'll tell Jackie that her studio is out of bounds because it is full of furniture from the house and the cottages. I'll say it is in the way of all these extra guests. Meanwhile you fill it up so it's actually impossible to even open the door. Then put a lock and padlock on it."

"What do you think she will say when you tell her this?" said his friend quietly.

"What do I care? You were right about her all along, Niko. What sort of wife would do this? She set me up."

Wearily he returned to the house to prepare for dinner.

As Nikos went about organizing the studio to be filled with recliners, small tables, plant containers, and other objects, he couldn't help but be curious about any visitor who might still try and enter this edifice through the secret sea entrance.

He felt sure that Ari had found her scent down there. Who was to say that it was just her head on that pillow? If he could find out that Jackie had a lover, that would be the end of her.


Jackie was unhappy. Guy had gone. By this evening there would be a surfeit of guests, including various strangers that Ari, suddenly moody and bad-tempered, was aggressive about the arrangements and their stay.

"They are important, after the weekend we are signing a big, big deal. Money doesn't grow on trees. The boss, Harnier, Pierre, he is very sympathique. In Paris we had a couple of dinners together, just the two of us. He's been fun to have in Athens and seems like a nice guy. The wife looks okay too."

"Well, the other wife looks like a hooker," spat Jackie.

"We can't all be born in a bourgeois bed, my dear. Give her a chance, she might be charming. Anyway, you won't have to worry about her; the star of the show is Rose. We shall fete her and make her love my island."

Jackie noted the "my." When he had gone she lay on the bed for a moment. She knew that a lace call had come but she wanted to wait until Ari was well out of earshot before she telephoned the States. Over the last few days, since Guy's arrival, she had lived on virtually no sleep. She closed her eyes for a second. By the time she got through to Harry he had been sitting by the phone for some nail-biting two hours.

Although he had intended not to worry her, his nerves had been rattled by the wait. Swiftly he explained the secret identity of four, possibly more, of her guests.

"Don't mention this to your husband. We have no way of knowing whether he knows the truth about them or not. He is in love with their deal, which they may be making as Russians.

"I don't think they will do anyone any harm, they are KGB but they aren't violent goons. But don't go back to the mooring under any circumstances and don't get into a situation where you are alone with any of them, even the women. Stick close to someone you trust all the time. The same goes for the children."

"The children!" Jackie suddenly sounded panicky.

"I am getting the Secret Service guys over to you as soon as possible. They should arrive sometime over the weekend. It's a little earlier than scheduled for the children's return home. Oh, and by the way, Guy didn't fly home. He is probably back, somewhere on the island now. He's known Vladimir for years, so he will be in heavy disguise, but he is going to be watching out for you. We are probably all worrying about nothing. The Russians will be gone on Monday. They may just be curious to see Ari's showplace and to meet you. Remember, we once did very well out of that. One more thing. From now on, if you get a message from me, please call right away?"

"And I moved here to feel safe," she muttered as she replaced the receiver.

Vladimir wasted no time. As soon as Ari's welcome was over and his host had retired to the Pink House he plunged into the sea.

"If they are trying to track down a submarine, they must have their equipment in the water or by the water's edge," he told Mikhail. "You take a look around the place on land. I will tell Sonja to say that we are having a siesta in case the old man comes looking for me. Regina should use her charms any way she can to extract information from the staff. See if she can find our beekeeper. We have three hours before cocktails; let's confer half an hour before then."

It was Regina who discovered the secret passage. Pretending to be casually mooching around the place in a demure white cotton dress that managed to show off all her curves, she sneaked into the kitchen for some fruit. A young boy welcomed her in and she feigned complete disinterest when she overheard staff complaining about being suddenly ordered to dump furniture that was in no one's way into the studio in the hot summer sun of the afternoon.

She made the studio her next port of call and insinuated her lithe body into a small gap while the staff took a break. As she crouched behind the furniture and listened, she could hear the man overseeing the proceedings sounding angry and irritated that it was taking so long. If it was not important why did he feel he had to stand there? Through a chink she saw him with a large lock and padlock in his hands. What was it about this place that made securing it so important? Why, in such a magnificent setting with many million-dollar paintings, sculptures, and ceramics on display, was there such heavy security for a place that contained no items of worth?

When he was sure that the door could barely be wedged open, she heard him putting the key in the lock and attaching the padlock. When she was satisfied that he was gone, she crawled out from under an occasional table and gingerly began trying to explore. Balancing precariously on the varied objects that had been hastily stuffed inside, she searched for over an hour before she found the hidden trapdoor. She was inside the staircase in minutes.

After examining everything, Regina took the only way out—she swam. The guests who had begun to assemble for predinner drinks thought Skorpios even more exotic as they spotted her racing across the lawn. Her dress had become transparent when wet.

Nikos was interested for different reasons.

Paranoid, Nikos decided to send his son to watch and see if anyone else came out or went into the tiny mooring. The lad was thrilled when his father gave him some binoculars and told him he could take one of the island's two small motorboats and keep watch from offshore until Nikos came to get him.

While drying herself and easing into her cocktail gown, Regina told Mikhail everything she had seen. "Very good work. This evening you will have to pretend you are what they call a wild child, a hippie. Say something like, the sea spoke to you and you had to go in. Tell them that you were swimming somewhere else though. I will go and tell Vladimir. Be outside in ten minutes."

Friday night on Skorpios never lasted too late. Many of the guests, especially those who had come a long way, retired quite soon after dinner.

The next morning Nikos wondered how he was going to tell his boss that both of the businessmen had taken a late-night dip in the vicinity of the hidden harbor. His son did not think they swam inside it, but since he had been told to keep away from the shore he could not be sure.

Nikos thought it best to keep this information to himself for the moment. Maybe it was coincidence. If the visitors were not who they said they were, Nikos knew Ari would be doubly heartbroken since his boss was still thinking this great deal would be going through next week.

He would keep an eye on them.

Vladimir was exultant. He had been right all along. He called his

KGB superior, who had flown to Athens as soon as their invitation to Skorpios was secured. The men spoke carefully, mentioning no names in case they were being listened to. The man rang back. He had disappointing news.

"I apologize. It has been decided not to tell the world about this. We have no idea what this machinery does or how long it has been there. It could make both the senior partner and their hosts appear far too clever."

Vladimir knew better than to complain. So the Americans and the Greek Colonels would not be associated with the technology.

"It has been decided that you should destroy it. Any way you can. But you must be very careful. No one must be physically harmed. Especially not the main person, however bitter you feel about her. The orders are clear. If it was ever found out that *we* had caused an accident in her vicinity, well, the international repercussions aren't worth thinking about. Unfortunately, our superiors do not think that we have had sufficient time in the area to cover our tracks. They are moaning as always that producing the contracts and the papers for the back story, to convince the old man that you are who you say you are, has taken enormous effort.

"Nonetheless, they believe that it is imperative that the message to our rivals be clear. We must make it difficult for them to use her in the future," he ordered.

It was agreed that as long as there was no loss of life, the secret harbor and its contents should be wrecked. Once again, Vladimir thought that Jackie led a charmed life. The Kremlin was far too soft.

It would not require much gelignite to blow the machinery and the secret harbor apart. Vladimir had been given details about the two Communist sympathizers working on the island. Two hours later they had been located. The Russian thanked them for all their support in the past and asked for their assistance.

By lunchtime they had enough explosive stockpiled in their cottages. Vladimir put another call in asking if these two could be trusted to destroy the American equipment and the hidden mooring after they left.

"Too risky. While you have the opportunity you must do it," said his superior. "Our experts have some suggestions. The ideal way is to tell Ari that today is your birthday. If Mama Rose does not feel upstaged, perhaps they will ignite fireworks. If you can't get them to do so, blow the place up at three tomorrow morning."

Jackie had tried to tell the children that they should stay close but they were so excited to see their grandmother they couldn't help running to and from her room.

Once again she warned the nanny to keep an eye on them and gave her orders that on no account should she leave them at any time, not even with their relatives. Jackie was nervous. She kept as far from the Russians as she could, using the excuse that both Rose and Janet needed her special attention.

She also altered the evening's arrangements. Usually she tried to be inclusive, using one big table to mix up old and young, rich and spectacularly rich. For the first time she split the huge table into two and all four Russians were put well away from her and her family.

When she showed Ari the new plan she could not resist trying to find out what he knew about their business guests. Still furious about that morning's discovery, he was anxious she should not spoil his big deal.

"Don't neglect these people. I don't know the wives but I like the men a lot," he replied.

Wary of being too aggressive and bearing in mind Harry's dictum, she said, "I couldn't put my finger on it but I think there is something fake about them."

"Of course," he said and roared with laughter. "For such a manipulator, Jackie, you are so naive."

So he knew.

"Sure they are," he continued, "so many Germans pretend they are Swiss nowadays, I wouldn't be at all surprised. But they are not charlatans, I've been in business long enough to have had them thoroughly checked out. They've also probably been to all the best parties from St. Moritz to St. Tropez so I want you to concentrate on giving them a good time."

Jackie pulled out a new Givenchy dress, deep pink silk zibeline. As she slid into the new shoes especially dyed to match, she thought them impractical. Ari's response had enhanced Harry's warning and tonight she might need to move fast. She hunted for a pair of silver pumps that were more comfortable. As she trawled through her evening shoe cupboard she thought achingly of Guy. She was missing him so much already. Where was he?

She must talk to Caroline on her own, make sure she stayed with the nanny and kept her eye out for John. Thank heaven the Secret Service men would be here either later tonight or tomorrow. She talked to her daughter while her hair was being done. Jackie was used to her difficult mane; it always needed straightening and could look unflattering unless it was teased and backcombed. Because she was hot and nervous tonight it took an age to get right.

When she emerged cocktails were being served but she thought it advisable to check the tables for herself. She was worried when she saw that one, her family's table, was half in shadow. As she called for more candles and lanterns, she noticed that the guest of honor had moved the placements.

About to return them, Jackie heard the Kennedy matriarch right behind her. "Please don't move those back, dear. Let me sit between Caroline and John?"

Jackie could do nothing but agree. As she checked the rest of the seating plan she saw that the two Swiss men, originally at the other table, were now placed next to her children. Pierre next to John, the other one next to Caroline.

Rose implored, "Those men are charming and they're from Switzerland. They can tell Caroline and John all about it. Now, Jackie, you and I have always agreed, that's how children learn, in real life as well as the classroom."

At that moment her husband and the Swiss group appeared, and Jackie had no choice.

The evening seemed to drag by. She knew that she was looking across to check on her mother-in-law and her children too often. Once or twice she went over to the other table ostensibly to see that her guests were enjoying themselves.

Her tiredness fed her fear. She hardly touched her food, supposing the Russians were intent on poisoning or drugging them all.

Finally the meal was over and the band struck up some of Ari's favorite Greek tunes. He was attempting to persuade some of the guests to join him in the Greek peasant dance traditionally done by Greek men. From time to time she looked behind her into the pleached hornbeams and the oleander bushes. Was Guy there somewhere? Would she recognize him if he were?

When the music ended the small orchestra struck up a Beatles ballad and Ari encouraged her to lead the dancing with Pierre while he swept onto the floor with Rose.

At the end of the dance Pierre did not relinquish her until a young John F. Kennedy Jr., excited to be staying up so late, raced up to her. "Mommy, Mommy, we're having fireworks. It's all because of Pierre. He told me he asked because they don't often have them in their country because of avalanches."

"I told you they would learn something sitting next to those men," Rose said, smiling, as she waltzed past.

Jackie knew that fireworks had not been planned. When she was arranging this evening she had vetoed them because no one knew when Rose would go to bed. It would be very inhospitable if their noise woke her up.

Intuition, instinct, and frayed nerve endings all suggested to her that the man had requested a fireworks display for a reason.

Jackie looked around; if only she could warn Guy. She tried to calm herself; perhaps she was being silly. She could see Pierre, smiling, cutting Ari's cigar. But as she peered across the lawn she could not see his sidekick or either of their wives. The frills of her dress swished against her legs as she walked around searching for them among the arrangements of deep wicker chairs on the lawn, on the dance floor, or by the bar where coffee and postprandial drinks were being dispensed.

In the guise of a concerned hostess, smiling at this one, having a brief chat with someone else, she spent several minutes hunting for them. The three of them were absent.

And, she suddenly realized, so were her children.

She called their names, first quietly and then louder, over the band, as she went through the crowd. Two or three times. Ari, in the center of things, finally heard her and told her that both they and their nanny were with Nikos's son. Apparently the boy had been out on the motorboat yesterday and had handled it so well, he had asked if he could take all the children, including hers, for a ride to get a better view of the fireworks.

"I don't want them out there in the dark," she shrieked.

"Relax, Jackie, what can happen? They can all swim."

He returned to the dance floor, now throbbing with disco music. The moment she left the melee she slipped off her shoes and automatically raced toward the promontory. If she could look down from there and see the children out at sea, she would tell them to come back.

As she ran she heard the first explosion.

A profusion of color, with stars shining red, white, and blue in honor of the late president's mother, lit up the sky. It was rapidly followed by another and then another.

Jackie was nearly above the promontory now. As the fireworks illuminated the landscape she saw Nikos's son, the nanny, and the children bobbing about in the boat below. Madly she started to use her arms to indicate they should come back. She shouted but her voice was drowned in the next explosion and the one after, which didn't come from the sky but from somewhere deep below her feet. She could feel the vibration. The other party guests, much farther away, did not yet realize the difference.

It took her some minutes to reach the edge of the hill to signal to the children again. The motorboat had vanished. She could see no children, only bits of wood on the sea. She had to get down there. She ran to the studio, forgetting it was locked. Frantically she ran back to the crowd. They were laughing and dancing, unaware of the extra explosives that had been used.

"Ari, Ari, something terrible has happened, the motorboat, the children's motorboat . . . it's broken."

Followed by a few others who had overheard, they raced to the shore. Now pieces of burning debris were visible.

From behind her Nikos appeared and Ari shouted, "Get the other boat, now!"

As they raced around to the port only the *Christina* was at anchor. The other motorboat was gone.

"My God!" cried Nikos.

"Get on the *Christina,* now," shouted Ari.

The three of them and two of the waiters who had heard her and been right behind them raced aboard. The engine roared to life.

No one spoke; they just scanned the sea for any sign of the motorboat or its occupants.

Jackie thought that hours passed but ten minutes later, as the yacht finally nosed around to where the hidden harbor had been, they could see a large gaping hole in the rock face.

Then they heard voices.

On a wide ledge, some two hundred yards from the hole that had been gouged out by the gelignite, sat the nanny and the children, all of them. Some shouting, some crying. Alive.

Nikos and one of the waiters jumped into the sea and brought them, one by one, down to the water's edge and swam alongside them until they reached the yacht's stairway.

The adults devoted themselves to calming the children. While waiting for dry clothes to be brought to the ship, the youngsters told Ari, Jackie, and Nikos how their great adventure had begun just as the fireworks were about to start. Two American sailors and an "old, smelly man who spoke American" drew alongside. They suggested that everyone would have a far better view if they went aboard their larger vessel.

"They were very polite and friendly, and because they knew our names," said Nikos's son, "I thought they were friends of yours and that you wouldn't mind if we went aboard their boat.

"The trouble was that even though they promised to tow our boat, the minute the first fireworks went off they drew away from the shore in such a hurry that our boat got left behind."

Ashen-faced, Jackie assured him that they had done the right thing.

Ari, so relieved that the hidden mooring with its American technology was gone, thought that this was not the moment to try and discover how deeply his wife was involved. What mattered now was that the whole thing remained secret.

Of course the Swiss were really Russians. Only the U.S.S.R. would want the minicave destroyed. It was possible they would try to unmask him and Jackie as part of a propaganda coup. Ari thought it unlikely. The Soviets knew that the Americans would emerge looking good. Not only had they got closer than anyone else to monitoring everything that was moving around the Mediterranean, but with President Nixon working on détente in both Moscow and Peking, it just might backfire.

Above all else, Ari was a pragmatist. If this story did become public, he would lose his ongoing trade with the Iron Curtain countries, but revelations about the secret mooring would succeed in making him, and especially Jackie, very popular in some quarters. The West would clamor to do business with him.

However, if the Russians didn't talk, the next twenty-four hours were vitally important if this caper was to be contained. It was up to him to see that this story didn't spread. One glance at Jackie's strained expression convinced him that she too wanted an information blackout. Ari guessed that she would wish to distance herself, and more importantly her children, from the whole affair.

He was right, but he had no idea how involved Jackie had been. She was nervous. Did the Russians have any inkling how long the secret mooring had been planned? She was not worried if they denounced her as a spy. She knew that her own country and the rest of the West would applaud her. But how would Ari take it? Did she care? He had betrayed her with Callas anyway. Still, she was in no position to sermonize. She waited for his accusations and was surprised when he broached the subject of the night's events with reserve and affection.

Standing on their private deck, he poured her a glass of warm Turkish coffee and gently said, "It would surely be in everyone's best interest to minimize this episode?"

Exhausted with relief, Jackie sank down on a couch and asked for a minute or two to think.

"Unless someone wants to make mischief"—she shivered as she remembered how long ago it had been since the Skorpios drawings were first spread on her New Jersey table—"this story will probably only get out if the children think it is fascinating. We can swear the older ones to secrecy. But we have to give the younger Kennedy cousins, and that includes my two children, something much more enthralling than a boat ride to talk about."

She looked up at her husband and whispered, "Ari, please ask the chef to come to the yacht's galley and have him make pancakes, flap-jacks, cookies, anything the little ones want. He should cook in front of them and they should be encouraged to help him. Then let them all sleep on the yacht. Let them have the full *Christina* experience, Ari," she said. "By tomorrow these treats will have made their great adventure on the other motorboat recede. I can't ask Caroline, John, and the others to lie to Rose and Janet, but it would be preferable if they bored them with how many pancakes they ate rather than the wild boat ride.

"Both my mother and my mother-in-law already worry too much about my children traveling around Europe. If they hear about this they'll unite to stop me taking them out of the country."

Jackie knew that her fears about Rose's and Janet's attitude to the children's safety were well founded. Both grandmothers made no secret of their desire for Caroline and John to spend more time at Hyannisport or Newport. In this they underestimated her. One of the plusses of being Jackie O was her ability to travel when and where she liked. She was determined that the events of last night should not hinder her freedom. One of her pipe dreams with Guy had been to settle down in Paris or Rome.

As the adrenaline subsided, Ari felt guilty about his part in the evening's drama. He was very fond of his stepchildren and was god-father to Nikos's son so he felt bad that his greed had nearly brought disaster to them. Jackie's idea was right. If the whole thing remained unexamined, he would never have to explain how two phony Swiss businessmen had fooled him.

As night turned to day the pair warily created the best story for public consumption. The rock-face explosion was caused by a fire-work that ignited a gas tank housed beneath the studio. The Swiss had been recalled to Zurich for urgent business reasons.

In the morning as many of the guests, unaware of the real action, left the island, Ari pursued the rest of Jackie's plan. A day cruise with the relatives would not only give all the in-laws something to do, it meant that the children would be busy with their cousins swimming and diving off the boat rather than chatting to the older ladies, who took up their positions beneath large hats on the upper deck.

Jackie guessed that "the old, smelly man who spoke American" was Guy. Caroline had told her that after he had carefully deposited them on dry land, he and his companions had headed swiftly out to sea. So he had been watching over them all along.

As soon as she had a moment, she put a call in to Guy at Langley. It was unsuccessful, as were the six that followed. She knew enough not to push it. He could be anywhere. She decided to wait until everyone was gone. Within a week she was alone on the island. The children accompanied her mother to Newport, Rose and the other Kennedys were Paris-bound, and Ari returned to his Athens office.

Finally, she called Harry Blackstone. When she could not reach him either she paced around the island. She even took the motorboat out to see the result of the explosion. Their bunk bed, the tiny mooring, their haven had been ripped apart. There was no trace of it. She felt doubly bereft.

When Nikos returned from attending to his master's business affairs in the Greek capital she read his cool politeness as subtle hostility. She could understand that he might blame her for the near-death of his son but wondered what else he knew. Her nervousness grew when she was sure that she heard two staff members talking in what sounded like Russian.

It seemed like Skorpios was telling her that it was no longer a safe sanctuary.

She wanted to leave, to get to America. Suddenly she didn't want to be alone with her thoughts and memories. Even though her intellect told her that Guy was probably on one of his typically complex and dangerous missions and couldn't call her, her emotions were shattered. Hadn't it been only a fortnight since they had declared undying love for one another? What was the point in waiting here for a man who did not even return her phone calls? Maybe she had just been useful to him while the agency needed the island and it was his way of telling her that this was it. It was over.

Her self-esteem at rock bottom, she found she couldn't bring herself to challenge Ari over Callas. All she wanted from her husband were his boats and planes to give her privacy as she returned to the security and love of her family and Hammersmith Farm.

As time passed and the Communists remained silent, Ari was delighted that his deals with Russia's allies were no longer in jeopardy, so he became more caring toward his wife. He could understand how extra precious the children were to her. If he was away he phoned her every night, long loving calls, promising her that during the fall he would spend as much time as possible with the three of them in New York.

Ari had never asked Jackie how culpable she had been in the covert American spying operation. After the initial shock subsided he found it easy to excuse his wife for her implication in the ruse. His ego convinced him that it was inevitable. Giving it some thought, he had assumed that after their marriage the CIA had, in the nicest possible way, put pressure on her. Arrogantly Onassis presumed that as a mere woman she would not have known how to negotiate her way out.

By mid-September Jackie had tried to write Guy off and was attempting to heal her broken heart with activity. So when the call finally came, from Harry Blackstone, under orders from Guy to apologize for his absence, she was, for once, overcome with emotion. Her cool demeanor shattered after Harry asked, as Guy was somewhere he couldn't phone, if he could write to her. She began to shake and emit soundless sobs while still holding the receiver.

For security reasons the agency arranged to have Guy's letters hand-delivered to the former First Lady. They were long, literate, ardent outbursts. Guy explained that for the next few weeks, maybe months, these weekly missives would be all they could have together.

"But, my darling," added Guy, "I've never forgotten that night at 1040 and your face when you told me how important letters are. How exciting it is to read the words of someone who is committed to you totally and longing for you every minute of every day.

"I shall be no slouch about writing and breathing love all over these pages."

These adoring tributes made her feel more relaxed about her husband's sexual infidelity. Instead of feeling a failure, as she had with Jack, she related Ari's behavior to that of her father's.

She realized that Black Jack had always exuded such an air of sexual danger and mystery, even to his daughters, that she had grown up thinking that adulterous misbehavior was the inalienable right of the attractive man in society. It had even made her more capable of understanding Jack when he first strayed, even though the thought of him in another woman's arms had made her jealous. Her father had successfully brainwashed her into thinking, This is what men do.

Always highly disciplined herself, she realized that she began to hate Jack when he failed to follow the rules that allowed a man his mistresses. They were very clear. For a man to deserve a secret life it was essential that he be adroit in its management. Jackie loathed Jack for not understanding that as commander-in-chief this was impossible. Agreeing to this role automatically relegated clandestine affairs off-limits. Jack couldn't postpone his adultery until such time as he was not in the White House because he was simply out of control.

Guy's passionate letters buoyed her up as did regular visits to the psychoanalyst David Goadshem, who with professional grace and generosity helped her accept happiness.

This joy made her a better wife. With Ari she could afford to be at ease, good-humored. Without sensing why, Telis began to spend more time with her. For a marriage without trust it worked well. From Rome to Capri, from Cannes to Naples, the couple continued to fascinate the press and each other.

Jackie kept away from Paris. She did not mention Callas but regularly reminded Ari how lucky it was that the loss of his "Swiss deal" had not embarrassed either of them because Ari had been so discreet about it.

Her comments acted as a cautionary restraint on him. He now met the diva more privately.

Jackie enjoyed being open in her letters to Guy. Honestly she told him about her fears for herself and the children, how just hearing Russian spoken still made her anxious. He told her about his son, his grandfather, and his ex-wife's financial demands, but remained quiet on where he was and what his current commission was.

In 1971 she and her children were invited by President Nixon to return to the White House to unveil the official portraits of her husband and herself. After the disastrous evening back in 1964, Jackie had promised never to go back to 1600 Pennsylvania Avenue, but Caroline, now fourteen years old, and John, eleven, were keen to revisit their famous old home. After some debate they persuaded Jackie that tourists should see a picture of their father.

Richard Nixon, his wife Pat, and their two daughters went out of their way to make the day very special. After the official business was over, Jackie and the children joined the family for lunch. With trepidation they entered the private presidential quarters. She was happy to see the Nixons' other lunch guests included Harry Blackstone, ex-President Johnson and Lady Bird, General Mo Dodsworth, and Hugh Mitchell.

As they sipped their drinks a six-foot man in his seventies accompanied by a tall teenager, obviously his grandson, arrived pushing a man in a wheelchair. It was Guy. Jackie was dumbstruck. He stopped right in front of her and smiled. She wanted to cry, to reach out to him, but in the presence of two U.S. presidents and her children she summoned every ounce of self-discipline. Courteously Guy shook her hand. She leaned over and kissed him on both cheeks.

"So your children thought I was smelly, did they? Old, yes, smelly, never!"

The group laughed and Caroline and John were introduced to their savior.

"I'd no idea, no idea at all, that you'd been hurt," said Jackie.

"Sorry, Jackie," interrupted President Nixon, "we've got a little piece of unfinished business here." The president then informed the gathering that Guy was being honored as he had been badly wounded by the Russians while chasing them to their freighter. He had been in one hospital after another ever since.

After lunch Jackie and Guy finally had the chance for a more intimate chat.

They rapidly realized that their feelings hadn't changed since their last night together on Skorpios.

"Why don't I help you recuperate? You can come and stay with me in New Jersey. There's no risk. Now that his Greek chanteuse isn't performing her sensual arias en route, Ari sticks to the city." Cautiously Guy decided it would be advisable to rent a farm nearby.

For some months she ably nursed him, devoting as much time to him as she could, when she wasn't with her children or performing as Mrs. Onassis.

When they were alone Jackie and Guy pleased themselves, rising late, driving out to buy local produce. In the morning they concentrated on his exercises. His right leg and shoulder had been badly hurt. She would teach him easy yoga positions and slowed her pace to accompany him on his halting walks. He would lovingly charm her in every language he knew, teaching her smatterings of Russian and Turkish. They pooled their knowledge of Greek, the language, the history, the literature.

As time passed she and Guy started making plans for a life together. At the beginning he encouraged her to follow his example and become single again. His wife was keen to remarry as soon as possible. But all too soon they both realistically accepted that for Jackie to divorce Telis would be too intrusive and embarrassing. His affair with Callas would be blazoned across the world's newspapers, and with her children now teenagers she could not face the scandal. Their love affair must remain their secret.

"Will I ever be free and be me?" she dejectedly asked Guy.

"Alone together, we are as honest as most people ever are," said

Guy. "We can, and do, say everything and anything we want to each other. We laugh and moan and I complain that I can't walk, the blond hairs are going gray, and you can't ride as fast as you used to. We have no no-go areas. Our bad luck is that we have to deal with your public."

She was not convinced that her only problem was the public. Especially once he recovered and finally returned to work.

So they could be together, he rented a country house just outside Langley in the rolling hills of Virginia. The agency converted a small cottage on the property for their surveillance purposes. They built gates and fences that would deter both press and burglars. In between doing her duties as a mother and as Ari's wife, Jackie found much happiness with Guy under the whitewashed rafters.

At first Guy planned to spend just three days a week at work, but within a fortnight he was back, fully involved in the CIA. "Sorry, I can't just sit around doing nothing. Once I am in the office, I'm involved. I can't do a proper job if I'm half-time."

A few days later Harry invited himself over and carefully explained that the agency desperately needed experienced officers out in the field. "Guy, we need you to go overseas, but only for another year or two, then my boy, you'll probably get my job!"

Soon Jackie was behaving like every other person involved with someone from the agency. She became used to long periods worrying and waiting for Guy's call. For the first time in her life she was not worried that the man she loved would be unfaithful or disloyal. All she fretted about was his safety.

Jackie had adapted to her double life with panache. If she occasionally blamed the children for her nonappearance at Ari's side, he only chided her gently. If her presence was important to him, since the Jackie effect garnered goodwill and sales, he would make sure that he gave her very early warning.

His own affair made him wary of discovering anything more about her life.

But everything changed in 1973 when Alexander, Ari's son, died in a helicopter crash. Bowed by grief, Ari started to hate her. He blamed Jackie, encouraged by his Greek friends, not to mention his daughter.

"She brings death everywhere she goes. Get rid of her," screamed Christina.

He couldn't yet bring himself to do so. His revenge was to use her, so when he called Jackie, it was to summon her across the world for angry bouts of sex.

If his aim was to make her feel like a highly paid prostitute, he succeeded. But, knowing how the death of a child would be the worst thing to happen to anyone, she could do nothing but accede to his wishes. She felt sorry for him.

For once she couldn't tell Guy. She guessed he would not understand.

This was easier than she imagined. Guy was working hard and often away. The letters of love never dried up and from time to time Harry Blackstone delivered them himself. A few months after Alexander's death he arrived, in one hand Guy's latest missive, in the other transcripts of radio transmissions that revealed a plot to eliminate Guy and Jackie. With no histrionics Harry explained how the one link between all this information was Vladimir Zerev.

"Over the last few years he has become very powerful," said Guy's boss.

Without any drama Harry continued.

"Without naming names, I asked some of my fellow officers to outline the risks that you two are running. You see, Zerev and others in the KGB seem convinced that not only did you work for the CIA but that you still are."

Harry pointed to the places in the translations that mentioned her specifically, and one which mentioned her children too.

"I hate to say it but you should know better than anyone that no one is impregnable," he warned.

"I know you and Guy only manage a few weeks a year together, a day here or a night there, but you have to be even more safety conscious now," said Harry.

"The press haven't found you out because, frankly, the combination of your activities in New York, the charities, the ballet, keeping Grand Central Station's landmark status to stop it from being knocked down by developers, keeps them fueled with new stories, new pictures. Not to mention your frequent photogenic trips with your husband. So they have not discovered your secret life in the Virginia countryside. They just think you are involved in riding and hunting there.

"But the Russians will use wiretaps, secret cameras, anything at all to tie you two together. I would think they have enough to expose you. But hey, now you are with a good-looking American spy—"

Jackie stopped him. Harry didn't have to paint a picture. Her countrymen would love it.

"The Russians don't want you to look good. They mostly want to stop Guy. He's been too successful for their taste lately."

Harry may or may not have heard a ghostly "Not again, not again" from her lips, but he thought it best to continue and to ensure she got the message.

"Let's be clear, I can protect you in the U.S. but from now on you will have to meet elsewhere and abort all established patterns of behavior. I can't be sure that I can keep you safe abroad."

When he returned from his latest assignment, Guy was so worried about her safety he suggested they return to letter writing for the moment.

Jackie would have remonstrated but she had other problems. Not only was Ari still furious with her because he believed she was cursed and responsible for his son's death, now that he was ill, he mistrusted her help. While in New York, Ari had had growing health problems after being confined to his suite at the Pierre Hotel. Even though his "flu" was diagnosed as myasthenia gravis, a progressive muscular disease, he was determined enough to head back to Greece. At first medication seemed to treat the symptoms— drooping eyelids and fatigue—but very soon his heart function was compromised. Concerned, Jackie turned up at his Glyfada home in Athens with a renowned American cardiologist. Suspicious of her doctor, he chose to fly to Paris. With his sister, Jackie accompanied him, but when it was suggested he should have an operation on his gall bladder, Ari refused to go to the American Hospital and holed up in his Avenue Foch apartment for three days. His recovery was complicated. His heart was weakened, his muscular disease was taking hold, but after a week of antibiotics he rallied enough for the doctors to tell Jackie she would be safe to return to New York to see Caroline and John.

A combination of the aggressive attitude of Ari and his coterie toward her and the lonely hours she spent in the French capital meant that Harry's forebodings started to have an effect. She began to see shadows in the Parisian streets. Once or twice she swore she had seen Vladimir Zerev across the road or in a chauffeur-driven car at the lights. She crossed and recrossed the Atlantic as Ari's stay in the hospital lengthened, while her fears for her personal safety grew stronger each time. She made the children spend their weekends with at least one family member and was glad that she had persuaded Harry to warn the Secret Service to be especially vigilant.

Once again she returned to the City of Light and the French doctors reassured her that her husband was making slow progress. Jackie was torn. She knew she ought to stay but by now she was very fearful for her children, so after a few days, when she was assured that her husband was in no danger, she left her bedside vigil and flew to the East Coast. Ari's situation suddenly worsened. He developed severe pneumonia, which would not respond to any medicine. He died without her there.

Guy sped to 1040 as soon as Jackie returned from the funeral in Skorpios.

"I am so angry that you are now being criticized publicly for leaving Ari. I feel so bad. You can't live your life feeling hunted because of me, and even if I give the job up the Russians will always have me in their sights.

"Darling"—he took her in his arms—"now we are both free, how I long to be with you. Always, in public. But it is too dangerous. Harry doesn't exaggerate. I couldn't let Caroline or John come anywhere near me now."

Swift shadows of fear crossed her eyes.

"I'm even keeping Lucas at arm's length."

Reluctantly he left in the early hours.

That night he left her a message: "Jackie, do you remember that famous night when I came to see you with the notebook and those lists. You might recall that at the time you felt very strongly that you wanted to surprise the world by doing something good. You did. You did years of working for the agency, but we could not let the world know. In fact, we may never be able to do so. If we do the enemy will assume that all of our first ladies are spies and that isn't very fair to wish on your successors.

"This isn't a farewell letter but I would never forgive myself if something bad happened to you or the children because Vladimir S. wants to dispose of me!

"This is just a short farewell note. You aren't going to get rid of me that easily. Somehow we'll have our moments together again. But think about what you said that night. Why not fill your day with a different stress and pressure, the one that comes of struggling and exerting yourself into doing your best, being creative, helping someone . . .

"Whatever you decide, I will always love you, Guy."

Not long after, the announcement that she was to work as an editor of a New York publishing house did stun the world.

Gradually she understood that work was as much about status as salary and that a hard day's work did help dull the pain of the forced separation from Guy.

Finally Mrs. Jacqueline Kennedy Onassis threw off some of the structures visited upon her by her mother. Like other women of her time who chose intelligent liberation, she finally realized that a husband was an optional extra, not a necessity.

She never married or spied again.

# ACKNOWLEDGMENTS

My first gratitude must go to Gilly Vincent who suggested that I should write something more about Jacqueline Kennedy Onassis. Both she and Elizabeth Sheinkman have been the most supportive and encouraging agents. I am also grateful to my editor, Alison Callaghan, and her sidekick, Jeanette Perez, who deftly handled someone working on the other side of the Atlantic.

Among the many others who supplied advice and information, I would like to acknowledge Peter Brown, Monie Begley, and Patrick McCarthy, Gloria Sheehan and DeLano Knox of *Women's Wear Daily,* Christopher Banks, Barry Winkleman, Barrie Penrose, Joyce Hopkirk, Wendy Steavenson, Wendy Miles, and not forgetting Wendy Payne and Jenny Moffatt for their technical expertise.

Those closest to me excelled themselves, especially Claudia Winkleman, Kris Thykier, and Oliver and Rachael Lloyd.

For his constant care, encouragement, and involvement in this venture, as in all my schemes, harebrained or not, my love and thanks go to my husband, Nick.

**EVE POLLARD** has had a long and successful career in both television and print journalism. She made her mark in the United States as launch editor in chief for American *Elle*, and makes frequent appearances on the *Today* show and MSNBC. She is one of the few women to have edited two British national newspapers. She lives in London.

Eve Pollard